Unexpected Peril

Alissia Roswell: Book Three

Tianna Holley

Unexpected Peril

ISBN 978-0-9894908-1-8

Published by:
Canton Walk Publishing

Mom, to see your eyes light up and to experience your support with each book I write will always put a smile on my face. Even as an adult, I hope to make you proud. You're my mother, and I love you more than words could ever describe. You'll never truly know how much you mean to me.

Chapter 1

Alissia Roswell jumped from the covered wagon as soon as it came to a halt. She pulled her arms behind her back and began to stretch out her chest, when something caught her attention. Dropping her arms, she cocked her head and began to stare out into the distance.

"It's eerie," Anika muttered.

Alissia nodded, her eyes not leaving the bare tree in the shape of a skull. The tree was only one of many standing above the unruly brush and weeds covering the long distance between the trail and thick woodland.

A cacophony of sounds, including bullfrogs and evening insects, could be heard from the direction of the unsettling trees. It reminded Alissia of the nights she had gone frog gigging and fishing as a child.

However, she had never seen a row of tall, barren trees in the shape of human skulls.

"Somebody had to carve those trees," Alissia said, matter-of-factly. "They didn't just grow that way."

"No, they didn't, and that's why we don't leave the trail tonight," Salvatore said, as he and Luke walked up behind them. "We rest, and then we leave first thing in the morning. Alissia, it would help if you made sure Shade and the dogs also understood this. Otherwise, I'll have to cage them."

Alissia nodded.

Anika turned to him with wide eyes. "Are you sure this is safe?"

"I've traveled this way more than once," the older man said reassuringly. "This trail is recorded on some of the earliest maps, and some people believe the stones beneath our feet were placed here before the land was settled. If so, the people that live in that bog have been here for a long time."

"How do you know it's a bog?" Anika asked.

"Look carefully around at the animals in the area and the trees, not to mention the sounds. We're also in the lowlands."

It had been over three weeks since she and her friends had left Pallen with Salvatore and his people. Since guards along the road often unexpectedly stopped them, Alissia spent most of her time traveling in the covered wagon.

Each time they were stopped, she hid in a secret compartment, and she was certain she would have already been found if not for her ability to control the guards' dogs.

By now, Salvatore and his people knew about her power over animals. When they had first met Alissia, they had kept the lion-like animal named Shade and their two dogs in a cage and away from her, fearing she could use the animals against them. Now that her friends and Salvatore's group knew each other better and some trust had been established, the animals were allowed more freedom around her.

Alissia still kept most of her abilities a secret from Salvatore and his people. He believed she was changed by a group of Lamians from her reality before entering this one, and he had no idea that she had never even met a Lamian.

She dreaded telling anyone the truth about her circumstances—that she was a mistake. The ancient people that have been hidden for almost two thousand years found her near death after being pulled into this reality.

Having heard footsteps running toward them, they scampered away after healing her, leaving her with a faint memory of two separate voices and their handprints branded into her abdomen.

Within days, her long, curly hair changed from dark brown to a deep purple, similar to that of a plum. Her eyes were now purple and glowed slightly. Her skin was soft and shimmery, and her blood was also purple.

Then there were the special abilities, although she often wondered if there were more than she knew about. Her body healed itself, she could see in the dark, charge solar-powered stones, heal animals, and tell them what to do. She could not eat meat or even stand the smell of it cooking without getting sick, and she had to wear dark glasses, as the sun greatly burned her eyes.

Although Mia often showed herself to Alissia's friends and the animals they traveled with, the mysterious creature sent to her by the Lamians continued to stay hidden from young Devon and Salvatore's people.

Luke and Alissia rarely ever had the pleasure of being alone together, so it had been a while since the pixet had resorted to growling or biting when she thought the couple were tempted to kiss—causing Alissia's purple blood to glow beneath her skin and her body temperature to rise for some unknown reason since healing Luke from severe wounds, connecting them in the process.

Alissia was no longer fooled by the tiny grey and black fur ball's cute and innocent appearance. Although only a foot tall when standing on her two raccoon-like back feet, Mia viciously killed one of the men trying to harm Alissia before they escaped Pallen, leaving a gruesome and bloody scene behind. Her round face, black nose, pointy ears, and big grey eyes easily disguised her fierce killing capabilities.

"This isn't something you normally see in your lifetime," said Grady, stepping up beside Salvatore.

While Luke and Salvatore had been driving the wagon Anika and Alissia had ridden, Grady had spent the day riding with Romeo. He and Luke had stopped hiding from the guards within the first week of their departure from Pallen. They now impersonated traders, even allowing their facial hair to grow out to help with their disguise.

Luke's black hair had always had an unruly touch to it, matching his piercing dark eyes, lean and toned body, along with his dominant personality. Being a skilled assassin, he was used to traveling and working with his hands. His olive-skin tone absorbed the sun naturally, and his transformation was not as extreme as Grady's.

As a government official within the Eldership, Grady had spent his entire life with a clean-cut appearance, wearing fine clothing and eating the best foods. Although his chestnut-colored hair was the longest it had ever been and his sun-kissed faced showed his many hours of driving a wagon, there was still a hint of formality about him. The way he sat, along with his speech, gave away his real lifestyle.

His cousin, Anika, no longer dressed in the extreme disguise she had worn when escaping Pallen. Her long, auburn brown hair was pulled into a braid, and the temporary tattoos were faded on her skin.

It was the same for her husband. Although Langley continued to wear the clothes Salvatore gave him, the fake tribal tattoos were now faded and the jewelry was gone.

However, he easily blended into Salvatore's group of foreign traders. He was tall and stocky, with unruly light-brown hair, and being a man that spent his days tending to horses, his hands and skin showed signs of a man accustomed to labor. If it weren't for his soft and kind face, his presence could easily be dominating.

Grady unconsciously lifted his hand and began to scratch at the unfamiliar hair on his face. Studying the strange landscaping in the distance, he said, "I've read about this place, but I never thought I'd actually see it."

"What have you read? Is it safe?" Alissia asked.

His hand left his face, and he nodded thoughtfully. "Seems so, at least, if we don't go near the trees. There are numerous records of people going insane after they got too close."

"Insane?"

He chuckled, while turning to meet her eyes. "The only people to lose their sanity are the ones curious enough to go near the trees—mainly researchers, teenage boys acting on a dare, and even hunters. Many warning signs are posted along the trail so people are aware of the danger."

"Most people don't even travel this way," Salvatore added. "They're too superstitious."

"Smart," Anika said.

He grinned. "Traders, such as myself, know this path is free of danger, as long as you abide by the rules."

"What rules?" asked Anika.

"Respect the ones that possibly built this path and trimmed those trees as a warning. It's obvious they don't want to be bothered."

He clapped his hands together and turned to go before adding, "We leave at daylight. I don't think I need to add how imperative it is for you to stay close tonight. This trail is saving us a week of travel and is worth the discomfort."

Before walking away, he said reassuringly over his shoulder, "Besides, we have Shade and the dogs to warn us of any danger."

As Alissia stared at his back, she shook her head. "So we're taking the fastest route, not the safest one. Where have I heard that before?"

Luke laughed as he placed his hand on her shoulder and gave it a playful squeeze. "Don't worry, Pixet. At least this time I don't have to worry about you trying to run away, getting yourself into trouble."

She scowled up at him, and he laughed even harder as he and Grady walked away to begin their evening chores.

"That's it!" Anika said, slapping her arm. "I've got to put on some insect lotion. They're horrible here."

"I wouldn't know." Alissia gave a smug grin.

Her friend shook her head and frowned. "You could at least try to get them to refrain from biting everyone else."

"You know it's not like that," Alissia responded as she watched Anika climb back into the wagon. "Insects are different than animals, and there's so many of them. I've found they leave me alone, so maybe I should leave them alone as well."

By now, a routine had been established among everyone. Since there were so many of them and they slept inside the wagons, it did not take long before their chores were completed each night.

The women prepared the meals during the day as they traveled, and as soon as a fire was lit, a pot of food was placed over it. Although traveling with wagons meant they had to stay on heavily traveled or constructed paths, it was much more convenient and pleasant than traveling by horseback.

They had already encountered many rainy days, and the wagons ensured that their belongings were kept dry. They also held a large supply of food so that they did not need to stop in a village to buy more.

The weather was getting much warmer, and many wild berries, other fruits, and edible plants grew along the trails.

Alissia learned that the horrible-tasting murdock root grew abundantly in the wild, and when she and Luke had traveled together, he had only stopped in villages for her sake. If he had been traveling alone, he could have easily lived off the land. Although he had seemed indifferent and uncaring to Alissia, she now knew he had subtly tried to make her less miserable during that time.

Since the night she had saved his life, their relationship had greatly changed. She had learned a lot from the bond she shared with him, and there was no doubt of his love for her. She had experienced it from within his own body during their bonding process—or whatever it was that had happened between them.

Her worry over what she had done to him had lessened over time. Other than their ability to mind speak and feel heightened emotions between them, they had not noticed any more changes. His hair and eyes had not changed color, and she was hopeful that the Lamians would have an explanation for why they could not share a kiss.

Alissia did not allow herself to believe she would never be able to be intimate with him, as those thoughts scared her too much. She had never loved anyone as she did Luke. Part of her desperately needed to believe that one day they would have all the answers to their questions, and they would finally be able to be together without fear and danger controlling their lives. Sometimes she even allowed herself to imagine a distant future with him, although she never allowed herself to go as far as thinking they could have children and live a normal life.

Everything about her future was uncertain, except for Luke. She knew he would never leave her side, and she found comfort in that.

"I love it when I catch you looking at me like that," came Luke's voice from within her head.

Alissia blinked and was brought back to her current task of stirring the pot of bean soup over the fire.

"I was just pondering whether I like this scruffy look of yours," she lied.

"Is that right?" She could hear the disbelief in his mental words. *"And by scruffy, I'm guessing that means hot?"*

She laughed out loud at his attempt to use one of the slang words she had taught him from her reality.

"What's so funny?" Anika asked, setting a box of dishes down near the fire.

"Oh, nothing," Alissia stammered. "I just had a strange thought. That's all."

Her friend crossed her arms and frowned. Studying Alissia's face, she said, "You've been distracted a lot lately."

Alissia gave a lighthearted smile, in an attempt to hide her guilt. No one knew about what had truly happened between her and Luke the night of their escape, and since then, she often got caught not paying attention to those around her.

Although she and Luke did not have many chances to be alone together, they spent a lot of time sharing mental conversations throughout the day. Some nights she even drifted to sleep with the sound of his voice in her head.

She knew her friend had a reason to be suspicious. Numerous times over the past three weeks, Alissia had rolled her eyes or laughed out loud during one of her mental conversations with Luke, only to realize Anika was watching her with a worried expression.

"I promise nothing is wrong. I just have a lot to think about. That's all." As she spoke the words, she glanced past her friend to where Luke was tending to the horses. His back was now toward them.

Anika's eyes followed, and she was smiling when she turned back around. "I see," she teased, before walking away to complete her next task.

"See what you made me do!" Alissia mentally said.

Luke's laughter filled her head. *"I can't help it you can't control yourself when it comes to me."*

"Anika's beginning to think I'm going crazy."

"Start closing your eyes, as if you're resting," he responded.

"Oh, that'll work perfectly while I'm tending to the food."

After everyone had eaten and the food and dishes had been put away, they all sat around the fire to relax. The animals sat with them, and Alissia noticed how they continuously turned their heads toward the eerie woodlands, as if sensing some unseen danger in the darkness.

In an attempt to lighten the mood, Salvatore began to play music from his viola, and the others from his family soon joined in with other instruments. Shortly thereafter, Alissia found herself resting her back against Shade as she watched Anika and her husband, Langley, dancing to the music.

Everyone in Salvatore's group played a musical instrument, and on the nights they camped in a private location and did not have to use extreme caution, they would entertain Alissia and her friends by the fire.

Alissia highly enjoyed the folk-like songs, much different than what she was used to hearing in her reality. Some of them were fast, and everyone would laugh as they stomped their feet or danced by the fire. Others were slow, the men chanting along with the music. However, Alissia loved the ballads sung by Edda and Bruna the most. The wives of Salvatore's nephews pulled emotions from her she never thought she could feel just from hearing a song. It did not help that each of the sad ballads were based on true stories of love and death.

She also enjoyed watching Devon's young face light up while listening to the music. Being only twelve and having raised himself on the streets, Alissia felt he was much too serious for a boy of his age.

He worked hard throughout each day and seemed like he was trying to prove his worth to Luke, and it pulled at her heart to watch. Yet when listening to the music, a smile would appear, his lanky body would begin to move to the beat, and the dark mop of hair on his head would flop around.

On this night, the music was fast and fun, in an attempt to lighten the mood of the eerie surroundings. Salvatore and Santo tapped their feet to the beat of the music, and their faces filled with pleasure.

Unlike Lita, with her green eyes, and long, honey-colored hair naturally highlighted by the sun, Santo was a smaller version of his father. Both men had the same sandy-brown hair, brown eyes, and chiseled facial features. However, Santo did not have his father's broad chest and build. He also had less tribal tattoos and did not wear an earring.

Alissia grinned to herself as she watched Langley give Anika a twirl. Then a set of legs stepped in front of her, along with an outstretched hand. "Will you dance with me?"

She smiled up at Grady and accepted his hand. Although they had not shared a slow dance on nights such as this, they had enjoyed playful dancing more than once during their journey.

Luke was not jealous of Grady, and Grady had not said or done anything to make the situation more uncomfortable than it already was. She knew he was still struggling with the end of their relationship, which was one reason she and Luke refrained from open displays of affection. The fact that she and Luke could be intimate through their thoughts had many benefits and helped them to get through each day.

In the middle of the second dance, Grady abruptly stopped. "Do you mind if we talk? Alone?"

Alissia tried to hide her surprise with a lighthearted smile. "Sure."

As she followed him to the wagon where she spent most of her time, she glanced back at Luke and met his curious gaze. *"It's nothing. He just wants to talk."*

Luke turned his eyes back to the musicians and did not respond, mentally or otherwise. Alissia forced a smile as she turned her attention back to Grady.

He helped her into the front of the wagon before hopping up beside her, and they sat down on the driver's bench.

"What's up?" Realizing she was talking in slang from her reality, she stammered, "I mean, is there something wrong?"

He looked down at his hands in his lap, and after a short moment, he lifted his head and smiled. "Nothing is wrong. I just wanted to wish you a happy birthday."

"It's my birthday?" Alissia asked, completely surprised.

He nodded. "I didn't think you knew, especially with the differences in how our realities track time, but..." He cleared his throat awkwardly. "But, when I watched the videos from your past, I remembered which day you visited the tree on your birthday."

Alissia did not know whether to be happy or sad at that moment. Life had been too crazy since she had entered this reality, and the thought of her birthday had never even crossed her mind.

She gave a weak smile. "Well, at least I now know what day to call my birthday. I guess that's a good thing since this is my new life and home."

He reached beneath the seat and pulled out a small, wooden box. It was handmade with intricate carvings.

As she took it from him, she said, "It's lovely. Thanks."

He chuckled. "You didn't open it."

"Oh, I thought the box was the gift," she said sheepishly.

He shook his head. "No, there's more. It's not much, as I didn't know what to get you that..." He frowned and paused before saying, "That would be acceptable with your new relationship status. Hopefully this will do." He tried to smile. "It's also one of the only things available on this journey. Luckily, Salvatore is a trader from a foreign land, and this is something he just happened to have with him."

Alissia slowly opened the box to find an assortment of small, brightly colored crystals. She picked out a red one and lifted it up to her eyes to get a better look.

"They're beautiful. Thank you, Grady."

He grinned and watched her for a moment before saying, "It's candy, Alissia. You're supposed to eat it."

She gave a small laugh before placing it into her mouth. Looking up at him, she playfully said, "You knew I wouldn't know what it was, didn't you?"

The foreign, sweet taste of the candy took her by surprise, and she began to rub her tongue around the small crystal. Although she had tasted many new things, some good and some bad, since being in this reality, a completely new flavor filled her mouth.

"Oh, my goodness. Have you tried one of these? It's like... I don't know. This is good, really good." She reached into the box and pulled out a green one. Ignoring his shake of the head, she forced a piece into his mouth.

"Am I right?" she asked, watching his face.

Grady nodded and said cheerfully, "They're supposed to be yours. And, yes, I tried one when Salvatore first showed them to me. They're from his land, made with a unique blend of spices." He turned his head away. "I thought you would like them."

She recognized the hurt he was trying to hide. Not wanting there to be an awkward silence between them, she tried to sound happy as she said, "You always know what I like." She paused, struggling with what else to say. "You spoil me."

As soon as the words left her mouth, she regretted them. He turned back to face her and said softly, "But that's not what you want. Is it, Alissia?"

She bit on her lower lip as she looked down and replaced the lid to the box of candy. When she looked back up, she said, "I will always love you, Grady. Unfortunately, my life is too complicated, and..." She stopped, remembering the last time she had told him he deserved better.

"I'm complicated. My new life is full of questions and all about survival. I'm sorry."

He abruptly stood and hopped from the carriage.

"Come. It's your birthday."

She accepted his outstretched hand and let him help her down, and when they began walking toward the fire, the music changed. Everyone stood and began to sing a birthday song in her honor.

Alissia smiled awkwardly and then accepted a friendly hug from Anika.

"I didn't know it was your birthday today," her friend said, pulling away.

"Neither did I."

Langley gave her a hearty embrace, with her arms trapped at her sides. Once he released her, he said, "So how old are you now?"

"I'm twenty-nine."

He glanced toward Grady, now standing near the fire with a thoughtful look on his face. "Grady didn't mention it was your birthday," he said in a low voice. "I guess he wanted to share this moment alone with you."

The music stopped, and Salvatore walked over. He gave her a warm smile. "I hope you've had a pleasant birthday. Since Grady informed me, I've taken time to ponder over a gift for you. The one I've chosen is something I don't have with me but will be able to acquire once we enter the port city."

Alissia smiled uncomfortably. "Don't worry about it."

"No worries, my dear. It is both an honor and pleasure to share this moment with you."

Salvatore's son, Santo, along with his nephews, Carlo and Romeo, joined them.

"Edda and Bruna have something for you as well," said Romeo.

Over the past three weeks, Alissia had learned that he and his older brother were complete opposites. Although they both were of medium build and shared the same dark brown hair color, Carlo did not talk much, whereas Romeo had a playful personality and spent a lot of his time joking around with his younger cousin, Santo. His wife, Bruna, was very pretty and shy, and she and Edda were cousins and seemed to be best friends, too.

Alissia often found herself somewhat envious of the family bond among Salvatore's group. It was obvious they all enjoyed each other's company. Even Lita's occasional temperamental remarks did not seem to bother them.

There was something among them she had never seen or experienced for herself, and although she was happy for them, she often found herself wishing things had been different in her own life. They reminded her of the one thing she would never have.

"So is it a bad thing if I ask how old you are?" Romeo inquired.

Carlo said, disapprovingly, "You don't ask women that."

"Don't tell me you're not curious to know how old she is," responded Romeo. "She could be over a hundred."

"True," said Santo, grinning at Carlo's frown.

"Guys," Alissia interjected, "I'm only twenty-nine. Do I look a hundred?"

"You really don't know much about your future, do you?" Romeo said.

Alissia felt Salvatore's hand on her back as he said, "I expect you will age differently now, although I'm not certain."

She shrugged her shoulders. "I don't know if anything is for certain when it comes to me."

"She's an enigma," said Santo.

"Really, Santo?" Carlo scowled.

Alissia could not help but laugh at Carlo's disapproval of his younger brother and cousin.

Romeo said smugly, "See? She doesn't mind."

Lita stepped into the circle. "Here. Happy birthday," she said, holding out a closed fist.

Alissia held out her hand, and Lita dropped the small gift she was holding. "I make them," she said, somewhat awkwardly.

"Thank you, Lita. It's very pretty."

Alissia stared down at the three-chord wrap bracelet. It was made of woven material, tie-dyed in various shades of pinks, purples, and blues. A hand-carved, wooden button was used for the clasp. "Did you make the button too?"

Lita nodded.

"Wow! Thank you," Alissia said, impressed.

"Aw, you did something nice, Sis."

Lita's elbow immediately went into her older brother's stomach, knocking the breath from him.

"I make them all the time," she said, as if it were nothing.

"We have something for you too," Edda said excitedly. She and Bruna both stepped into the circle now around Alissia, and they each held something behind their backs.

Alissia placed the bracelet into her back pocket. "Y'all didn't have to give me anything."

"But we want to," Edda answered. Bruna nodded in agreement. She then turned to her cousin, urging her to go first.

Edda grinned and held out an old leather bag. "You have to look inside to find the gift."

Alissia took the bag and opened it to find one of Edda's knitted projects. When she pulled it out, she realized it was a grey, thick sweater in an open-front style, and she immediately noticed the amount of detail in it.

"Oh, it's beautiful," marveled Anika.

Edda grinned proudly. "I grabbed one of my smallest ones. Try it on to see if it fits," she said, taking the bag from Alissia.

As she put her arms in the sleeves, Alissia said, "You made this?"

"I sell them, and I can teach you." Edda motioned toward Bruna and added, "We can teach both of you."

The sweater was thick and warm, and although Alissia would not need it any time soon, she loved it. She wondered how much time it had taken her new friend to make it.

"There's more," Edda said, reaching into the bag.

It took a moment for Alissia to realize what it was Edda was holding out. The knitted, black hat was big, much too big for Alissia's head.

Edda and Bruna both laughed at the confusion on her face.

"Here, let me show you how to wear it," Edda said, passing the old bag to her husband. "It fits like this."

The woman placed the hat on Alissia's head and pulled her hair up into it. Once finished, it not only held her hair, but it covered her ears and the top portion of her forehead.

Bruna held out a mirror, and Alissia took it from her. As she stared at her reflection, Edda said, "See, it's supposed to fit like that.

You can also wear your hair down with it. It's tight enough at the edges, either way."

Alissia grinned. "I love it."

"I know you won't need to wear them for a while, but they'll definitely keep you warm next winter. I mean…" Edda glanced at Salvatore before adding, "unless you're on the island. You won't need it if you stay on the island."

Alissia shrugged. "You never know. I may have other places to be." She passed the mirror to Edda and began to take off the sweater. "It's definitely warm."

After removing the sweater and hat, Anika took them, and Bruna held out another used leather bag. She smiled and said, in her usual soft voice, "Sorry. I didn't have anything else to put them in."

"That's fine. Thank you, Bruna," Alissia said, accepting the bag. She then opened it to find a knitted pair of leggings, along with a pair of boot socks.

"They'll keep you warm next winter, and you can wear the leggings under your pants or with a dress," Bruna said.

Alissia grinned. "I love them. In fact, all of this would be very expensive where I come from, and I've never owned anything like this before." She looked into the eyes of Edda and Bruna as she emphasized, "I really love and appreciate the gifts."

Edda said, "We can teach you." She looked at Anika. "Both of you, if you would like."

Anika nodded excitedly. "I know how to do the simple stitches, but I'm not near as talented as the two of you."

"I would love to learn how to make something, although we probably should start out with something small," Alissia said, causing the two women to laugh.

A short while later, everyone began to say goodnight, and Alissia glanced toward Luke to find him sitting alone. He was staring into the fire, and she thought she sensed a bit of anger coming from him.

She asked Anika to carry her gifts to the carriage they shared with Langley, and as everyone began to get ready for bed, Alissia walked over to Luke. She stepped in front of him and began to study his face.

"Are you angry?" she asked.

"No."

"Are you sure? Because I think I can sense it."

He glanced toward Grady before standing. "I'm not angry, Alissia. I'm just a little bothered that I wasn't told it was your birthday."

"I didn't know either."

"Someone knew," he said, eyeing Grady—who was now crawling into his bedding in a corner of Shade's barred-carriage.

Then he turned back to Alissia and gave a determined shake of his head. "No problem," he said, smiling. He picked up her hand. "We have many years to celebrate together."

Luke pulled her in close before lifting her from the ground, and she gave an involuntary laugh when he playfully nuzzled her neck. Then he stopped to place a tender kiss near her ear. After setting her back down, he kissed her on the cheek. "Happy birthday, Alissia." He grinned and gave a wink before walking away.

She stared at his back for a moment before realizing she was being watched, and then her eyes met Grady's. After giving a quick smile, she turned away.

"You did that on purpose, Luke," she mentally said.

"Did what?"

"You knew he was watching."

"Can I not give you an innocent kiss without being accused of anything?"

As Alissia began to walk toward the carriage she slept in, she rolled her eyes. *"You're not innocent, Luke, and you know it!"*

She heard the smugness in his tone as he responded, *"I gave you the only gift I had on such short notice. What else was I to do? Maybe if Grady had not kept it to himself..."*

Alissia began to get ready for bed, and it was not long before she was wrapped snugly in her blanket. While Anika and Langley slept in a corner closest to the front of the carriage, Alissia curled up at the opposite corner, near the closed back flaps.

The air smelled strongly of the lungona plant used to keep insects away. The leaves of the plant simmered in a small container set on top of a tiny cooking stone.

"Are you sure we're safe?" Anika whispered to her husband.

Not wanting to eavesdrop on their conversation, Alissia began a mental conversation with Luke.

"Are you sure we're safe?"

"As long as no one enters the forest, we should be safe. People have been traveling this way for many years, and nothing has happened on the trail. We also have Shade and the dogs, and I'm taking the first watch of the night. We should be fine, so you should get some sleep."

Mia crawled under Alissia's blanket and snuggled up next to her. The tiny creature did not seem worried about their surroundings, which gave Alissia some reassurance.

"I would help to distract you tonight, but I need to stay focused while on watch," Luke mentally said.

Alissia grinned mischievously and decided to send a quick thought of her own. She began to imagine they were standing together on a beach under a full moon. *She wrapped her arms around his neck before pulling him down for a heated kiss.*

Then she abruptly ended her thoughts and began to laugh to herself.

"Nice visual. Now get some sleep before I get too distracted. You've given me enough to think about for the night."

"Goodnight," she thought, happily. Alissia pulled Mia in close and drifted off into a peaceful slumber, thanks to Luke.

*****

"She's waking!"

The unfamiliar voice was raspy and in the old language. Alissia let out a small moan before noticing the sound of bullfrogs and night insects was much louder than it should be. Her head felt foggy, and she struggled to open her eyes as she realized she could feel water moving beneath the hard surface under her back. She recognized the sound of paddling. She was in a boat.

A hand immediately covered her eyes, and something was placed at her nose, causing her to cough from its stench.

"Shh... Rest now. It's not time for you to wake."

Suddenly, it became impossible to keep her eyes open, and her mind drifted into darkness.

Chapter 2

Alissia smacked her parched lips, in an attempt to get rid of the strong, unpleasant taste in her mouth. Her mind felt foggy.

"Hello, dear," said a hoarse voice, in the ancient language.

Alissia slowly turned her head, and when her eyes met the creature sitting at her bedside, terror instantly replaced her confusion.

Although the creature resembled a human in many ways, there were also drastic differences. She looked like a plump, elderly woman with a wild mass of pale grey, knotted hair. The sackcloth dress she wore was stained and grungy, and her stubby fingers were wrinkly, with dirt beneath and around each of her short nails. She held something in her bottom lip, reminding Alissia of her grandfather and his dipping habit.

Her wild human features were no comparison, however, to her large, round eyes, situated within deep sockets. They were solid black, without any white or other color around them, and they were glossy, giving them the likeness of glass.

The woman was smiling, but it was unsettling, as the teeth left within her mouth were pointed and looked as if they had never been cleaned. The dip, resembling green sludge, coated her teeth and the creases of her lips. Alissia noticed, with disgust, that she swallowed the slimy substance instead of spitting it into a container.

"The fenton will leave your body soon, and you'll feel much better," the old woman said. She then cocked her head. "Are you aware of our kind? Do you know of our ancestors' relationship many years ago?"

Alissia tried to speak but nothing came out.

"Ah, yes," said the woman, bending down to pick up a bowl from the floor. "You need to drink. This will help you. Can you try to sit?"

For a moment, Alissia struggled with her weak body before she was able to sit up in the small bed. The woman then lifted the bowl to Alissia's lips, but she refused and shut her mouth tightly.

The woman pulled the drink from Alissia's mouth. "It's a sweanut, nothing more, and it was picked from the tree this morning." Holding it up for Alissia to inspect, she added reassuringly, "It's fresh. I just cut it for you."

What Alissia had first thought was a bowl, she now recognized as something resembling a halved, yellow coconut with a pale-green milky liquid inside. She studied it for a moment before the woman began to lift it toward her own lips.

"It's safe. I'll show you."

Alissia quickly reached toward the exotic fruit. The idea of drinking from the same container as the sludge-mouthed creature disgusted her, and she made a hasty decision to try it.

After taking it from the woman's hands, she held it up to her nose. It smelled sweet and fruity, and wanting to get rid of the horrible taste in her mouth, she took a small sip.

She held the juice in her mouth for a brief moment, taking in its unpleasant and somewhat bitter flavor before swallowing. She then forced down most of the liquid before returning the sweanut to the creature.

"Where..." She cleared her throat and began again. "Where am I, and where are my friends?"

"You're safe. Don't be frightened, child." The woman hefted her body from the chair. "Let me inform Gore you're awake. He's more familiar with our history, and he's eager to meet with you." She shuffled, with a limp, to a door made of thatches and reeds. Once alone, Alissia studied her surroundings.

Green and white bella flowers grew along the ceiling and all four walls of the small room. Clay pots were placed in each of the corners, holding their roots. The floor was old and worn, with many cracks between the wooden beams.

A large chest was set along one of the walls, and an old, wooden chair and stool were the only other furnishings to be seen, along with a shabby nightstand and bed.

Unlike the elaborate craftsmanship she had become used to since arriving in this reality, the furniture in the room was nothing special to look at. It was as if each item was made to serve its purpose, nothing more. Instead of heavy, dark stained wood, they were made with stripped wood, reeds, and thatches.

Alissia turned her head in alarm when one of the walls began to lift. As she stared at the moving wall, she sat up straight and tried to force clarity into her mind.

She was still wearing the same clothing she had gone to sleep in, and her hands hastily traveled over her body. An uneasy feeling came over her as she realized all of the daggers she normally wore beneath her clothing were gone. She glanced over the edge of the bed to see if her abductors had brought her boots, but they were nowhere to be seen.

Once the wall stopped moving and was transformed into an awning, a group of elderly men began to walk through the opening, and soon there were seven of them staring down at her. Some were bald with long, scraggly white beards, while others had a head full of wild, grey and white hair with matching beards.

Each of them had the same frightening, black eyes and pointed, grimy teeth, and they were all tall and stocky. However, they ranged in skin color, as there were tan, chocolate, and even a green tone represented within the group.

Their clothes were a variety of long sackcloth dresses to skirts made of animal skins and cloth. Jewelry made from bones and teeth seemed to be highly fashionable, and all of them had many tribal tattoos along their wrinkled bodies.

A dark brown man wearing a sackcloth dress sat down in the chair beside Alissia. Although he was somewhat bald, he had a mass of white hair pulled onto the top of his head. A piece of bone with a band held it in place, and he did not have a long beard like most of the others. He wore a necklace and bracelets decorated with bones and sharp teeth, and he held a wooden staff with a handle made of bone, intricately carved into the skull of an unknown animal. Tribal tattoos circled some of his fingers in place of rings.

He smiled at her, revealing more teeth in his mouth than the elderly woman. However, they were also grimy and pointed, as if they had been neglected for many years.

Alissia looked into the large, solid black eyes of each of the men staring down at her. Even with their mouths curled up, somewhat into a smile, they all had a savage appearance to them. With their creepy eyes, sharp teeth, tribal clothing, and jewelry, along with their lack of hygiene, they looked like they belonged in a horror movie.

Her pride quickly overruled her fear, and even with her heart beating wildly, she forced herself to make eye contact with the man sitting next to her. A calm façade came over her as she stared at him expectantly.

"Hello. My name is Gore, and we mean you no harm. You have nothing to fear," he said, in a raspy voice that she was beginning to expect from the creatures.

She mentally screamed Luke's name, but there was no response. Her fear grew even more as she realized she did not feel his presence within her, which she had grown accustomed to since they had bonded.

The man continued, "Our ancestors shared a strong friendship, and they did much trading before all the great races went into hiding." He paused and gave a curious look before adding, "We were not expecting to ever see your kind again, and you can't imagine the excitement your presence has caused, especially with me. I've studied the ancient scrolls my entire life and know many stories of our ancestors. Is it true you do not know of our people?"

Alissia shook her head. "I don't know anything about your people."

"Ah... I can easily understand. Not many of our own know all of our past. It's a shame, as there are many lessons to be learned from history."

A movement on his left shoulder caught her attention, and she began to stare at what at first appeared to be a tiny stick. She then realized it had a face, arms, legs, and wings.

"It's a felium." The old man held out his hand, and the creature flew to his palm. It seemed as curious of Alissia as she was of it, and they both studied each other for a moment.

It was about two inches tall, and it had dark green wings attached to its back. Matching green antlers were on top of its head, giving the creature the appearance of a small twig with pine-like foliage attached to it. The creature could easily blend into a tree, completely camouflaged.

Alissia leaned back defensively when it abruptly flew up to her face and began buzzing around her head in a frenzy.

"Skatonia, you're scaring our friend," Gore said.

The tiny creature quickly flew to his ear, and Alissia heard a buzzing sound before it settled back onto his shoulder.

"She's intrigued with the glow in your eyes."

Alissia instinctively raised a hand to her face as she realized she did not have her sunglasses on.

"Don't worry about your eyes. There's more shade than sun in our land, and you won't need your glasses."

"Why am I here?" Alissia asked, lowering her hand back into her lap.

"I would like to ask you the same. Why are you traveling with humans, and what is your business with them?"

Alissia mentally screamed Luke's name again. When he did not answer, her fear grew even stronger.

"What have you done to my friends?" she asked, accusingly.

The man cocked his head and studied her face for a moment. "So you claim these humans as your friends? I thought your people didn't want anything to do with humans ever again. Did they not learn from the past?"

Alissia thought for a moment before answering. "My people haven't forgotten, and we still live in hiding. Now tell me what you've done to my friends."

"We've done nothing to your *friends*, other than give them some fenton to induce a deep sleep. They're safe and are still sleeping, including the pixet we had not planned for. In fact, one of our men almost lost his life from that mistake, and he'll be wearing the scars from that encounter for the rest of his life."

Remembering what she had been told, she asked cautiously, "And what about their sanity? Will they be the same when they wake?"

Gore glanced at the men behind him, and they all laughed. "It seems we've achieved our goals." Turning his attention back to her, he said, "Do the humans fear this place?"

"Should they?" she asked.

The laughter in the room stopped, and the man became serious. "Yes, they should greatly fear this place, enough that they'll never enter our bog. You see, our relationship with humans has worked out much better for our people than yours. We knew from the beginning not to trust them, but your ancestors didn't listen to our kind. For that, they greatly suffered the consequences.

"I've read the scrolls and know of the many slaughters committed by the humans. They are savages, ruled by their greed for power. They came to our land in droves and claimed everything for themselves. Your ancestors easily trusted them, and because of that, it was not long before they were being hunted down by the humans."

As Gore leaned in close and looked hard into her eyes, a sickening odor slammed into her, causing her to hold her breath. "Your race would be extinct if it were not for them going into hiding."

Leaning back into his chair again, he let his words sink in before continuing. "From the moment the humans arrived on this land, my ancestors made the decision to claim this swamp as ours. We are happy here, and this is where we belong. However, if any humans make their way into our home, we send most of them out with a message. It seems that message has gotten around and served its purpose if the humans fear this place."

"What about the others? You said most of them," Alissia said.

"Some don't make it out as lucky."

Her eyes left his stare, and she tried to sound casual as she asked, "Why did you kidnap me?"

"My dear, we only want to speak with you. When the feliums informed us you were here—and within the company of humans—we became worried for your safety. If your people are still in hiding, why are you and a pixet traveling with a group of humans?"

Motioning toward the small creature on his shoulder, he added, "And Skatonia informs me you seem comfortable with them, even enough to have been kissed by one of their men."

Alissia scanned the faces of the elderly men in the room as she carefully considered her words.

"Alissia! Alissia, where are you?"

Luke's faint mental scream was filled with fear, and it sent shivers throughout her entire body. She immediately looked down at her hands, in an attempt to hide her reaction.

"Luke! Where are you?"

"I'm coming for you, Alissia! Are you hurt?"

Although she physically longed for him in a way she did not understand, she mentally yelled, *"Don't come! You can't come, Luke!"*

"I'm not losing you, Alissia!"

Gore cleared his throat, and she looked up.

"Um... I don't feel well suddenly. I'm sick on my stomach," she stammered.

One of the men stepped forward and handed something to Gore.

"Are you hurt?" Luke asked.

"No," she mentally answered.

"Here. This should help to relieve some of your discomfort," Gore said.

Alissia stared, repulsed, at what looked to be a root in his outstretched hand, dirt beneath his fingernails and in the creases of his skin.

Shaking her head, she said, "No, I don't want it." She caught herself from adding that she just needed some rest and wanted to be alone. Although she desperately needed to talk to Luke, she also needed to learn more about her abductors.

"Luke, I'm in a room with a bunch of old men, and I can't talk right now. Let me ask some questions. Just wait."

She turned her attention back to Gore. Looking him directly in the eyes, she asked, "When will I be returned? What are your plans for me?"

He set the root on the nightstand before answering. "We mean you no harm and have no wrongs with your people. However, recently we've noticed a lot more human guards and officials traveling our roads, and it has us questioning if a war among the humans is coming. Then we see you traveling with them, and our confusion is even greater. Are you or your people in danger?"

"No," she answered with certainty. "Although some people know about me, they believe I'm from another reality and am the only one of my kind among them."

"Are you the reason we've seen more officials traveling lately, or is there unrest among the humans?"

Alissia furrowed her brow as she looked away, not knowing how much information she should give. When she turned back to face him, she said carefully, "People are curious about me, but I'm not in danger and can trust the humans I'm traveling with. They keep me hidden and safe. As for war, there has been peace for well over a thousand years, and a civil war is not something the humans want."

"A war is rarely ever wanted. However, with the right circumstances, it can easily happen," he said. "What is your name, little one?"

"I'm Alissia."

"Well, Alissia, we'll return you safely to your friends soon, but we have many..."

"Alissia!"

As Luke's desperate scream entered her mind, an uncontrollable terror slammed into her, and she gasped out loud. Her body froze as the surroundings around her transformed. No longer in the room filled with the elderly men, she was now standing deep within a bog. Dark, thick mud covered her bare feet, and a layer of early morning mist obscured the swamp in front of her.

"Alissia, run!"

She turned her head to find Luke racing toward her. "Run!" he yelled, with urgency.

She quickly pulled her feet from the mud and began to rush toward him. Just as she was about to catch up to him, a spear flew past her head and landed directly into Luke's chest.

"No!" she screamed.

His eyes locked with hers for a brief moment before his body crumpled to the ground.

"No! Oh, no!" she cried, falling onto her knees beside him. She quickly scanned the surrounding area but saw no one.

"Please, Luke." Alissia wept, as her trembling hands touched his face.

His dark eyes stared out in front of him, lifeless. As soon as she looked down at the spear piercing his heart, she knew there was no way he could survive such a blow.

Her body began to shake uncontrollably as a feeling of great loss swept over her. In a small, trembling voice, she whispered, "Please. Please don't leave me."

As she tenderly stroked the wild lock of hair on his forehead, she felt herself being ripped away from him. She was soon back in the room with the men. Gore's face was inches from hers, and he was gripping both of her arms tightly.

"Child, look at me!" he demanded, the stench of his breath filling her with nausea.

Alissia blinked in confusion before she noticed the mud covering her feet.

"You killed him!" she screamed, jerking away from his grasp. "Why did you kill him?"

She jumped from the bed, ready to fight everyone around her. Her pain quickly turned to fury, and something within her told her she had nothing to lose.

"You might as well kill me too. I'll give you nothing," she hissed, her hands tightly balled into fists at her sides.

At the sound of movement coming from behind, she turned around to find two men standing beneath the awning. Unlike the elderly ones, these were in the prime of their lives. They were completely free of hair, wearing nothing but a loincloth, and various weapons made from bone and flint were strapped to their powerful toned bodies.

Both of them were covered in frightening tattoos of the skeletal system, even their faces. Nothing seemed to be unmarked, and with their black, glossy eyes, they looked like warrior creatures from the pits of Hades.

They said nothing as they stared at her for a moment, their hands behind their backs. One of them smiled, displaying his pointy teeth. Then he proudly revealed what he had been holding behind his back.

Darkness immediately overtook Alissia. As she fell to the ground, her last thoughts were of Luke's lifeless eyes staring at her from his severed head.

Chapter 3

When Alissia opened her eyes again, memories of what had happened to Luke immediately flooded through her mind, and she stared numbly out in front of her. Even when she realized she was lying in a cage made of thick rope that was hanging from a massive tree, fear did not come.

Someone had replaced her outer clothing with a short skirt and a wrap that only covered her chest, yet she did not feel self-conscious about the skimpy clothing or worry about who had undressed her.

She felt nothing.

Last night she had fallen asleep with a smile on her face, only to wake up and lose everything. She did not even know if her friends were dead or alive.

"Ah, I see you're awake now."

Alissia looked toward the low, raspy voice, and chills immediately crawled up her spine. An older creature was standing outside of her cage, and his massive body was entirely covered in tattoos of bones and muscles. Unlike the two men she had seen in the hut, this creature's tattoos were richer in color. He was completely free of hair, and brains were etched in colored ink onto his large head. Two small horns were atop his head, and he wore a gaudy necklace made of bones and teeth. He was wearing a loincloth, and although covered in tattoos, she noticed many pronounced scars along his face and body.

The various-sized knives strapped to him, along with the frightening tattoos, set him apart from the two other men standing beside him.

She sat up and faced the three creatures, and noticing their look of disdain, she defiantly looked each of them in the eyes before locking onto Gore's.

"You lied to me," she accused.

"What do you mean?" Gore asked, mockingly.

"You told me I would be returned to my friends, and you meant me no harm."

He nodded. "That was before we knew you're a human. You deceived us."

Fury filled Alissia. "How did I deceive you? If you don't recall, I was minding my own business before I was kidnapped! We didn't do anything to deserve this!" Her voice cracked as she added, "Luke didn't deserve to be killed like that!"

He cocked his head and studied her face for a moment.

"And which one is Luke?"

"The one your people beheaded! Or did they behead all of my friends like that? How many did they kill?" she hissed, while reminding herself she would not give them the pleasure of seeing her cry.

The three creatures stared back at her in silence, and she shook her head defiantly. "You might as well kill me too. I'm not going to answer any of your questions."

The warrior smiled. "You may find that we have many ways of getting our answers—ways you could never imagine."

He pulled a large knife from the long shoulder strap he was wearing and stroked his thumb along the sharp edge for emphasis.

Alissia forced herself to hide the terror that slammed into her as she met his creepy eyes. "Do what you want. I'm already dead," she challenged.

He laughed heartedly. However, Alissia thought she noticed a look of unease appear on Gore's face.

The warrior began to tamper with the cage, and Gore whispered something to the man standing between them. The man then responded with authority.

"Stop! Not yet, Gafeen."

The eager warrior scowled in disapproval. He obeyed the command but looked at Alissia with a leering grin. "You hear that? Not *yet*, little one, but soon. And I will show you there are some things worse than death."

She silently glared back at him, hoping her face did not betray her true emotions.

Gore's face softened, and he asked, as if suddenly concerned, "This Luke you speak of, was he your zeer?" When she did not answer, he added, "How long before you die too?"

Alissia pretended to ignore his question, not wanting him to know she was clueless as to what he was talking about.

Although he frowned, his voice held no anger. "Are there others like you?"

Gafeen turned to Gore. "She's not going to answer your questions without force," he said angrily. "I should be allowed to question her on my own."

The other man said, "You will have your chance."

The warrior turned his attention back to her. He glared at her for a moment before a malicious grin came to his face. "This should be allowed."

Staring at her intently, black streaks appeared beneath the skin around his eyes. It was not long before his entire face was covered in the streaks, as if revealing the veins beneath his skin.

He put his hand through a space in the roped cage, and it shook tremendously as he held it out toward her. Alissia was under the impression something was supposed to be happening.

He seemed to be straining when Gore said, "It won't work on her, Gafeen. You've seen her blood."

She looked down to inspect her body, but there was no sign of any wounds or dried blood. She wondered what had been done to her while she had been unconscious.

Gafeen pulled his hand back from the cage, and the streaks left his face. He scowled in frustration. One side of Alissia's mouth curled up as she smugly stared back at him.

"She's still human," he spat out, angrily.

Gore calmly responded, "I agree." He turned to Alissia. "I can tell you about your friends—where they are, and if they're safe." He paused. "If you answer some questions for me, I can answer some of yours."

When she did not respond, he said, "I'll start with an easy one. We've noticed a lot more traffic on our roads by human guards and officials. Is there unrest and a threat of war among the humans in the land?"

"Why do you care so much about what the humans do? How does it affect you?"

"Other than possible battles on our roads, it doesn't. That's why it's an easy question. You're not betraying anyone by giving an answer."

When she did not respond, he said, "I can tell you the location of the woman that was sleeping in the same cart as you. I'm sure you would like to know if she is safe or in harm's way."

"And how do I know you won't lie to me?"

"I have no reason to lie."

Alissia chewed on her bottom lip in thought for a moment before answering, "There's talk of a war, but no one really wants it. Now, what about Anika? Where is she, and is she safe?"

He smiled and nodded. "She is unharmed, and I will tell you where she is, once you give me a little more detail about this war. Why is there a threat of a war and between whom?"

A small amount of relief filled her, knowing her friend was safe. Although by now, she had given up on her own life. The only happy ending she could foresee at the moment would be to know that all of her friends were safe before she joined Luke in death. However, the glowering look on Gafeen's face led her to believe her death would be slow and painful.

"Alissia, why is there a threat of a war and between whom?" Gore repeated.

"The people of the North are unhappy with the leaders of the South. Now where's Anika?"

"You mean it would be a war between the North and South?" he asked.

"Yes, now where are Anika and my other friends?"

"She is exactly where you remember her to be, in your covered wagon."

"Unharmed?" Alissia asked.

"Yes, completely unharmed." He nodded and said something in a low voice to the man next to him before all three of them turned and walked away.

"How about the others?" she yelled, at their backs.

Gore turned. "We'll talk again."

Alissia watched as they walked a short distance and sat down on a group of logs. While they began a heated discussion, she stood and did a quick inspection of her body for scars and dried blood. Although she found neither, her feet were no longer covered in mud.

That thought brought a sudden memory of Luke falling to the ground with a spear through his heart, and the pain she fought not to feel came bursting through.

The cage was round and had no corners to hide in. She went to the opposite side, only to find more warriors with their bulky bodies covered in frightening tattoos, and she realized she had no privacy.

In an attempt to hide her tears from all the strange eyes staring at her, she leaned back against the cage and hugged her knees, burying her face into her legs. Alissia let her emotions take over, and the tears began to pour from her eyes.

She could not believe after all she had overcome in life, this was how it was going to end. She had survived all of her father's drunken abuse as a child, even a date rape as a teenager. Once she had left her parents' home immediately after graduation, she had worked hard to build a successful career.

After nearly dying from being pulled into this reality, the Lamians had risked exposing themselves just to save her life. Now she would never find the answers to all of her many questions. She would never know why her hair, eyes, and blood were now purple, and why her wounds healed on their own. She would never learn of everything she was capable of doing with her new powers. Yes, she knew she could see in the dark, heal and speak to animals, and charge the solar stones in this reality. But what if there was more she could do?

Then there was the star on her hand. What was it, and why did the tiny creature in the forest give it to her? It had helped her to heal Luke when he was almost killed by Ian and his men, but that had added more questions she needed answers to. Although now they could mentally talk to each other and physically feel each other's presence and heightened emotions, they could not share a kiss without frightening things happening to her body.

Alissia had watched Fang kill two of her kidnappers, and she had dragged their bodies behind horses to conceal their deaths. She had escaped the Eldership in Pallen and even saved Luke's life after killing Ian with her own hands.

Grady, Anika, and Langley's lives had been destroyed in their attempts to help her. She had also broken Grady's heart—the first man she had ever loved, and he truly loved her still.

It was over. Within an instant, Luke was dead, and she did not see a way out of her new nightmare. Honestly, she was tired of fighting. It felt as if she had spent her entire life fighting, and although she would change nothing from her past—it had made her the person she was today—sometimes she just wanted to give up.

After a while, Alissia closed her eyes, and the tears stopped. She said a silent prayer, and instead of asking for an escape, she asked for strength to withstand the torture she knew she would likely have to endure before her death.

Chapter 4

"Human! Look at me, human."

Alissia cringed at the sound of Gafeen's voice. She had nothing to wipe her tears with, and she scowled, knowing her pink and swollen face would be seen.

She ignored each of his demands for her to look up, and as she listened to him open the door to her enclosure, she made a rash decision that it would be in her best interest to get him to kill her quickly. To do that, she would need to provoke him into a rage strong enough that he would forget about his orders to wait.

As soon as she felt his presence inside the cage, she jumped to her feet and rammed into his massive body. Although he did not budge, she was able to pull one of his knives free. However, he swiftly grabbed it from her hand before she was able to stab herself with it.

"She believes she'll die soon from the connection," said Gore, still standing outside of the cage.

Alissia glanced over at him, and then she turned her attention back to Gafeen. After spitting on him, she rammed into his body again, and he effortlessly shoved her to the floor. She immediately scrambled back to her feet, and knowing he was too tall for her to throw a successful punch, she ran up to him and snatched the necklace from around his neck. As she scattered the bones and teeth across the floor of the cage, she hoped it held sentimental value. Then she glared up at him with pure hatred, daring him to hit her.

Fury immediately flashed into his eyes, and he knocked her to the ground before delivering a hard kick to her stomach. Intense pain shot through her body as he began to deliver more blows, and she instinctively curled into a ball.

"Alissia! Alissia, are you alive?"

Luke's frantic voice screamed into her head, but her mind was too focused on the pain she was receiving with each blow.

"Stop! Stop hurting her, you animals!"

At the sound of Luke's audible shout, Gafeen stopped kicking, and he took a few steps back.

"Leave her alone! Come for me! Leave her alone, I said!"

Although the screaming sounded desperate, it was definitely Luke's voice. Tears filled Alissia's eyes as she mentally called out to him. *"Luke? You're alive?"*

"Yes, Alissia. What did they do to you? Why are you in so much pain?"

A sob left her throat, and her body trembled uncontrollably with emotion, as a wave of hope passed through her. *"I thought you were dead. I saw you die, and then they cut off your head."*

"No! I watched you die, and I thought you were the one dead."

She wiped at the tears on her face and tried to sit up, but her body would not cooperate. Pain was everywhere, and she closed her eyes and moaned, wondering if she suffered from broken bones or internal bleeding.

"They're going back to their seats," he mentally said. *"How badly are you hurt? What happened?"*

"I got into a fight with the big one, and I think he won."

"Why would he attack you?"

She focused on her breathing for a moment before responding. *"I don't think he liked being rammed or spit on, and I think his bone necklace was important to him."*

"What?" asked Luke, incredulously?

Even in pain, Luke's reaction brought a slight smile to her face. *"In my defense, I thought you were dead."*

"And that was your plan of escape?"

"Who says there was an escape plan?" she snapped, as a spasm of pain went through her body. She immediately regretted taking her pain out on Luke, and she added softly, *"Have you really looked at these creatures? They have skulls tattooed onto their faces. I have one tattoo, and I know how painful that was. These creatures are covered in them, and they're evil. I was just hoping to end it quickly."*

"You were going for suicide?" She winced in pain instead of responding. *"Alissia, please don't try that again."*

"I feel your sadness seeping into me," she mentally said.

"And I feel your physical pain. You're hurt badly."

"You can feel my pain?" she asked, in surprise.

"Yes. What was he hitting you with?"

"I think just his foot. He stomped on me a couple of times. How did you get here? I saw a spear pierce your heart, and I saw your decapitated head."

"I woke up to Mia slapping my face, and when I realized you were nowhere to be found, we came for you."

"Who?"

"Mia and I. I woke Salvatore before I left and explained I was going after you."

A fresh set of tears began to stream down her face as the realization that Luke was alive hit her again. *"And how did I get taken from the camp with Mia and all the animals around?"*

"They used blow darts on everyone."

"Where are you now?" she asked.

"I'm in a cage hanging from a tree, and I think I know where you are. There's a wall of reeds hanging down outside the left side of my cage, and I believe you're on the other side of it. I can see the three main creatures sitting on a group of logs. They're watching both of us."

Alissia turned her head in the direction of the wall, wishing she could see through it. *"Why?"* she asked.

"I don't know. What have you learned so far?"

With the throbbing pain distracting her, it took a while for her to explain how she had awoken in the hut. She described everything that had happened and been said.

Once done, he asked, *"So you felt an immense amount of fear, and then you witnessed my death?"*

"Exactly. What about you?"

"Mia was on my shoulders, and we weren't far into the bog when I suddenly felt your presence again. That's when I called out to you with my mind, and you told me to wait while you asked questions. I continued walking, and it wasn't long before I saw smoke. Then I crept to the edge of a camp, and I saw..."

Alissia felt a strong wave of sorrow go through her.

"What? What did you see, Luke?"

"You were being burned alive. I watched you and heard your screams, but there was nothing I could do to save you. I couldn't put out the flames, and you were desperately calling my name. You died right in front of me, and it was a painful and slow death."

His mental words were filled with grief, and she could feel his strong emotions, as if they were her own. After a moment, she asked, *"How did you get here?"*

"I'm guessing another dart. My last memory was of the fire, and then I awoke here, wearing very little clothing. They've stripped me of my knives. I was convinced you were dead until I suddenly felt your presence again, along with a great, searing pain. Just when I realized you were still alive, I feared I was losing you again."

"I'm sorry," said Alissia.

"For what?"

"For the suicide mission. Now you're in pain."

"But not as much as you, I'm sure," he said.

"I think I'm healing already. I didn't think all of it through. Apparently, I can be beaten over and over without dying. He would have to finish me off to kill me. Otherwise, my body will heal."

Luke said, *"I wonder if he knew that."*

"Gore knows a lot about the Lamians from the scrolls of his ancestors. He said their people used to trade with them before the Lamians went into hiding. He asked if you and I are zeers. What does that mean?"

"I've never heard of it. However, they left you alone as soon as I began to yell for them to stop. They may be wondering how I knew what was happening to you."

"Do you see Mia or know where she is?"

"No, I haven't seen her since the fire."

"Do you think she's free?" Alissia asked.

"I hope so. That would help."

"Do you think we'll be able to get out of this?"

"Not if you keep attacking their chief warrior!" Luke warned.

"Why do you say he's their chief warrior?"

"The others I see are much younger, and their markings are different. He's also one of the three making the decisions right now. The necklace you took from him could have been a symbol of his power, although I'm not sure."

"Well then, I chose the right thing to do if I wanted to get him angry. It worked."

He sent a mental groan, and she grinned, imagining the look on his face she was accustomed to seeing when he disapproved of her actions—which was quite often.

"Never do that again, Alissia," he said sternly.

"Yes, dear. I won't attack the chief warrior again. I promise." Always hesitant of commitment, she then added, *"Well, I take that back. I may have to attack him again. You never know what the future holds. I'd rather say I'll try not to attack the big, scary beast than to give a firm commitment. I do heal, you know. We can always say this was a test as to how much my body can heal itself. Oh, and now we know that you can feel my physical pain when it's intense. That's something we didn't know."*

"I also feel your presence physically," he said.

"I do, too. It's as if a part of me was missing when I woke up without you in the hut. Do you think the others will try to come for us?"

"No, no one has ever entered this place and come back the same, Alissia. I knew the risk when I entered, and I told Salvatore that no one was to come for us. He agreed and promised he would not allow anyone to leave the trail."

"Even if we never come back?"

"Even if we never come back," he answered firmly. *"Do you want them to come?"*

The small amount of hope that had built up since realizing Luke was alive disappeared, and she let out a resigned sigh. *"No, but how long before they leave us? And what if these creatures decide to kill them?"*

"I don't know how long they'll stay before giving up on us. As for their safety, I believe these creatures are only interested in you."

Her eyes went to the three main creatures sitting on the group of logs. Gore was staring at her, while Gafeen was talking. The third creature seemed to be listening intently to his words.

Turning her attention back to the wall separating her and Luke, she mentally said, *"That was before they decided I'm a human, and they seem to loathe humans, which means we won't make it out alive or with our sanity."*

"You give up so easily?"

"I prefer to call myself a realist," she answered. "Do you see a way out of this?"

"Not yet. However, things may go more in our favor if you don't try to provoke them. Pixets are supposed to appear cute and adorable before they go on a surprise killing binge."

"I'm not a pixet!"

"No, but you sure act like one."

"Are you trying to annoy me right after you found out I'm alive?"

"I'm actually trying to take your mind off the pain, and the easiest emotion to draw from you is anger. It seems to come naturally for you. And truthfully, I think you're hot when you're angry with me."

Alissia could not help but smile again. Out of all the slang words she had taught him from her reality, he seemed to enjoy using hot the most.

The two of them were able to share a long, uninterrupted mental conversation while her body healed, and Alissia was eventually able to stand again. She immediately began to study her surroundings.

The tree her cage was hanging from was massive and looked similar to an oak tree. She guessed it to be very old, as it had many thick and winding branches.

Although there were no bella flowers growing along the tree, green moss covered the majority of it. Dark brown clusters similar to the appearance of Spanish moss hung down from many of the branches.

It would have been a beautiful place if it were not for the rope cages hanging down, along with the sight of many tattooed warriors standing around. Some of the menacing creatures were even resting in hammocks hanging from the branches.

The tree provided much shade, which seemed to be the perfect habitat for a variety of insects. None of them bothered Alissia, but she could see them flying in swarms and climbing along the tree.

After doing a mental search of the area for animals, she only found small, scurrying ones.

Luke told her the swampland was much larger than she had imagined. The road they had been traveling on was only one of many surrounded by trees carved into skulls, and with the variety in skin tones of the creatures, he guessed their population to be substantial.

This was an ancient civilization, and from what Alissia had seen so far, they still lived in the old ways. Their clothing and weapons were crude, their warriors looked like horrific savages, and simple hygiene did not seem to be important to them. Alissia could not help but imagine them as headhunters and cannibals, and fear was strong within her.

Even if they did escape from their captors, they did not know where they were. She remembered how she had awoken for a short moment in a boat, and she imagined they were deep within a swamp. She knew from living near swampland as a child that people could easily get lost and die in this type of ecosystem. Even if Luke could forage for food and she could get an animal to lead them out of the bog, she was certain the warriors could easily hunt them down.

Although Luke was trying to be optimistic, she did not foresee a happy ending to their situation. To her, a quick death was the best thing they could hope for, but she kept those thoughts to herself.

Chapter 5

lissia's gaze followed the three main creatures, along with a small group of warriors, as they walked to where she guessed Luke's cage to be. Gafeen was holding a lit torch, yet it was still daylight, and this greatly worried her. Once she could not see them behind the wall of reeds, she immediately reached out to Luke.

"What do they want?"

"I don't know. I don't speak this language."

The third man that had not yet spoken to Alissia walked over to her cage and stared at her. He was about the same age as Gore and was dressed in a skirt made of animal skin. He wore many necklaces made of bones and teeth, and a black tribal tattoo covered most of his tan face. Large ones covered his right and left shoulders and traveled down both arms.

"What do you want?" she asked in the ancient language.

He said nothing, while continuing to stare.

Hoping he was different than Gafeen and Gore, she said, somewhat pleadingly, "We didn't enter your swamp, and we haven't done anything to you. *Please* let us go."

The creature turned his gaze toward Luke's cage, and Alissia's eyes followed. She could barely see Gore at the edge of the reed wall, and he was staring into what she believed was Luke's enclosure.

She began to hear scuffling noises, and she mentally asked, *"What's going on? Are you okay?"*

"Fine," came Luke's clipped response.

Something was wrong, and Alissia grabbed the roping of her cage and pressed her face into it, in an attempt to see past the wall.

The sound of fighting worsened, and she yelled out to Gore. "Tell them to stop! Luke hasn't done anything! Leave him alone!"

Gore glanced over at her before he took a few steps, and she lost sight of him past the wall.

"Luke, what's going on?"

Anger and fear all at once slammed into her, and then a fierce, burning pain shot through her right hand. She screamed out loud and fell to her knees.

"You experienced that?"

Holding her hand to her chest, she glared at the creature standing outside of her cage. She could barely talk, as her hand was throbbing greatly.

"What do you want?" she asked, between ragged breaths.

Gore was soon standing beside the unknown man. "Is he your zeer?" he questioned.

"I don't even know what a zeer is!" Alissia yelled angrily.

Luke's voice entered her head. *"Are you in pain?"*

She responded, *"What did they do to you?"*

"I've been burned. Are you in pain?"

Anger flared inside of her, and she turned to Gore and demanded, "Why are you doing this? We didn't do anything to you! I didn't enter your precious swamp, and he only came to find me!"

Gore cocked his head to one side and seemed to be studying her as Gafeen walked up to stand beside him.

"So you know he's alive? I thought he was dead," said Gore.

She answered, "I don't know what game you're playing, but I saw him die. He saw me die, and now all I know is you're torturing him for no reason."

"The torture would not be necessary, my dear, if we believed you would talk to us. However, I can see the stubbornness within you, and we'll have to find the answers on our own," said Gore.

"What answers? I don't know what a zeer is, and that is the only question you keep asking me."

He frowned. "Did you steal your gifts? You don't seem to know much about yourself. Explain how you came to be. How did you change?"

"I didn't steal anything. The Lamians—"

Rage flashed across Gore's face, and he spat out, "You dare to call them by that name! Only a human would dishonor them in such a way. That's enough proof in itself! Lies and dishonesty! You stole from them!"

The pain in her hand was severe, and she worried for Luke.

"I didn't steal from them. They chose to save my life," she said, through clenched teeth. "I had never even met them, yet they made the choice to save me, which leads me to believe they are an honorable people, unlike you and your kind."

She practically screamed, "You're savages! Kidnapping and torture! We've done nothing to you, and we just want to go on our way. Leave us alone and let us go!"

"Ah, but you know no human has ever left our home alive or mentally competent. That's how we do things," said Gafeen with a leering grin.

"Yes, but we didn't enter your swamp freely. This is your fault, not ours!"

Gore said, "Cooperate with us, and we may consider your release."

Alissia shook her head in disbelief. "How am I not cooperating with you? I don't even know what you want."

"How did you change?" asked Gore.

She gave a frustrated sigh before answering, "I was about to die, and the La—and *they* saved me. However, someone interrupted them, and they unexpectedly had to leave me. That's why I never got to ask questions. Now I'm on my way to get those answers."

"You're going to them?" Gore asked.

"Yes, that's where we're traveling to now."

"And these humans? You're taking them with you?"

She began to rub her hand, in an attempt to lessen the pain. "Not all of them, but some of them are friends of theirs. They've already met and traded with them."

"Traded with them?" asked Gore, not hiding his confusion.

"Yes, years ago when they went into hiding, they used some humans to help. Throughout the years, the human descendants have continued to protect them, and they do a lot of trading with each other."

"Power stones," said Gore thoughtfully. "The humans still have use of the power stones?"

"You mean jade? It's rare and only used by various government officials, but only a select few of the humans know where they truly come from."

By now, all three of the creatures had scowls on their faces. Gafeen shook his head and said, as if to himself, "So after all the humans have done, they still have use of the power stones."

"Luke, are you okay? How bad are you?" she mentally asked.

"It's just my hand. I'll survive. What have you learned?"

"They're finally talking to me. Hold on."

Turning her attention back to the creatures, she said, "I didn't say everyone had use of the power stones. What do you mean by power stones? Are we talking about the same thing?"

Gore answered, "They wear them around their necks throughout their entire lives so the stones can absorb their power, and many of them were tortured and killed for those stones. It's hard for me to believe they continue to give them to the humans after all that happened. Why would they do that?"

Alissia shook her head. "I don't know. Maybe if you let me go, I could ask them."

Without a word, Gore turned around, and the other two creatures followed him back to the group of logs. They sat down and began to talk, and although she strained to hear their conversation, their raspy voices did not travel far.

Just as she finished telling Luke all that had been said, a tattooed warrior walked over to her enclosure. He hung a bag made out of sackcloth on a limb, and she watched as he reached inside before pulling out a large snail about the size of his hand. He sneered at her while ripping the poor creature from its home. After tossing the empty shell aside, he grinned and bit off the animal's head.

As she watched his sharp teeth tear through the flesh, Alissia began to feel nauseous. The creature seemed to enjoy her reaction, and he continued to make a show of his meal.

Once finished, he reached into the bag and pulled out another snail. He held it out to her, and she shook her head violently. "I don't eat animals."

He laughed heartily and tossed the snail back into the bag. Then he pulled something similar to a piece of sugar cane out. He cut off a portion for himself and popped it into his mouth before slicing a piece for her. She accepted his offer and began to study it.

The warrior cut off more for himself and motioned for her to eat as his teeth ripped into the cane. She frowned. In an attempt to clean it after it had been in his grimy hands, she peeled the outer layer of the cane before tentatively chewing on the end of it.

It tasted plain, but it was edible. After witnessing the assault on the snail, she did not know when she would be offered something else she trusted herself to eat. She continued to gnaw on the meager bit of food as she watched the creature walk over to Luke's cage.

"I think the cane is safe to eat. I'm eating it," she mentally said. Her hand still burned severely, and she instinctively held it up, as if it were truly injured.

She guessed Luke took the food, because the warrior soon returned to retrieve his bag. Without a word, he walked away. As Alissia ate in silence, she could feel Luke's anger seeping into her, and she decided against trying to make conversation. He was in a lot of pain and not happy about it.

The same warrior came back after a while. He held a long rope with a noose on it, and as he walked into her enclosure, she scooted away from him.

He smiled, as if amused by her fear. "I'm not to hurt you. I come to give you privacy. Come. I must tie you before we walk out."

She frowned, knowing she had no choice in the matter, and he put the noose over her head and secured it.

"Now we go." Like a dog on a leash, he led her toward the entrance.

Alissia took that opportunity to step out of the enclosure and dart to Luke's cage, hanging not far from hers. The guard did not stop her, and as soon as Luke saw her, he rushed toward her. Pressing his body into the ropes, he reached out with his uninjured hand. She eagerly grabbed it and stared up at him.

His face was swollen, with some bruising, and there was blood over his right eye, where there was a small gash. However, it was nothing compared to the skin peeling from his burned hand.

"Why do you have a noose around your neck?" She could hear the fear in his voice, as well as feel it seeping into her own body.

She reached through the roping of the cage and caressed his cheek with her unharmed left hand.

"I don't know. He said he's not going to hurt me and something about privacy. If anyone is going to kill me, Gafeen will be the one to do it."

Her voice cracked as she looked down and added, "Your hand looks bad. You need a doctor."

Luke's eyes never left her face. "It will heal."

"Yeah, but I feel your pain, so I know how much it's bothering you." Alissia turned her head and met the eyes of Gore, Gafeen, and the other man, still sitting on the group of logs. They were watching her and Luke.

"He needs a healer for his hand!" she demanded. "Why did you torture him?"

"Do you feel his pain in your own hand?" Gore asked.

Her eyes widened with understanding. "You did this to see if I would feel it as well. You're doing experiments on us, aren't you?"

"Do you feel the same pain?" he asked again.

"And why should I give you the satisfaction of an answer?"

"We can always do more experiments until we understand things better," said Gafeen, somewhat eagerly.

She glared at the creatures but admitted, "Yes, I feel his pain. Now you can leave him alone."

"And you can mentally speak with each other. Correct?" said Gore. When Alissia nodded, he added, "Yet, he still has human blood and eyes, and his marking is different from yours. You're branded with two tiny handprints, and he only shows one larger handprint. Why is that?"

She clenched her jaw and hissed, "I don't know. Maybe that's one of the reasons why we need to see the Lamians." She did not care if the word offended them. Her anger was strong.

"Who branded him?" Gore asked.

Alissia glared at him for a moment, the pain in her hand, along with Luke's strong emotions, affecting her mood. She let out a frustrated sigh and said, "I marked him to save his life, but I don't know how or what I've done. In fact, we don't know all of the consequences, and that's why we're eager to visit the Lamians—or whatever you call them. We don't know a lot of things, and we want answers too."

"So he doesn't share your gifts?" asked Gore.

"No."

"Yet he is your zeer," he said thoughtfully, as if to himself. He motioned to the guard, and the noose tightened around Alissia's neck as it was given a swift tug. She stared back at Luke as she was forced away.

Once out of Luke's vision, she mentally reassured him she was not in any danger. After a quick stop at a crude bathroom, she was led back toward her cage but was surprised when the guard stopped in front of Luke's enclosure and opened it. He released her from the noose and motioned for her to step inside.

She immediately rushed to Luke's side, and he pulled her into his arms tightly, with his injured hand held out behind her.

Tears threatened to break free as Alissia clung to him. With her head against his chest, she listened to his heartbeat and said a thankful prayer he was still alive. They lay in silence for a long while, both of them all too aware of the excruciating pain they shared.

"She's here and will help."

At the sound of Gore's voice, Alissia turned around to find the three creatures now standing outside of the cage with a female. She looked to be in her early twenties, but appearances could easily be deceiving when it came to the ages of the foreign creatures.

The girl had wild, knotted dark hair. She wore a simple dress made of sackcloth, and dirt was smeared across her face. Her skin was tanned, and she had the same frightening black eyes as all of the others. Alissia noticed the look of hatred upon the girl's face as their eyes met.

"This is Selona. She's a healer and will help with his hand," said Gore.

Alissia stared at the girl for a moment before turning her attention to Gore. "So now you want to heal him? Why'd you have to burn him in the first place?"

"It's up to you whether his hand is to be wrapped for the night. She has a mixture that will ease the pain and will help with the healing. Do you accept or not?"

Turning to Luke, Alissia explained the situation. He frowned in discomfort as he pulled away from their embrace and stood. Then he walked to the edge of the cage and sat down, holding his hand through one of the gaps in the netting.

"You trust her?" she asked in surprise.

"I don't trust any of them, but I know you can feel every bit of the pain I'm feeling. And I don't want that for you tonight."

Her hand was throbbing, and she wondered if the pain was worse for him.

She sat down beside him, and they both watched as the girl slathered a green pasty substance all over his hand.

"What is it?" Alissia asked.

Selona answered, without looking up, "A mixture of plants and algae that will aid with the healing." She reached into her basket and pulled out two large, bright-green leaves about the size of an elephant's ear. She wrapped the wound tightly with both leaves before turning to Gore.

"It's finished."

He turned to one of the guards and nodded. After picking up her basket, Selona silently followed the guard away from the tree. She never looked back.

Alissia stared at the three creatures, and they stared back at her in silence for a long moment. Then Gafeen jeered, "We shall resume in the morning."

As they turned to leave, she yelled to their backs, "Resume what?"

They continued on without even a glance back, and Alissia let out a groan as she got up and walked to the other side of the cage. She sat down, and Luke joined her, picking up her left hand with his. He gave it a quick kiss before setting their hands on his leg.

She noticed his clothing, or lack of clothing, and tried to smile. "They've adopted you into their tribe," she teased, looking at his animal-skin skirt.

"Have you looked in the mirror?"

She followed his stare beneath his raised eyebrows and realized how little she had on. Luckily, these tribal creatures did believe in covering the females' breasts, even if it was only with a tight wrap.

Although it was not yet dark, the nocturnal frogs and insects were beginning their nightly chorus, and the air was getting cooler. The insects around them were much bigger than what she was used to seeing, and Luke's body seemed to be covered in welts from their bites and stings.

"It's not so bad when you're around." At her confusion, he added, "The insects. They don't come near me when you're around."

She tried to smile, but it didn't come. "What if this is our last night together?"

"Then at least I'll get to spend it holding you. I'd rather die tomorrow having loved you, than die of old age without ever having known you, Alissia. You've brought that much happiness into my life."

"I thought I made your life miserable."

Luke chuckled lightly. "Yes, you did in the beginning." Shaking his head, he became serious. "And yet, now I could never live without you."

"What do you think will happen tomorrow?"

He let go of her hand and carefully positioned his body onto his side. Then he gently pulled her down beside him. Although he was careful not to let anything touch his injured hand during the process, he winced, and she felt a jolt of pain shoot through her own hand.

Once settled, with her back against his chest and his injured hand resting in front of her, he said, "Tomorrow we shall learn more about our situation. And you never know. Your little pixet friend may even decide to show herself."

"You're not worried?" Even as Alissia asked the question, she knew the answer. She could feel his fear, along with hers. He was trying to be strong.

Luke let out a small breath. "Yes, I'm very worried about what they'll do to you. However, this morning I watched you die a gruesome death, and I was completely powerless in saving you."

His body trembled, and a wave of grief flooded into her, causing her eyes to fill with tears. "It was the worst pain I've ever experienced in my entire life."

They shared a moment of silence before she asked, "Luke?"

"Yes?"

"I love you."

"I love you too, Alissia."

She closed her eyes, realizing how weary her body felt. Even her restless mind and throbbing hand could not keep her from drifting into darkness, and her last thought was how she wished she had more time to spend in Luke's arms.

All through the night, she awoke from the pain but took some comfort in Luke's embrace, as she drifted in and out of sleep. It was barely dawn when she let out a frustrated sigh, and her eyes opened wide.

"This could be a problem for us." Luke slowly sat up and leaned his back against the enclosure.

Alissia followed his lead and rearranged her body so that she was sitting between his legs, with her back against his chest. His wound reeked of the plant-based salve beneath the leaves on his hand, and she gently set it away from her.

"What could be a problem?" she asked, while trying to stifle a yawn.

"With my lifestyle, I've never really cared about certain consequences," he said hesitantly. "However, I now worry about how my actions will affect you." After a pause, he added, "If I get hurt during a sword fight, or even a simple fight, you'll share my pain, which is what I want to protect you from—pain. Any pain."

She shook her head. "I didn't feel anything when they did that to your face or when Grady hit you in the barn, so I think it has to be severe."

"What about if I get killed? How will that affect you? I mean, physically, not emotionally."

As Alissia laced her fingers through Luke's left hand and set it on her stomach, she remembered that Gore had mentioned something about her dying because of the connection. She chose to ignore that thought. "It would kill me, either way. I don't want to even think about that. Remember? I've practically experienced your death twice already. I mean, I've never imagined us having a normal life together. Now I just want us to *be* together."

"I've been thinking about what happened to us yesterday. Those visions we had."

"And?"

"The people that have entered this land and come back alive lost their sanity. They went mad and spent the rest of their lives tormented by visions, and I think that's what we were experiencing yesterday. We both saw things that didn't happen, and it was the worst thing that could happen to us. Our biggest fears."

She thought for a moment. "That would make sense, and I don't think they planned it to happen like that. When I first met Gore, he was being nice to me, but when I woke up after the vision, everything was different. They knew I was human, and they suddenly hated me."

"They also knew about our connection," said Luke. "Which leads me to believe I was somehow infected with the visions, and you contracted them from me."

Alissia closed her eyes as a wave of pain shot through her hand. "Did you get any sleep last night?"

"No, and neither did you," he answered. "I tried to take my mind off the pain by thinking through everything that happened. I also spent most of my time watching them yesterday, and although I can't understand their words, it's obvious Gore and Gafeen disagree about something. They also seem to do a lot of explaining to the third creature. He didn't talk much and spent most of his time listening to the other two."

"Yeah, Gafeen is eager to get rid of me, I think. As for Gore, I don't know. They all despise me because I'm human."

"And they want to know more about us being zeers," Luke added thoughtfully.

"Whatever that means." Alissia frowned. "I don't understand how I suddenly know the ancient language but don't know this word."

"There are a lot of things we don't understand."

A chopping sound startled them both, and they turned their heads and watched as one of the guards set a sweanut down in the enclosure. His large hand was wet from the fresh liquid.

Alissia retrieved the fruit and took a sip of its bitter juice before sitting back down to face Luke.

"They call it a sweanut. I drank some yesterday morning." She held it up to his mouth. "Let me help you."

His stomach growled, and she was reminded of how hungry she was as well.

Shortly after they emptied the drink and set it aside, they noticed the three main creatures walking toward them. Alissia's entire body tensed, and she instinctively lifted her chin defiantly.

They stopped outside of the cage, and the first thing she noticed was Gafeen's malicious grin.

"Shall we try this again, little one?" He reached his hand through the cage toward Luke. Meeting her eyes, he said, smugly, "Remember yesterday?"

He turned his attention to Luke, and black streaks slowly began to appear around his eyes, beneath his skin. As the streaks began to travel along his face, Alissia felt a tight grip around her neck.

Her eyes widened with fear when she noticed Luke gasping for air, and she began to claw at her neck, in a desperate attempt to remove the invisible vice.

By now, Gafeen's head was covered in the black streaks, and an evil grin filled his face.

"Enough!" commanded the man that had yet to be introduced. When Gafeen did not listen, he slipped his hand through the cage and took ahold of Gafeen's, pushing it down. "I said enough. It's not time."

Alissia fell to the ground, gasping for air, and Luke did the same. After regaining her breath, she glared at Gore and said coldly, "If you're going to kill us, just kill us! Stop playing games."

He shook his head calmly. "We still have questions."

"Well, you're not asking any! What was that all about?" she demanded.

"You've already informed us you don't know all the answers."

She stood, and Luke did the same. "And what question did that just answer?"

"It confirmed your connection. We now know that if we kill the man, you will also die."

Terror slammed into her, and knowing her face betrayed her true emotions, Alissia turned toward Luke. He stepped up and took her by the hand.

"What's wrong?" he mentally asked, giving a light squeeze.

She quickly recovered her composure and turned back around. Meeting Gore's eyes, she sneered, "If you want to kill me so badly, I'm sure chopping off my head would do just fine."

He chuckled to himself before answering, "Yes, I'm sure that would work too."

Looking at Gafeen, he nodded. "It's time. I have all I need."

Luke's mental voice was firm when he asked, *"What's wrong? I need to know."*

Alissia turned and met his eyes, and with all of her willpower, she tried to disconnect herself from her feelings. She mentally answered, *"I think our day is about to end."*

She had to look away quickly, as a sudden wave of emotion flooded through her, like an open dam.

Until that moment, she had never cared so much about dying. With her faith in the Creator, she was certain of where she would go after death, and at times, she had even longed for an end to all of her worldly struggles.

Yet things were suddenly different. For the first time in her life, she truly had something to look forward to. Although nothing had ever been certain about her and Luke's future, she had believed they would be together, and now their time was up.

Luke grabbed Alissia and shoved her behind him. He then stood protectively in front of her, and a tear rolled down her face, knowing his fight would be futile.

She watched three massive warriors enter the cage, and with tears streaming freely down her face, she mentally said, *"I love you, Luke."*

Her loud scream filled the air as they knocked him to the ground, and she nearly collapsed from the pain that shot through her hand. She watched in terror as one of the warriors sat on Luke's back and shoved his face into the woven floor of the enclosure.

A blinding pain shot through her hand as they forced both of Luke's hands behind his back. One of the creatures put his knee on top of the injured hand, and Alissia screamed in agony before darkness overtook her.

Chapter 6

The searing pain in her hand immediately brought Alissia back to reality when she regained consciousness. She winced at her throbbing headache before noticing Gafeen leering down at her. With her hands tied tightly behind her back and a noose around her neck, it took a while before she was able to maneuver herself into a sitting position.

She found herself in a large, wooden canoe with a warrior paddling in the front and Gafeen paddling in the back. They were deep within a swamp, and although her surroundings were somewhat similar to the swampland around her childhood home in Southeast Georgia, the massive trees shooting out of the water were much larger than the cypress she was used to seeing.

Their many large and winding upper branches were covered in greenery, creating a canopy that left the entire swamp in a deep shade. The water itself reminded her of Georgia swamps. It was pitch black, and although her head hurt too much for her to reach out with her mind, she imagined it to be filled with numerous foreboding animals.

"Luke? Luke, are you still alive?"

Although she heard a faint whisper within her mind, she could not make out the words, and she could barely feel his presence. She anxiously scanned all of the many boats in the water that seemed to be filled with warriors, but Luke was nowhere to be found.

The throbbing in her hand was worse than it had been that morning, but she took comfort in the pain. To her, that meant Luke was still alive. She squinted while staring at the crude boat Gore rode in, knowing it was large enough to conceal a body.

"Looking for someone?" asked Gafeen, with an evil grin.

Alissia glared at him for a moment before turning her body so that she was facing the front, with her back to him.

He laughed heartily and taunted, "Your time is almost up, little one."

While clenching her teeth, she chided herself for having attacked him, as she now regretted achieving her goal of making him angry with her.

The trees were filled with intriguing animals. Strange looking birds rested on their branches, and there was an unfamiliar humming noise within the swamp. At first, Alissia believed the noise to be coming from insects. However, she soon realized the strange sound was caused by the voices of many feliums. The tiny fairies seemed to be everywhere, and they zipped through the air with great speed. Like Skatonia, they were curious little creatures. Some even darted around her head to get a closer look.

As their boat passed the hollow base of a large, cypress-looking tree, Alissia's eyes unexpectedly locked onto another set of eyes.

Unlike the solid black ones of the other creatures, these were big and completely round. Their black pupils were surrounded by gold.

Although most of the creature's body was submerged in the dark water, its upper torso and facial features led Alissia to believe it was a female. Her thick, green skin was shiny, and although she was not wearing any upper body clothing, her breasts—along with the rest of what Alissia could see—looked like she was wearing a tight-fitting rubber suit. She had long, brown hair that looked like thick, leathery ropes coming down, as if each strand could be used for a whip. Her ears were big and pointy with gills beneath them, and she had a flat nose.

Ignoring her headache, Alissia reached out with her mind, but she immediately realized she could not connect with the creature or the feliums. By now, she was coming to the conclusion she could only connect with simple animals, not advanced beings.

Alissia twisted around and continued to stare after the boat passed, and the creature seemed just as curious about her. She left the hollow portion of the tree, and they watched each other for a long moment before the creature suddenly dove under the water. When a large fin came up, Alissia realized she had just seen a mermaid. Except, instead of a beautiful one resembling a human—like those she had read about in fairytales—this one lived in a swamp and looked somewhat menacing.

By now it was impossible to ignore the throbbing in her head and the intense pain shooting into her hand, and she was more than uncomfortable with her hands tied behind her back. She tried to reach out to Luke again, but there was no response.

They traveled for a long while in silence before trees along the bank of the water began to thin. Grim statues of skeletal creatures in various positions with outstretched hands adorned the swamp here.

Long, swinging ropes hung down from some of the trees, where barely clad children were lined up to playfully drop into the water. Simple boats were tied to docks, and there were many huts with outside fires and dead animals cooking over them. A large, open shelter with a thatched roof was filled with people, and Alissia guessed it to be a market.

Most of the creatures wore sackcloth clothing or animal skins, and unlike the warriors, their bodies were marked with tribal tattoos instead of the hideous ones that looked like the insides of a person.

A small female child was sitting on a white animal similar to an alligator. She was holding onto a harness that was attached to its mouth, as if it were her pet horse.

Some of them noticed Alissia and the many warrior-loaded boats in the water, and they stopped what they were doing and stared. However, many of them did not even look her way.

The sight of three dead bodies hanging from a tree over the water caught her attention, and terror slammed into her. Her mind went to thoughts of her friends being tortured, and it was not until they got closer that she realized none of the bodies were human.

Their bulky frames and the few tribal tattoos she could see in what was left of the rotting skin told her they were the same barbaric creatures as her captors. Large black birds were fighting over their meal, and as Alissia's boat got closer, she could smell the rotten stench. She had to fight with her body not to gag. However, it had been over a day since she had eaten a proper meal, and she knew her stomach was empty.

A menacing laughter came from behind. "Now we'll learn of your fate, little one, and I'm very confident you'll be given over to me."

Dread filled her, and it took her a moment before she could force a cool smile. She turned in her seat and looked back at him. Trying to sound casual, she said, "Is this about the necklace? To be fair, you kidnapped me first."

He shook his head and glared at her. "You're a human and don't deserve to live."

Alissia turned back around. There was no arguing with that. It was obvious these creatures despised humans, and after what she knew about the torturing of the Lamians, she could understand why.

She began to wonder if the Lamians felt the same way but did not have time to dwell on those thoughts. As the boat slid into the muddy bank, Alissia struggled not to fall. The warrior in front of her hopped out and grabbed the end of the rope tied around her neck.

Once she was standing on land, her eyes searched each of the boats as they pulled up to the bank, and relief filled her when she finally saw Luke's body crumpled between two warriors. Although she desperately wanted to run to him, her captor pulled her away.

Alissia walked barefoot along the dirt paths of the community, and as she passed, everyone stopped what they were doing and stared. Her senses were in overload as many repulsive odors filled the air, and if it were not for her empty stomach and the intense pain distracting her, she imagined she would have retched the entire walk.

Almost every fire was cooking meat, and one large cauldron was overflowing with what looked like snakes, frogs, and a large alligator head sticking out from it.

Although she had eaten frog legs and alligator tail many times as a child, she had never seen anything as disgusting as these creatures' meals. It seemed they did not waste any part of an animal's body.

None of them seemed to care about basic hygiene either. Their hair was wild and knotted, dirt covered much of their clothing and body, and many of them filled their mouths with the same green sludge she had seen earlier.

Gore, Gafeen, and the third man led the procession, and they stopped at a large hut with many young warriors surrounding it. One of the warriors knocked on the door, and a plump old man answered it. When he noticed Alissia, he nodded and stepped out.

She immediately knew something was different about him, as none of the other creatures were dressed anything like him. He wore a long, brightly colored skirt made of tiny beads, and the tribal tattoos along his upper body were red, not black. His face was covered in bright red paint, and he had a bone spiked through his nose, with smaller ones in his ears. He wore a headdress with red feathers at the front, and his chest was covered in a large necklace made of carved bones.

He walked straight to Alissia and studied her for a moment.

"So this is her?"

Gafeen answered, "She's human, and there's no value to her."

The man nodded without taking his eyes off her. "And she speaks our language?"

"Yes, and I have much to tell you," said Gore.

He turned to Gore. "And you've brought a witness?"

The third man that had never been introduced stepped forward. "I'm their witness."

"Very well. Let's get started." He motioned to one of his guards. "Take her away."

Alissia was taken to an enclosure similar to the one she and Luke had spent the night in. However, her new surroundings were much more populated, and many eyes turned her way.

The noose was removed and her hands were untied, leaving patches of purple, dried blood against her skin.

She was in a lot of physical pain, and her body was exhausted. In an attempt to fall asleep, she stretched out on the floor of her new prison.

"Where are you?"

Excitement and relief filled Alissia at the sound of Luke's voice in her head. She eagerly answered, *"I'm safe. Are you still in the boat?"*

"I'm getting out now."

He then began to describe his surroundings, and it was not long before he was standing in the cage with her. The guards were not gentle when they pulled the noose from around his neck and cut his wrists loose. Alissia shuddered in pain throughout the entire process.

Once the guards left, she and Luke ran into each other's arms, and both of their bodies trembled with emotion as they clung to each other. After a long moment, she kissed his chest and pulled away.

She wiped the tears from her eyes and looked up into his battered face. "You're hurt badly. Let me help you sit down." Once they were settled, she said, "Let me see your hand."

He leaned his head against the enclosure and closed his eyes before holding out his injured hand.

"Does your head hurt too?" he asked.

"Yes, ever since I woke up."

Although the leaves that had been tightly wrapped around his hand were nearly falling off, it took a while for Alissia to remove them. The process was extremely painful for both of them.

"Oh, wow. It doesn't look good," she said, staring down at the mix of blisters and peeling skin.

He opened his swollen eyes and tried to smile. "Remember the first night I met you outside of the inn?"

"Yes. How could I forget?"

Luke picked up her left hand with his and tugged on it. She took the hint and carefully arranged her body so that her back was resting against his chest, with his injured hand off to the side.

"You lied to me and gave me leo to knock me out."

He chuckled as he put his other arm around her waist. "I eased your pain, and I never lied to you."

Entwining her fingers into his, she said, "Yeah, but you didn't tell me you were knocking me out either."

Alissia could tell he was falling asleep. Even through the pain, his battered body was fatigued, and it was not long before she joined him in a deep slumber filled with a series of vivid dreams. Each time her eyes shot open with a start, they would unwillingly close again, resuming the troubling visions.

The sound of nearby voices woke her with a jerk, and Luke's grip on her waist tightened.

An unfamiliar warrior entered the cage, and although he looked young, his body was already covered with gory tattoos. He had horns attached to his shiny head, and she caught herself wondering if they were natural or somehow added to make him appear more intimidating.

"It's time we talked, my dear."

Alissia met the eyes of the brightly dressed man she had seen earlier. He was standing outside of the cage. Gore and her usual captors were nowhere in sight.

Luke's arm tightened even more around her waist. *"He says it's time we talk. I think he's their leader,"* she mentally said. She looked down at his injured hand, and then she turned her attention back to the eccentric looking man.

"I'll talk to you, but he needs medicine for his hand," she said with more assertiveness than she felt.

He nodded. "I'll have my healer come." He paused thoughtfully. "I can also give you something for the pain."

"He's the one that needs it, not me."

He shook his head. "No. It's not for humans. Your body will take it, and from what Gore has told me, both of your bodies will feel the effects."

"How do you know it won't kill him, if it's not for humans?"

"It will not kill you, and as a result, it will not kill him. Now come," he said with authority.

Alissia lifted Luke's arm from her waist. "He says he'll send you his healer. I'm going to talk to him."

"Please be careful."

"I will." She stood and gave a reassuring smile before walking out of the cage.

"You'll join me for a meal, and I'll hear what you have to say," he said. "But first, let me speak to my healer while you prepare."

Without waiting for her response, he turned and walked away. The young guard with the horns said, "This way."

A small group of guards led her a short distance away to a hut, and then the young guard pulled back a flimsy wall of reeds. It took her a moment to realize she was staring at a primitive bathroom before she nodded and stepped inside.

A short while later, she stepped out of the hut feeling a bit refreshed, having splashed cool water onto her face and redone her ponytail. Although the pain in her hand was still intense, she realized her headache was gone.

If the leader was going to send his healer to Luke and was willing to listen to her, she decided she would make the attempt to be on her best behavior.

"Where are you, Alissia?"

"I'm safe. They just took me to a very interesting bathroom, and now I think I'm going to eat." Her stomach growled, and she added, *"I'll bring something back for you."*

The guards led her to the back of the leader's hut, and beneath a small pavilion, the old man was sitting on a large, woven mat. Some baskets and other picnic items were arranged near him, and he was talking to another man sitting next to him. When he noticed her, he motioned for her to join him, and the other man stood. The unknown man watched her for a moment before turning to leave.

"Come. Sit," the old man said, pointing in front of him. Alissia sat down and smiled politely. "My name is Tolden, and I'm the chief of my people."

He picked up a clay decanter and poured two drinks before motioning for her to take one of the mugs. She obeyed and took a cautious sip, and realizing it was a sweet and fruity drink, she quickly gulped it down. He laughed and poured more.

Tolden opened a basket and pulled something similar to a large crawfish from it. It was about the size of her hand, and she immediately noticed it was still moving and very much alive. She watched as he licked his lips before turning it over, revealing a mass of black eggs attached to it. After scraping them off with his grimy tongue, he closed his eyes in pleasure and chewed slowly.

Then his eyes flew open, and he wasted no time in popping off the head of the helpless animal. He sucked the brains out, tossed the empty head aside, and then ripped open the body's exoskeleton to get at the meat within.

Alissia stared into the mug she was holding, fighting her sudden nausea.

Once finished, he threw the shell aside before slapping his hands together. "It's been a while since I've enjoyed such delicacy. The eggs are only available a few weeks out of the year."

Alissia took a sip from her drink and tried to smile.

"Ah, but you can't eat meat. Is that correct?"

"That's correct."

"Hmm… There should be something here for you." Tolden peered into each basket before selecting one and setting it down in front of her. "You can eat what's in here." He pushed another one toward her. "You can choose from this one as well."

Each basket contained an assortment of raw fruits and vegetables she had never seen. As she went to reach into one of them, a sharp pain shot through her hand, and she cried out while pulling it back.

"What happened?" she mentally asked.

"The healer's here. Get ready for some pain."

Tolden smiled. "I believe my healer is with your man." Alissia clenched her teeth in pain and nodded. "Tonight I'll give you something strong to help you sleep."

She let out a shaky breath. "Why did they do this to him?"

He was sucking on something resembling a chicken's foot. Although it was not moving and appeared to have at least been cooked, it made a crunching sound when he bit it.

"Nothing personal against you," he said, while chewing. "Gore and Gafeen have two very different ideas when it comes to you."

A jolt went through her hand, and she winced. It took her a moment before she said, "And what are those ideas?"

He finished off the foot before answering, "Gafeen has probably given you hints to his desires. For him to be one of our head warriors, I'm surprised at how simple it is, as he seems set on torture and death."

"And Gore?"

Tolden took a few loud gulps from his mug. "His is a bit more complex. He's the keeper of our ancient scrolls, and he has a greater knowledge when it comes to the past. He sees you as an opportunity to make things better for our people. He seeks improvement."

"So why all the torture?"

"Torture?" He took a large grub out and placed it on his tongue. "I wouldn't take Gore's experiments personally. He's spent his entire life reading those scrolls, and then you suddenly appeared. You can't imagine how excited he is, although I admit he's not very happy about finding out you're actually human. Then there's this connection between you and your man. Gore was only seeking answers."

A cool, tingling sensation went through her hand, and she looked down. *"What's going on?"* she mentally asked.

"He's slathering some horrid smelling goo over my hand. What have you learned?"

"Still working on it. Hold on."

Alissia looked up at Tolden, only to witness another large grub going into his mouth. "Are you going to kill me and Luke?"

He chewed thoughtfully before answering. "Right now I have two choices set before me, and I have to decide which is best for my people. You see, every human that has ever walked into this swampland has either died a gruesome death or left with the poison of a felium in their blood. Those are the rules, and our ancestors established them the very first time a human entered this swamp. They've never been broken, and those rules have protected us all these years.

"I imagine you're not that old, even in human years, and Gore tells me you're ignorant of the great races. You don't know that our land was once inhabited by many powerful beings, yet they lived in peace until the humans arrived."

Tolden shook his head and frowned. "The scrolls say it was the Medicians that trusted the humans first. They talked some of the other races into showing themselves, and eventually, the humans deceived them all.

"Our land became filled with war and death, all because of humans. Yet, this swamp was preserved and untouched by their deeds—well, almost untouched. When all the great races went into hiding, we lost those relationships and trade. Each great race became isolated."

Alissia looked down at her hand. It was beginning to feel numb, which was much better than the throbbing pain. She pondered over Tolden's words for a moment before looking back up—just in time to see his sharp teeth rip off the leg of a shiny black salamander. She quickly turned away. However, his chewing and smacking were too great to be ignored, and she began to ramble, in an attempt to drown out the sounds.

"So the Medicians changed me, which makes sense, with them being healers and all. And they were the first to trust the humans, and then the humans took over the land, started populating, making wars and dividing the land, and they got greedy and started killing the Medicians. Right?"

He belched loudly. "That's correct."

Alissia heard a tiny squeak, along with more ripping of flesh, and she felt herself getting nauseous again.

"What's wrong?" Luke mentally asked.

"It seems these creatures love to eat animals while they're still alive, which is now making me quite happy with becoming a vegetarian—even if it wasn't by choice."

"Are you safe?"

"For now, and he's actually talking to me so I'm getting some answers. You should try to get some rest."

"Not until you're back with me."

Alissia risked looking at the chief again, and she thought she noticed a look of amusement on his face before he tore off another leg from the helpless creature in his hand.

Pretending to be interested in the basket of fruit in front of her, she said, "So no human has ever left this swamp alive or mentally competent, and Luke is a human. Is that the problem?"

"We also consider you a human," he replied, matter-of-factly.

She looked up and said, somewhat pleadingly, "But we didn't enter this swamp on our own. I was kidnapped, and Luke came to get me. We never had any intentions of leaving the trail and going past those skull trees. We're innocent in this."

Tolden nodded, and she looked back down after inadvertently catching a glimpse of the dismembered body in his slime-covered hand.

"So Gafeen wants to kill us. What is it that Gore wants?" she asked, while mentally saying a quick prayer that his plan did not involve her and Luke's deaths.

"He wants to reestablish trade among the great races." The chief put the rest of the lifeless body down in front of him and picked up a cloth. While wiping his hands, he said, "Gore has informed me that you're on your way to see the Medicians. Is that correct?"

"I am."

"Then one of our people can travel with you to meet with them. Everything can then be explained to the Medicians. We even know where another great race is hidden. In the end, I believe they'll be eager to find them."

Both fear and relief filled her. "Um… there's only one problem with that," she said, hesitantly.

"And what is that?"

Alissia looked into his strange eyes and answered, "The Medicians risked a lot to save my life. In return, Luke and I have both risked our lives more than once to protect their secrets. I've been kidnapped more than once, Luke was tortured and nearly killed, and then I somehow saved his life."

She looked away and frowned. "Your people kidnapped me, Luke and I nearly went mad, and then Gore and Gafeen tortured and almost killed us."

Meeting his eyes again, she added, "After all I've done to protect the Medicians, now I'm supposed to take my captors to them and put their lives in danger?"

Tolden laughed heartily, and she stared back at him in surprise.

"My dear, I understand your fear, but you won't be taking your captors to the Medicians. If I choose this course of action, you'll be taking a young female healer with you, and you'll be delivering something to the Medicians they'll definitely want.

"You see, the Medicians were once considered the great healers of our land. That's where their true name comes from—not Lamians, which the humans gave to them out of fear. They're not witches or vampires. They're healers. However, they're not perfect beings. None of us are.

"The scrolls state that the Medicians live a long life, yet their females are only fertile a limited amount of times throughout their entire lives."

Alissia thought of how she had not had a period since being changed by the Medicians, and he continued, "Although my people are not known as healers, this swamp is filled with many plants and animals that cannot be found anywhere else. We have access to things available to no one else, and our ancestors had a recipe to improve the fertility of a Medician woman. This recipe was greatly sought after by the Medicians."

Tolden took a sip from his drink. "If I choose this course of action, you'll be delivering this gift to them."

She considered his words for a moment. "Why are you talking and being nice to me?"

"Why not? I've been given the details, and now it's up to me to determine the outcome of this situation."

The chief poured himself another drink. "Do you realize this is the first conversation between my race and a human that has ever happened? You will go down in history, and your name will be written into our records."

He clapped his hands together excitedly. "Tell me about you. And tell me some things about humans. What have they done with this land they now control?"

Alissia cleared her throat, nervously. "Well, there hasn't been a war in over a thousand years. They have a very complicated government made up, and kings no longer rule them. It's more like one big group of people rule them all."

"But there's now a possibility of a war?"

"Yes, but no one really wants it."

"And what about you? How did you come to meet the Medicians?"

She chewed on her bottom lip for a moment before answering, "That's a bit complicated."

"Tell me."

"Well, I pretty much just woke up with these handprints branded on me. I didn't know what happened, and it took a while for me to figure it out. I almost died, and they chose to save my life but were interrupted at the last minute. They fled, and I was left behind. My physical appearance soon began to change, and I noticed strange things happening to me.

"Because all traces of the great races were removed from the humans' historical records, it wasn't easy for me to find out who was responsible for saving my life. Other humans realized I was a Lamian before I did, and I was soon being kidnapped and things like that. People wanted answers."

"And what answers did you give them?"

"I told them I'm a true Lamian, but I'm from an alternate reality. There are no other Lamians in this reality."

"Ah, so you protected their existence," he said, sounding pleased.

"Yes. They've been in hiding for almost two thousand years. I'm not going to thank them for saving my life by giving away their secrets."

Tolden nodded. "And the people you're traveling with?"

"Luke and some of the others have been with me from the beginning. They've almost lost their own lives protecting these secrets. As for the others, they found me and told me they're protectors of the Lamians—I mean Medicians. Their ancestors hid the Medicians, and they've been protecting them ever since."

"And they've been giving power stones to the humans?"

"Not a lot. They're extremely rare and illegal to have. The human protectors are the only ones that know the truth. They have this extremely complicated trade business that was designed many years ago by their ancestors."

The chief said nothing for a moment, as if in thought. Then he motioned to one of his guards. As the guard came forward, Tolden picked up a small bag and opened it, revealing a group of mushrooms.

To the guard, he said, "I need you to prepare a drink for Alissia here. With her size, I would say to use only half of what you would use for yourself. The human man does not get any."

As the guard took the bag of mushrooms, Tolden added, "Hurry back with it."

He turned back to her and said, as if amused, "You gave Gore quite a shock when he met you. Medicians are immune to the bite of a felium, and when your man entered our swamp and was bitten, the effects traveled to you. It wasn't until the male human was brought to him that he realized the two of you are connected. He had to heal your man to heal you."

"Felium? Isn't that one of those tiny twig looking creatures?"

"Yes, they're one of the many creatures that can only be found in this swamp, and as I'm sure you've noticed, they're also one of the protectors."

"And one bite did that?"

"It only takes one bite. This swamp is filled with many things a human could not survive. It's not a place for them."

"So I see. Will Luke suffer any more side effects?"

"No, he's been healed. However, you forget that I still have a choice to make by tomorrow morning, and although I find your story intriguing, I must make the best decision for my people."

At that moment, everything within her wanted to help reestablish trade among the great races, even if she and Luke could never settle in one place. She was desperate.

He peered into both of the baskets in front of her and then selected a bright pink fruit, about the size of a tennis ball. As he began to peel it, he said, "The food is safe for your man to eat, if you would like to take the baskets to him."

Alissia nodded and pulled a matching fruit from the basket. Following his lead, she attempted to peel it. However, she immediately realized her mistake, as it was a difficult task with her main hand being numb. Luckily, her long nails could be used as a tool, and although it was a bit messy, she soon ripped through the outer skin.

The inside looked similar to an orange, except it was dark blue. She remembered how she had once read that the healthiest foods were those richest in color and thought how healthy this new fruit must be. But she may be dying the next day, and all of her years of healthy eating and exercise would be for nothing. She frowned, thinking she should have enjoyed more dark chocolate during her brief lifetime.

She tore off a small piece and placed it into her mouth, immediately regretting it. The fruit tasted nothing like an orange, as it was highly acidic and bitter.

With Tolden watching her, she smiled and tried to look as if she was enjoying the calamity within her mouth. She even forced herself to take another bite.

When the guard walked over with the bag of mushrooms in one hand and a drink in the other, she was grateful for the distraction. He set the bag down by the chief and held out the mug. Tolden took it, and the guard walked back to his watchful post.

"Here you go, my dear," he said, holding it out. She set the unpleasant fruit down, and as she carefully took the drink from his hand, he added, "I would love to join you, but I'll need all of my wits with me tonight to make my decision."

Alissia set the steaming mug down in front of her and stared at the floating pieces she recognized as bits of mushrooms.

"I can help to reestablish the trade with your people and the Medicians," she said, looking up.

The chief nodded. "Yes, you can. However, the two choices are not as simple as you think. As a leader, I have to listen to the people, I have to abide by the rules of our ancestors, and I have to discern what's best for the future of this land." He stood and motioned at her mug. "Drink up. Tonight will be busy for me, but there's no need for you to suffer. I'll meet with you again in the morning to inform you of your fate."

There was no arguing with his assertive tone, and the last thing she wanted to do was offend him. With a smile, she lifted the drink and blew on it, before taking in its earthy scent. She then took a sip, realizing it had a meaty flavor.

"No meat?" she asked, pulling it from her mouth.

He shook his head and chuckled. "No meat. That's the flavor they produce. Now drink, and I'll have the guards carry the baskets for you."

She reluctantly lifted the drink to her mouth and forced it down. Then she set the cup on the mat, telling herself she had just sealed her and Luke's fate—hoping she did not just poison them. However, she thought death by poison would be much better than Gafeen's torture.

Chapter 7

Once inside the cage again, Alissia set both baskets down in front of Luke. "Here's some food, but I advise you to stay away from the pink balls. They're disgusting."

As she sat down beside him, she noticed his freshly wrapped hand. "Want me to peel anything for you?"

He grabbed something she guessed to be a root and bit into it before making a face.

"It's edible," he said, devouring the rest of it.

She laughed and shook her head, remembering the food he had prepared when they first met. "Says the man who eats murdock root."

"What have you found out?" he asked, picking up another selection.

"I thought you didn't trust other people's food."

He looked hard into her eyes and said sternly, "Poisoning us would be too easy. They didn't go through all this trouble for it to end like that. You need to tell me what you've learned, and I need to try to regain my strength."

As he spoke, a floating sensation began to come over her, and all of her current worries seemed to disappear. Luke abruptly stopped chewing his food, and a strange look appeared on his face.

"I was wrong. The food is poisoned."

Alissia laughed, suddenly feeling giddy. "Oh, Luke, you always assume the worst. I feel *so* alive." She stood and smiled down at him. "Don't you feel alive right now?"

A surge of energy came over her, and she began to pace in front of him. "I mean, we've beaten death more than once. We have, Luke! We're a team, you and I—together!"

Grinning wildly, he looked up and said, "Have I told you how hot you look in that outfit? I mean, you always look hot, especially when you're angry—which is often. Your forehead gets all wrinkly, and your eyes look as if you want to kill something—usually me. I think you're the hottest woman I've ever seen."

Luke shook his head vigorously. "No! You're *definitely* the hottest woman I've ever seen. *And* you're mine!" Turning to one of the guards, he yelled, "Did you hear that? She's *all* mine! *And* she's hot! You beasts don't even know what that means, do you? Because that's the natural language of my woman."

Turning back to her, now pacing the floor with a crazy look in her eyes, he bellowed, "Woman! Sing to me! I've never heard you sing before, and tonight, I want to hear your music. The music of love."

Alissia stopped abruptly in front of him. "You wanna hear me sing? I'll sing for ya." She scrunched up her face in thought, as he began to wolf down more food.

"A love song. Uh..." After a moment, she grinned excitedly. "Hah! I do know a love song, and this one doesn't involve punching a window out of someone's car or taking a baseball bat to their truck."

She pulled her hand up to her mouth, as if holding a microphone. "Ready for this, babe?"

"Ready," he said, shoving more food into his mouth.

A confused look slowly came over her face, and her mind went completely blank. After a quick shrug, she plopped down beside the baskets. Without considering her choices, she picked up one of the food items and took a large bite.

"I'm *so* hungry," she said, filling her mouth. "And for some reason, I don't even care that this tastes like a raw onion." She swallowed and took more bites.

Luke's voice sounded sluggish as he said, "I can barely understand you. Your accent's too thick. Talk normal."

Alissia swallowed what was in her mouth and set her unfinished food aside. Scowling at Luke, she challenged, "Who says I'm the one who talks strange?"

Luke shrugged. "I love you, but you do have some odd ways. Make that a *lot* of odd ways."

"Oh, really? So you think I'm strange?"

She stood and crossed her arms, glaring down at him. As she started to speak, a movement outside of the cage caught her attention, and she noticed the young guard with the horns staring at her.

"I'm *so* misunderstood. Do you have that problem?" she said, in the ancient language, shaking her head slowly.

She walked over to the edge of the cage and stared into his eyes. Cocking her head to one side, she scrunched up her face in a look of disgust.

"Is there a reason you look like you've just crawled out of Hades? I mean, why would you people do this to yourselves? I don't need to see your insides tattooed onto your outside. It's just wrong in so many ways!"

Pointing to the butterfly tattoo on her abdomen, she added, "This is what a tattoo is supposed to look like. See this! This is pretty." She took a few steps back and shouted, "You look like the walking dead!"

When the guard did not flinch or respond, she turned her attention to Luke and noticed his struggle to keep his eyes open. A flash of concern went through her, but as she began to walk toward him, she realized the cage made for a great wrestling ring. She abruptly turned back to the horned guard and screamed, loudly and slowly, "Let's! Get! Ready! Tooo! Ruuummble!!!!"

Then she slammed, face down, onto the woven floor of the enclosure.

*****

Someone was shaking her shoulder, and they were not being gentle. Alissia struck out with her hand before opening her eyes.

It was early morning, and her body was damp from the mist in the air. The young, horned guard was squatting down beside her, and she was positioned flat on her back.

Memories of what she had said the night before flashed through her mind, and she closed her eyes and groaned. When she opened them again, the guard pulled her to her feet. "You're still in Hades, human."

She turned to find Luke sitting in the same spot he had fallen asleep. He was now awake and staring at her. The throbbing in his hand was back.

The guard pointed at a fresh basket of food. "You need to eat quickly."

He walked out, and she moved the basket in front of Luke and sat down. As she reached for some food, Luke grabbed her hand.

"Not after last night. Don't eat anything."

She shook her head and pulled her hand from him. "It wasn't the food. It was the mushrooms, and you need to eat. You need your strength."

"What mushrooms?"

Alissia tried to ignore his question by popping a berry into her mouth.

"What mushrooms?" he asked, determined.

She let out a frustrated sigh and looked him in the eyes. "I was given a drink to help us sleep last night and to help ease the pain."

"You accepted mushrooms?"

"In my defense, it worked. We got a peaceful night's rest, and we needed it."

"You tried to pick a fight with the guards," he accused.

Alissia frowned. "I thought you were asleep by then."

"You were screaming!"

"Let's eat," she said, pointedly examining the contents of the basket. "We may get to live. I don't think they'd feed us and then kill us."

Luke said firmly, "As long as we're physically connected, don't put anything into your mouth that's promised to be medicine unless I know about it."

She shrugged. "Okay. Now can we eat and forget about last night?"

He filled his mouth with berries. "I need meat, not berries."

They had just finished eating everything in the basket when Tolden walked up to the cage. Gafeen, Gore, and their witness were standing behind him.

"I heard you slept well, and I see you have some food in you," the chief said pleasantly.

Alissia nodded and smiled, in an attempt to hide the sudden fear rising up within her. Luke took her by the hand.

"After much consideration, the fate of you and your man has been decided."

By now she could barely breathe.

"Although you and your man are humans, you'll be released to meet with the Medicians and help establish our trade once again. One of our young and best healers will be traveling with you, along with our gift, to the Medicians."

Relief filled her, and she knew Luke could feel it coming from her body. Alissia had to fight to keep the tears of joy from breaking free.

"As a cautious measure, to protect our healer, one of your people will be bitten by a felium, and he'll keep the poison in his body until our healer is safely delivered to the Medicians."

Alissia's heart dropped.

"What's wrong?" Luke mentally asked.

"We're safe, and they're letting us go. Hold on."

Tolden continued, "This person has already been chosen by the feliums. From what they've witnessed, they believe he's someone important to you. Therefore, you'll want to fulfill your bargain to see him healed."

Alissia remembered how Grady had given her a birthday present the last night she had seen him. She then imagined him being extremely distraught over her disappearance.

"Will he feel the same effects Luke and I did?"

"Yes, he will. Our healer will attempt to make the situation better, but even at the risk of her own life, she will not remove the poison from his body until our agreement has been fulfilled."

"And when will we be released?"

"You leave now and will be back with your own people by tonight. I'll also give you a powerful salve to take with you to aid in the healing of your man's hand."

"And there's no way to avoid my friend being poisoned?" she asked. "I volunteer myself if I have to."

"No," Tolden said firmly. "This is how it will be done. You'll protect our healer, and in return, she'll heal him once she's with the Medicians."

Alissia nodded and stood. Arguing would only get Luke and her killed.

After a quick stop at the bathroom, they were herded back to the boats. However, this time they were not bound. It had been determined that they were not a threat. If they tried anything, the bargain would be void, and their lives would be forfeit.

Their seating arrangements in the boats were the same as before, and she soon found herself with her back to Gafeen. His hate for her had not lessened, and he continued to taunt her.

As they traveled, Alissia mentally described all that had happened the day before, and Luke listened while taking in the strange scenery.

She continuously scanned the water, hoping to get another glimpse of a mermaid, and halfway into their journey she noticed one staring at her. He was watching from a distance.

"Look to the left. You see him?" she mentally said.

"I do."

The merman sunk into the water and disappeared.

"Tolden said this swamp is filled with creatures that aren't found anywhere else." An uneasy feeling came over her, and she added, *"Luke, do you think something could have gotten to Mia? We haven't seen her, and she entered the swamp with you."*

"We don't know yet so try not to worry. You know she's stronger than she looks."

"You dare to break the laws of the ancients!" shouted a high-pitched voice—much different than the whispered ones she had grown accustomed to.

Alissia turned to find a line of mermen blocking the path of the boats. Gafeen stood and said with authority, "These humans are ours, and Tolden has an agreement with them."

"Since when do we bargain with humans?" the merman demanded. His teeth were sharp and pointy, and his black, leather-like hair was short and stuck out like spikes on his head.

"This does not concern you or your people, Viscal," said Gafeen.

The silver-colored merman did not back down. "This swamp *is* of our concern, and Tolden has overreached his power. Why weren't we informed of a Medician and human in our land?"

Gafeen shrugged and said dismissively, "I didn't consider that a priority."

"You dare to mock me?" spat the creature, with fury in his eyes.

"You're in our territory. Are these two insignificant creatures worth a war? You need to think—"

Alissia screamed as a pair of hands shot out of the water and snatched her by the neck. As she was being hauled over the edge of the boat, Gafeen grabbed her arm and jerked her out of the merman's grasp.

The merman let out a high-pitched screech, and his nails, sharp as knives, sliced through her skin as he tried to regain his hold on her.

As Alissia cried out in pain from her new wounds, more pain shot through her right hand, and she turned to find Luke's guards shoving him to the floor of their boat. Both of them were standing over him, defensively, with large knives in their hands.

Gafeen's body shook with fury, and Alissia winced from his tight grip as he shouted, "Call your men away, Viscal, or the truce among our people will officially be over."

She looked down and closed her eyes, not wanting anyone to see her face, and hastily reached out with her mind. It was not long before she found a large animal similar to a crocodile. Without wasting any time, she urged the animal from his resting place on land. He obeyed and slipped into the water.

Alissia felt a sense of fear rise up within the animal, and she focused on calming him while leading him to Luke's boat. She told him to get under it, and then she felt an unexpected pain along her back. Many sharp, pointy blades covered the bottom of the boat, and as the crocodile's back touched them, they easily pierced through his thick skin.

She ignored their shared pain and continued to push her will into his mind, but her eyes soon shot open as a new set of hands snatched her ponytail, forcing her head back.

Tears of pain came to her eyes as the merman fiercely tried to wrench her free of Gafeen's grasp. Although the massive warrior fought to keep his hold on her, there were too many to fight off, and he was soon forced to let go.

As she felt her body being pulled from the boat, she mentally shouted, *"Finish it! Quickly take the boat to land!"* Then darkness surrounded her as she hit the water.

"Alissia!" Luke's voice screamed into her mind.

She felt herself being hauled through the water at a rapid speed. Out of fear of drowning, she mentally locked onto the crocodile again and told him to save her.

The merman dragging her through the water lifted her up for a quick breath of air before she was pulled back down. As he took off again, the crocodile swam between them and bit down on her kidnapper's arm, giving Alissia the distraction she needed to pull away.

Her only thought was to get to land, and although she had night vision, her eyes were not made for the murky water. Nevertheless, she desperately swam through the darkness in the direction she assumed the bank to be located.

A monstrous scream from within Alissia's head stopped her cold, and her entire body began to convulse in agony. Shortly thereafter, the pain ended, and as her body began to sink, she felt a small sense of satisfaction in knowing it was all over. She would never have to fight and endure life's challenges anymore.

<h1 style="text-align:center">Chapter 8</h1>

"Alissia, please wake up. I need to know you're still with me."

The sound of Luke's soft, pleading voice, along with his fingers stroking her hair, soothed her. She moaned and opened her eyes to find Luke staring down at her with glistening eyes. His battered face and the pain in her left hand immediately brought her back to their shared reality.

"You're crying, and I feel your sadness," she said, as Luke turned and quickly swiped at his eyes. Noticing the thatched ceiling of a hut, she asked. "Where are we?"

His hand went back to her hair, and he looked down at her. "I don't know. I woke up next to you in this bed, but that was a while ago. You've had me worried."

Alissia tried to pull him down next to her, but he shook his head.

"No, I want to look into your face." He stood up and tugged lightly at her pillow. "Here, I'll sit down, and you can rest with your head on the pillow in my lap."

Soon he was sitting on the bed, with his back against the wall and his freshly wrapped hand off to the side. Alissia was positioned on her side, with her head resting on the pillow in his lap.

Luke began to stroke her hair, and she closed her eyes.

"What happened? The last thing I remember was being in the water, but my clothes seem to be dry now."

"I have a theory."

"What?"

"After my guards pushed me into the bottom of the boat, I reached out with my mind to you. That's when I felt a strange sensation go through me, and I've just realized what happened. I believe you were reaching out to a crockphillian in the water." He let out a shaky breath, and she opened her eyes and looked up at him. "You had the animal push my boat to safety when it should have been yours."

She closed her eyes again. "And then what happened?"

"When I made it to land, you were nowhere in sight. I immediately knew you were in the water, but it was too dark to see anything.

"The guards in the boats were too distracted with fighting off the water creatures. Both of my guards left me and started running along the bank. Then I heard this horrible sound within my head and an immense amount of pain. My last thought was that you were dying, and there was nothing I could do to save you."

She felt the tears behind the lids of her closed eyes, as she shared Luke's struggle to regain control of his emotions. The image of his decapitated head filled her mind, and her lids tightened, in an attempt to hold back the tears.

After a long moment of silence between them, Alissia sat up and carefully arranged her body so that she was sitting on the pillow in his lap. She wrapped her arms and legs around him and rested her head on his shoulder, holding him close.

"It's almost over," she said.

Luke's left hand came up, and he began to trace lines along her back. "I've never cared about losing anything until you came along, and these past few days have nearly destroyed me."

She placed a light kiss on his neck. "I know."

"I've never been this incapable of protecting someone. I'm just..." His voice trailed off, and he let out a sigh, dropping his hand to his leg.

"Shh." She began to trace her fingers along his arm, in an attempt to calm him.

"And then there's you. You make it difficult when you try to protect me over yourself. How do you think I could live knowing you died to save me? You keep trying to do that."

"I know."

He shook his head in frustration. "No, you don't know. I'm a member of the league, and I should be the one doing the protecting."

She sat up and looked into his eyes, and an overwhelming sense of love filled her. She smiled as she realized he was also feeling that same powerful emotion.

Alissia never imagined she would ever feel this way about anyone, and knowing he felt the same about her eased all the fear and lack of trust that had haunted her throughout her entire life.

Even if she had not experienced his feelings for her the night she had bonded with him, she could clearly see he loved her. At that moment, it was written all over his face.

She slowly placed light kisses on his forehead and both cheeks. Then she placed a quick peck on his lips before she went back to his forehead.

"You're trying to distract me, aren't you?"

"Why would you think that?" Alissia grinned and pulled away.

"Because I know you." Luke smiled and pushed her hair from her face, most of it having come loose from the ponytail. "You're sly. You're sneaky. You're—"

"And this is your way of telling me you love me?"

He grinned. "This is my way of telling you that you drive me mad. I'm madly in love with you, Alissia Roswell."

"I hope so, because you're stuck with me for the rest of your life."

"I think I can live with that."

She smiled. Her eyes went to his lips, and she wrinkled her forehead with concern. "Does it hurt?"

"Does what hurt? My hand?"

Alissia shook her head. "I know your hand hurts. I feel it." She lifted her fingers to his chin. "It looks like they used your face for a punching bag."

Before he could respond, the door swung open, and she jumped from Luke's lap, landing awkwardly next to him.

Gore shook his head with a frown. "Now I see why humans are overpopulating our land. I left the two of you wondering if you'd survive, only to return to find you procreating."

She scowled up at him. "We weren't procreating. We were only talking. What happened, and how did I get out of the water?"

"One of our guards got to you just in time. He had to fight off one of Viscal's men while pulling you from the water, and it's a miracle he was able to save you."

"Why did I lose consciousness? The last thing I remember is that my entire body felt like it exploded in pain."

He thought for a moment before responding. "Did you attach yourself to one of the animals in the water?"

"What do you mean by attach?" she asked, not wanting to give away any secrets.

"I know about the abilities of the Medicians with animals. My people have our own, as do the water dwellers. The water dwellers can destroy an animal with pain, and my guess is that you were mentally connected to one during that process. Did you connect to the crock-phillian the guards told me about?"

"I don't remember," she lied, not trusting him. "When are we leaving? I was told we'd be out of this place by tonight."

"That was before we were attacked. We can't risk taking you by boat, and now you'll have to walk."

Alissia stood. "Then let's go. We're ready."

Gore frowned. "So I've seen. Do you two need more time for your breeding before we leave?"

She smirked. "Your people should try to enjoy each other's company more often instead of scaring and torturing things. It's called making this world a better place." Luke stood up beside her, and she added, "Are we leaving now?"

"It's a long walk, and it would be best to leave in the morning."

Alissia shook her head. "Luke told our friends to leave us, and tomorrow may be too late."

Gore motioned for them to follow him out of the room. Shortly thereafter, Luke and Alissia were standing with a group of warriors at the edge of a community of huts.

They were given food, along with moccasins. She slathered most of Luke's body with a horrid smelling green goo, having been told it would help to repel insects.

His body was already covered in welts, cuts, and bruises, and his hand was badly burned and wrapped in leaves. She could not help but think it was a bit late for the creatures to take an interest in his wellbeing.

Turning to Gore, she said, "He needs a shirt to cover his mark. No one knows about it."

"I thought you trusted the humans you travel with," he said, accusingly.

"I do, but some things are too intimate to talk about. What happens between me and Luke is our business and *only* ours."

Gore nodded and walked away, and it was not long before he returned with a shirt made of sackcloth.

As she helped Luke put on the loose shirt, he said, "I need my knives and ring back. They need to understand if they expect me to protect their healer, I'll need them."

After relaying the message to Gore, he responded, "All your items will be waiting for you a short distance up the trail from where your carriages are now. They're traveling with a separate group of men that have already left, and you'll find them in the middle of the trail a short time after your people begin traveling."

As he spoke, the sight of a young man with regular tribal tattoos walking toward them caught her attention. He was carrying a small cage, and it did not take her long to realize Mia was in it.

He set the cage down in front of them and opened it. Then he grabbed a piece of fur at the back of Mia's neck and pulled her lifeless body from the cage.

"What have you done? Give her to me!" Alissia demanded, grabbing Mia from his hands.

"She's asleep for the journey and will wake in the morning," he said. Alissia stared down at the limp body and took one of the tiny hands in hers. "We've been feeding her, but we've had to keep her semiconscious." He frowned. "She's more violent than she looks. Here's a sling to carry her."

She took the sling, and Luke helped to get it over her body. With both of them trying to avoid the use of their right hand, it took a bit of patience, but Mia was soon resting snugly against Alissia's chest, giving the appearance of a mother with a newborn.

The healer turned out to be the same girl that had wrapped Luke's hand the first time, and she had a lot of bags with her. Gore explained that as a healer, Selona would need to take many supplies with her, and most of them were living organisms.

"With your abilities, you can help with the plants."

"What do you mean?"

"You can use your power to help the plants thrive so they don't die during your travels."

Alissia stared back at him with a blank look in her eyes. "And how am I supposed to do that?"

He frowned. "I guess you don't know all your capabilities." Motioning for her to follow, he took a few steps and squatted at the base of a wild flower. "Concentrate on it and see if you can make it grow. I don't know how it's done, but you probably have the power to do it."

Luke stood behind Alissia as she squatted, and Gore grabbed her unharmed hand, setting her fingers on the flower. "Now concentrate."

She stared down at the flower and mentally told it to grow, and it was not long before she felt a warm, tingly sensation in her body. She could feel the power as it left her hand and traveled along her fingers, entering the small flower.

Although the difference was subtle, she noticed the flower's petals lifting and its color becoming more vibrant, giving it a healthier appearance.

Gore stood. "You have the ability with plants. You just need to practice and help Selona with what she brings with her."

Alissia nodded and stood, secretly amazed by what had just happened, and Luke smiled as she passed by.

When Gore informed her that he and the witness would not be traveling with them, dread filled her. Gafeen gave her an evil grin, and as Gore began to walk away, she asked, "How do I know Gafeen won't kill us before we get there?"

"He has his orders." He then walked away, leaving Alissia, Luke, and Mia to their fate. It was now in the hands of the head warrior that wanted her dead. And not just dead! He wanted her tortured.

If there was anything in her life she now regretted doing, it was attacking the head warrior of a bunch of sadistic creatures. She now considered that to be one of the biggest mistakes she had ever made in her entire life.

Chapter 9

It was nearly dark by the time they reached the less shaded marshland of the swamp, which meant Alissia did not have to worry about protecting her eyes from the sun.

As they walked, many animals scampered away, and any time she connected with one of them out of curiosity, she noticed their extreme fear of the creatures she traveled with.

Well after midnight they finally stepped past the eerie trees carved into the shape of skulls and stopped walking. The warriors set Selona's bags down and then helped to arrange them on her body.

More of her belongings were traveling with the same warriors that carried Luke and Alissia's knives and clothing, and they would be waiting for them along the trail.

By now, Alissia was exhausted and covered in mud. Her hand was throbbing in pain, and she was miserable. She and Luke had not even been able to enjoy a mental conversation during most of the walk, as there had been too many obstacles to distract them along the muddy terrain.

Luke helped her unpack the sling from her body, and to conceal Mia's presence, she arranged it so it looked as if she was carrying a bag.

The distant sight of their camp filled Alissia with excitement, and she had to push back an unexpected wave of emotion. Just as she was about to reach out with her mind to Shade and the dogs to let them know she was back, a piercing scream filled the air, followed by Grady calling out her name.

Within seconds, the peaceful camp lit up with glow stones, and Grady's screams became frantic. As she took a step toward the camp, Gafeen caught her by the arm, and she turned around. She glared back at his leering grin with a cold and defiant look on her face.

"I look forward to our next meeting, little one." He leaned down close. "And next time, there won't be a reason to keep you alive."

She snatched her arm free and said, between clenched teeth, "I don't plan to ever see you or your people again." She turned and started walking toward the camp, ignoring his menacing laughter.

As they neared the camp, she warned Shade and the dogs of their presence. With her night vision, Alissia could see Anika trying to console Grady in Shade's caged carriage. Lita and the men had their weapons drawn, and they were staring at the three figures headed their way.

"Here. Take Mia and hide her." Alissia gave Luke the bag and called out, "It's me and Luke. Don't kill us!"

Once they could see her face in the light of the glow stones, her friends lowered their weapons. However, they kept them at the ready while staring at Selona.

Alissia left Luke to explain things as she ran toward Grady, still screaming wildly. As soon as she entered the cage, Anika grabbed and embraced her.

"We thought you were dead." She released Alissia and turned to Grady, now standing near his bedding in the corner of the cage. "Look, Grady. Alissia's not dead. She's right here."

Alissia noticed he had a black eye as he fell to his knees crying, not even looking their way.

"Please don't leave me," he pleaded, in a whispered voice.

Alissia walked toward him, and in a soothing voice, she said, "I'm here. Shh. It's okay."

For a brief moment, she thought he saw her, but then he began to sob, staring at something only he could see. She turned to Selona, still standing at the edge of their camp. "Do something!"

The creature answered firmly, "I will not heal him."

"I didn't tell you to heal him, but if you want any sleep after all the walking we just did, you need to help calm him down. I'm exhausted and can't do this tonight. If you know of *anything* that can soothe him, now would be a good time."

Selona hesitated for a moment before setting her packs on the ground.

"What's happening to him?" asked Anika, her eyes wide with fear. Everyone but Luke and Selona were now entering the cage. Alissia could see fear and concern, along with confusion, in their eyes.

"He's been bitten by something, but he'll be okay. Let me see if I can get through to him," Alissia answered.

Tears were now streaming down Grady's face, and he cried out, "Alissia's dead! He killed her!"

She sat down in front of him and lifted her hand to his face, forcing him to look into her eyes. "It's okay. I'm right here."

He shook his head fervently. "No, you're dead!"

"How did I die then?"

Grady closed his eyes and whispered, "He killed you."

"Who killed me, and how can I be dead if we're talking now?"

His eyes shot open. "I see your body!" he shouted. "You're dead! Ian raped and killed you, and you're dead! I see the knife in your stomach! It's the same place your father stabbed you as a young girl! There's no butterfly! It's gone!"

Exhaustion and the pain in Alissia's hand made it hard to think, but she was more than aware of everyone standing behind her, hearing his words. She suddenly wished she had demanded more clothing from Gore for herself. The short skirt and chest wrap did not conceal her tattoo or the handprints branded into her abdomen.

He continued on with his ramblings. "It's not your fault either. You've always blamed yourself, even as a young girl. I watched you all those years blaming yourself for the evil of others."

Alissia turned to the healer and yelled in a threatening voice, "Do something *now*, Selona! Help him to go back to sleep!"

Grady reached out and turned Alissia's face his way. Leaning in close, he said intensely, "You didn't deserve to be beaten like that, and your father was wrong about you. I remember one night under that tree you cried so hard, telling yourself you deserved everything that had happened to you—even being raped. That's not true."

She froze at his words, and he began to gently stroke her face.

"Grady," she said, desperately trying to sound calm and reassuring. "I'm right here. See, I'm not dead."

"I loved you, Alissia. I still do."

Without warning, his mouth was on hers. When she realized what was happening, she gently pushed him away. "No. We talked about this. Remember?"

He nodded. "You still love me, but you think I deserve better." He shook his head passionately. "I love you, and—"

Selona shoved a small, crude mug through the bars, and Alissia eagerly grabbed it. Ignoring the rest of Grady's words, she asked, "Will it hurt him?"

"No, he'll sleep."

She held the mug out in front of her. "Here. I have something to help you feel better. Drink this." He stared at it for a moment, and she smiled. "Please. Drink it for me."

Grady frowned but reached out to take it from her, and she shook her head and pulled back. "No. Let me help you." When she lifted it to his mouth, he turned away, with a look of disgust. "Please," she said, begging with her eyes.

He gave in, and she lifted the mug back to his lips. Once finished, she set it aside and helped him into his blanket. As she went to get up, he wrapped his arm around her waist and pulled her back down.

Alissia frowned in defeat and mentally called out to Shade, and she was soon sitting with her back against the large creature. Grady's head was in her lap, and she gently stroked his hair.

When he closed his eyes, Anika asked worriedly, "What happened to you, and what's going on?"

Alissia let out a long breath, staring back at the group of eyes on her. When Luke and Selona entered the cage, everyone turned curiously to the newcomer, and Alissia was thankful for the distraction.

Luke sat down beside her, but Selona remained standing. She ignored everyone's curiosity, while staring down at Alissia and Grady. After a while, she grinned, and her face lit up.

"His nightmares are of you, aren't they?" Selona asked, in the ancient language. She looked at Luke in amusement. "They're both in love with you, yet only one of them is connected to you." Turning to the swamp, she added, "I wonder if Gore knows of this."

"He knows," snapped Alissia. "Why do you think Grady was chosen?" Turning to Salvatore, she said in the modern language, "How soon can we leave? We're not safe here."

Everyone's eyes went to the skull-shaped trees, and Salvatore answered, "The horses only need to be hitched."

"Good. Can we ride through the night? We really need to get away from here. Luke and I will explain everything, but right now, we just need to leave."

"What about her?" asked Lita, pointing to Selona.

"Unfortunately, she's going with us. Grady dies without her."

"What?" screeched Anika.

"He's been bitten by one of their creatures, and he won't be cured until Selona is with the Lamians."

"She can cure him now," Anika said angrily.

"Stop!" Alissia warned. She added pleadingly, "We're being watched, and I'm doing the best I can to get us out of here alive. Luke and I are covered in mud, exhausted, and in a lot of pain. I cannot stress to you how important it is that we get out of here as fast as we can."

Langley took Anika by the hand before turning to Salvatore. "Let me know which shift you need me to drive the carriage, and I will."

Salvatore nodded and turned to his nephews. "We won't stop until we've put much distance between us and this trail."

"Our clothes and belongings should be up the trail, so you'll need to look out for them," Luke said. "When you see them, you'll need to stop and get them."

"Does your hand need to be cleaned and bandaged? How bad are you hurt?" asked Edda.

Luke looked down at his throbbing hand, and Alissia answered for him. "They burned him with a torch, and it's bad. If you can bandage it while we travel, that will work. Knowing him, he won't take anything for the pain until after we're safe and away from here."

Edda nodded, and then she and Bruna turned to leave.

Alissia looked at Salvatore. "Do Luke and I need to stay in the covered wagons while we travel, or can we sleep here?"

Salvatore answered, "You should be fine where you are, especially at night. Once it gets light, we'll have the dogs travel ahead to warn us if there's anyone on the trail. We'll wake you if there is." He glanced at Luke briefly before turning back to her, concern in his voice. "Are you hurt?"

"I'm fine." She looked down at Luke's injured hand, forcing herself to appear calm as an unexpected wave of emotion came over her. "It's just been a rough few days, and I'm ready to get out of here."

He turned to Selona and studied her for a moment. The creature stared back at him with a look of disgust.

"I guess she can sleep in the corner there," he said, turning back to Alissia. "My carriage will travel behind this one so we can watch her."

"Perfect," said Alissia. "I don't trust her at all. These creatures are evil."

He frowned. "I'm not sure we can take her to the Lamians, if she's dangerous."

"Apparently, they only hate humans—I mean, they *really* hate humans. They used to trade with the Lamians, and she's bringing a gift they'll supposedly want and love." She yawned. "I promise I'll tell you all about them when we stop, but right now, we just need to get out of here. And everyone needs to stay alert while we're on this trail. We're being watched, and they could easily change their minds."

He nodded before ushering out his group of people, leaving Anika and Langley anxiously staring down at her.

"You look like you're in pain," Anika said. "And from Luke's appearance, I'm wondering what happened to you. I know you can heal, but I see some dried blood. Did they beat you too?"

"I'm fine. Thanks."

"Well, we're glad you're back. We've been worried," said Langley. "We'll let you rest now." He tugged at his wife's hand, but she resisted.

She stared down at Alissia for a moment before stammering, "I... I'm sorry to hear about what happened between you and your father. If you ever need to talk, you know I'm here for you, and you can tell me anything."

Alissia could feel the heat rising to her face. "Thanks," she said smoothly, behind the mask of a smile. "That was years ago. It's no big deal."

Anika nodded, and she and Langley left the carriage. Alissia turned to Selona. "We're leaving. You can move the stuff out of that corner and put your bags there for now. We'll find a spot for them later."

Selona smugly asked, "We leave so soon?"

"We're on a time schedule," snapped Alissia.

She looked down at Grady's face, still resting in her lap. He appeared to be asleep, so she lifted his head and gently moved it to his pillow.

Although her right hand was throbbing, using it did not worsen the pain. However, she could feel every movement Luke did with his hand, and she could not help but treat her own as if it was injured. Holding it off to the side was her natural response to the pain.

Luke lifted his left arm, and she shifted her body so the side of her face was resting on his chest. They snuggled into Shade's large body and closed their eyes.

"Where's Mia?" she mentally asked.

"She's in a corner, next to my pack."

She immediately let her weariness take over, and she fell asleep. However, it was not long before a sharp pain shot through her hand, and her eyes shot open.

"Ahh!" she cried out, sitting up in alarm.

"What's wrong?" Anika asked. She and Bruna were working together to carefully remove the leaves from around Luke's hand.

Alissia's eyes began to water from the severity of the pain. She looked at Luke's face and was surprised to find him still reclining peacefully with his eyes closed. He looked as if he was asleep, but she knew better. No one could sleep through that much pain.

"I'm fine," she said, noticing Anika's worried look. "Y'all startled me. That's all."

"You sure?" Anika asked.

"Yeah," she answered, resting her head back on Luke's chest.

"Ooh, this looks horrible," said Bruna. "Why would they do this to him?"

Talking was out of the question. By now, Alissia could barely breathe. She closed her eyes and hoped the two women would believe she was falling back to sleep.

Luke's voice entered her head. *"Focus on something else to take your mind off the pain."*

"Like what? You're hurt badly."

"I've been worse."

The memory of him being tortured by Ian's men in the dungeon came to mind. *"I'm sorry."*

"For what?"

She tried to imagine a passionate moment between her and Luke, but her mind could not get past the pain. Her hand felt as if it was on fire.

"You're scared of Gafeen," he mentally said. *"You know you shouldn't have taunted him and gotten him angry with you. You picked a fight with someone much bigger than you, and now you regret it."*

"I don't regret anything," she responded.

"Oh, but you do. You're angry with yourself."

"I'm not mad at myself. He deserved it, and I hope that necklace was over two hundred years old, given to him by his dearest great grandfather, and something he had planned to pass to his favorite son."

"You can't admit it, can you?"

Alissia cringed in pain. *"Admit what, Luke?"*

"That you were wrong to pick a fight with their head warrior. You know that's pride, don't you? You're the most prideful person I've ever met. Stubborn. Prideful. You can never admit when you're wrong."

"I'm not wrong! He deserved it!"

"Remember the night you drugged me with leo before running away?" he asked. *"You know you never should have left like that. Look at how you almost got yourself killed."*

Fire shot through her hand as something was poured over Luke's wound to clean it, and Alissia clenched her teeth, hoping the two women would not notice.

"You need a man's protection, and you know it," Luke continued. *"Women, especially one as tiny as you, need a man. You do know that, don't you?"*

Alissia clenched her teeth even tighter, and her mental words were slow and deadly. *"I have never, nor will I ever need a man, Luke."*

"Really? Are you saying you don't need me?"

She mentally screamed in frustration. *"Do you need me?"*

"Hmm... I don't know. Sometimes."

By now, tears of pain threatened to break free from behind her closed lids.

"What are they doing?" she mentally cried out.

"They're cleaning it."

Suddenly, a cool sensation went through her hand, and it began to feel numb. Just as she began to feel relief, an image filled her mind, taking her to another place.

She was lying on a blanket, looking up at the stars. A nearby fire warmed her skin. Luke was next to her, staring down into her face.

He smiled before lowering his lips to hers, and she responded readily. After a long, gentle kiss, his lips traveled to her ear, and he whispered, "I do need you, Alissia, and I always will."

The image left just as abruptly as it appeared, and she was immediately brought back to reality. However, she noticed the throbbing in her hand was less severe.

"Are you angry with me?" he asked.

She could still feel his touch on her lips, as if they had shared a real kiss.

"You did that on purpose," she accused.

"I did."

"Why do you play mind games with me?"

"I told you to think of something to distract yourself from the pain, but you needed my help."

"Why didn't you just distract me with a kiss in the first place, instead of messing with me?"

"Because I was in just as much pain as you, and no matter how much I crave a forbidden kiss from you, Alissia, that's a hard emotion to focus on while a searing pain is shooting through your body. Besides, I've learned anger is the easiest emotion to pull from you. It requires less work, and you get so passionate."

No longer fighting back tears, Alissia opened her eyes when she overhead Bruna mention Luke needed something for his pain.

"Yes, I think he does," she agreed.

Luke opened his eyes. "I don't need anything for the pain."

"Yes, Luke," she argued while sitting up. "You need something for the pain."

"No, Alissia. I need to be alert in case we're attacked."

"Then at least take something mild that won't put you to sleep."

"I don't like the idea of taking anything while there's a threat around us."

She scowled. "We're always in danger." In a threatening voice, she added, "Take something for the pain."

Luke shook his head. "Not while I need to stay alert."

"If you don't take something for the pain, I'll take care of it myself, and we both know how that went last time," she mentally argued. *"I bet Selona has some of our favorite mushrooms."*

"What if I need to fight?"

"Really? If they wanted us dead, we'd all be dead by now. The walking dead and their flying demon fairies surround us. I don't think there's much we can do if they want us dead, or insane for that fact. Take some meds! I need meds!"

He frowned. *"This could be a lesson of pain endurance for you."*

"I don't want pain endurance!" Alissia mentally screamed. *"I've survived years of PMS. I think I've earned a trophy when it comes to pain endurance. Now take some meds, Luke!"*

"You're talking in your foreign language again. I don't even know what PMS means."

The sound of a throat being cleared brought her back to her surroundings, and she immediately realized that she and Luke were glaring at each other in silence. Anika and Bruna were staring blankly at the two of them.

Alissia smiled at the two confused women and said calmly, "I believe Luke will take something for the pain." Turning to him, she added, "Isn't that right, dear?"

He glared at her for a moment before letting out a frustrated sigh. Turning his attention to the women, he said, "Yes, I'll take something *mild*. But I need to be alert in case we're attacked."

Chapter 10

lissia slowly sat up, still feeling groggy. The first thing she noticed was that someone had taken the time to put her sunglasses over her eyes.

Shade let out a yawn before standing and walking to the middle of the cage, where he began to go through a series of stretches.

While smacking her lips, she scrunched up her face and looked around. She frowned when she noticed they were still on the ancient trail. The sun was shining brightly, and she guessed it to be early afternoon. Grady was still asleep next to her, but Luke was now sitting beside Salvatore in the carriage traveling behind them. Anika had taken his place next to Alissia, and Selona was sitting in a corner of the cage. The lone creature stared at Alissia beneath her wild mass of hair, and she truly looked like a displaced savage.

"Here. Luke said you'd be hungry," Anika said, pushing a basket toward her. She pointed to a pail. "There's also some soap, water, and towels to clean your face and hands."

Alissia eagerly crawled to the pail that had been placed near the bars of the cage, away from the bedding in each of the corners. With mud covering most of her body, along with the horrible taste in her mouth, she felt grimy.

She took off the muddy moccasins before grabbing the bars to help steady her as she stood. The moving carriage made it somewhat difficult to stand up so soon after waking.

The tribal clothing she was wearing made it easier for her to clean her scantily clad body, and by the time she was finished with the sponge bath, the towels and water were filthy.

Luke was doing most of the talking between him and Salvatore, and she guessed he was describing what had happened during their captivity. She wondered how he would explain his torture without mentioning the two of them being connected.

Since he did not speak the ancient language, Luke did not know Selona had mentioned their connection in front of Salvatore. Alissia frowned, thinking how much more difficult her and Luke's secret would be to keep, especially with Selona around and her sharing in Luke's pain. Even now, she had a hard time forcing herself to use her throbbing right hand.

As she bent down to pick up the mouth cleaning solution, she noticed Anika staring at her tattoo, and she cringed. She turned around and ferociously swished the liquid in her mouth for a long moment before spitting it out and adding more.

By the time she finished scrubbing her mouth, she wore a scowl on her face. How would she explain to Salvatore that Grady had watched her before coming to this reality? And why didn't Langley and Anika try to distract Salvatore and his people when Grady was rambling on about her past? They all just stood there, listening to him.

Their knowing about her abusive father did not bother her so much. However, there were some secrets from her past she had never shared with anyone. No one needed to know about her father stabbing her or the night of her date rape. Those were her private memories.

She tried to pull the scowl from her face before turning back around.

"I'm starving," she said lightheartedly, while carefully walking back to her spot beside Anika. She sat down and opened the basket before devouring a hefty amount of bread, fruit, nuts, and cheese.

"Here's some chet," Anika said, lifting a pitcher from a heat stone. She poured the liquid into a mug, and Alissia eagerly accepted the hot drink she had grown addicted to in the recent months.

"Do you think she'll want anything?" her friend asked.

Alissia took a few sips of her drink before looking over at Selona, staring at each other for a moment before she turned back to Anika. "No, she can eat later."

"She's that bad?"

Alissia looked hard into Anika's eyes. "You have no idea. They're evil. They enjoy hurting people."

She went on to explain what had happened to her and Luke during their captivity, leaving out the details about their connection. Although she no longer thought of it as a big secret and knew she would soon tell her friend everything, she did not feel like explaining everything at the moment. She would leave that for another day.

"So Grady is going to see horrendous visions until she heals him?" Anika asked.

"I don't know. I don't know how it'll work over time. I just know Luke watched me die a horrible death, and I did the same with him. It takes your worst fears and brings them to life. It's horrible, and it seems so real. Last night I have no doubt he was staring at my dead body in front of him, and it was graphic."

Anika blinked back tears as she stared down at Grady.

"What happened to his eye?" Alissia asked.

Her friend looked up. "Langley did it. When Grady realized you were gone, he was bent on going after you. Salvatore tried to reassure him that Luke had already entered the bog, but Grady didn't care." She swiped away a tear on her cheek before continuing. "He became frantic and was determined to find you, even if he had to die to do it."

Alissia looked down and stared at Grady's face. After a while, she let out a deep sigh and turned back to Anika.

"This will be over soon," she said confidently. "Salvatore told me only one person can join me on the boat going to the Lamians, and that person will be Luke. I'll somehow get Selona to cure Grady once we get to the boat, and then y'all can go back home."

Anika looked confused. "Why didn't you tell us this before? We thought we were traveling with you."

"Because I knew y'all would have a problem leaving me with a bunch of strangers, and I hoped that by the time we reached the boat, we would know Salvatore and his people better."

"That was selfish." Anika crossed her arms and frowned.

Now Alissia was confused. "What? How was that selfish? Y'all would be able to go back home, and all of this would be over for you."

Anika shook her head. "I feel like ever since you've chosen Luke, you've been pushing us away. We don't talk like we used to, and I knew you were keeping things from me. I just didn't know what. Now I know you were just waiting to get rid of us. That way you could be with Luke without having to worry about Grady."

Alissia stared back at her friend in surprise and shook her head. "Wait... No, it's not like that. I can't wait for you to get back to Allure so your life can go back to normal. You and Langley can go back to your ranch, and now that Morton won't be telling the Elders that Grady committed treason, he can go back to the Eldership. Life will be great. No more danger, and it will be over."

"And what about you?" Anika uncrossed her arms.

She shrugged. "What about me? I'll meet these Lamians and hopefully get a lot of answers, and then I plan to travel back to the mountains to meet the other Lamians." She smiled. "I could even stop by your house along the way since you live near them."

Anika looked skeptical. "And what if these new Lamians don't accept you? They didn't change you. Remember? And what if they don't let you leave their island because that would put them in danger? Ever thought about that?"

She nodded. "Yes, I think a lot about those things, but I'm not going to let myself worry about any of it. I learned a long time ago not to ask 'what if.' What happens happens, and I'll deal with it then. That's all I can do with the craziness in my life."

Alissia leaned in closer. "But it's *my* life, and you and the others shouldn't have to ruin yours because of me. How do you think that makes me feel? Selfish? No, I only want y'all to be safe."

Her friend's face softened, and she nodded. "Just promise to tell me things, and don't keep secrets from me. I thought we were closer than that."

Alissia swallowed hard. She wondered if she should tell Anika about her and Luke's connection now or wait until a better time.

That thought ended abruptly when Grady began to stir. He opened his eyes and smiled when he saw her. "Alissia?"

She bent down and began to stroke his short beard. In a soothing voice, she said, "Shh. I'm right here. How do you feel?"

He sat up slowly, and she set the basket of food down in his lap. He grinned and tore off a large chunk of bread.

"Breakfast in bed? You spoil me," he said, before taking a bite.

She glanced at Anika and smiled, both relief and confusion filling her.

"Would you like some chet?" Anika asked, pulling a mug from a box.

He took another bite and nodded. "Yes, please. And thank you for taking care of the children so that Alissia could take care of me."

"Children?" Anika asked, carefully holding out a cup of chet. Although Shade's wagon had shocks built in, it still bounced slightly along the road, causing the liquid to slosh around in the mug.

He accepted the drink, and after taking a few sips, he set it down and took some fruit from the basket.

"Elsie didn't cry, did she?"

Anika shook her head and glanced at Alissia, who responded by shrugging, and the two women silently watched as he finished eating his late breakfast. Once he set his empty mug aside, he unexpectedly grabbed Alissia and pulled her into his lap.

"And how is my wife feeling today?"

Alissia's eyes briefly met Anika's before she smiled. "Great. How do you feel?"

"Much better. Thank you for taking care of me while I've been con- fined to this bed." He kissed her cheek and pulled her messy hair back from her shoulders. "You look beautiful."

His words made her wonder what he was actually seeing, and she stammered, "Um... do you know where you are?"

Grady laughed. "I'm not delirious with fever, my love, and you don't need to worry about me. In fact..." He placed a light kiss on her neck before whispering at her ear, "I can't wait to get you alone. I'm raven- ous for you."

As he began to nibble on her ear, she froze, while staring at Anika.

"And we're married?" she asked weakly.

He chuckled lightly. "If—"

"What's going on over there?"

Luke's voice within her head drowned out Grady's words. *"Well, it seems I'm not dead today. He thinks we're married."*

"At this moment, I prefer you to be dead. What next? A honeymoon?"

"I think we have kids together."

"Get out of his lap, Alissia, and get his lips off you!"

A flash of anger went through her, and she immediately knew she was feeling Luke's emotions.

"I'm working on—"

Before she could finish her response, she realized Grady's tongue was exploring the inside of her mouth, and she pulled away.

"Oh, my," she said, gently pushing him back. She scooted out of his lap. "Look... honey. We have company. Anika's here. Remember Anika?"

Grady laughed and looked at his cousin. "Ah, yes. Our former chaperone is watching us. Where are the children?"

Anika cleared her throat. "They're with Langley. I thought I would check on you. Do you need anything?"

He shook his head. "No, thanks to my lovely wife, I have everything."

Alissia felt a stress headache making its way to join the dull throbbing in her right hand. When she looked at Selona, a surge of her own anger soared within her, joining Luke's. The vile creature was grinning smugly, clearly enjoying Alissia's discomfort.

"Logically, not emotionally, Alissia," said Luke sternly within her head.

"I got this!" she snapped back.

She spent the rest of the day pretending to be Grady's loving wife. His current reality was much different than his true one. He saw himself resting in a comfortable bed in an elegant home he shared with Alissia and their two young children.

He believed they had been married for six years, and they lived in Allure. He was about to become an Elder, and no one cared that Alissia was a Lamian. The life he imagined sounded perfect, and it tore at her heart how happy he seemed to be.

When she noticed movement coming from the bag Mia was in, she retrieved it and set it in her lap. Mia remained concealed in the bag, while Alissia gave her food and spoiled her with petting. Grady seemed oblivious to the strange creature, as with everything else that did not fit into his dream reality.

Although they made a few quick stops throughout the day, it was late in the evening when they finally stopped for the night. A sense of relief seemed to fill the air, as they had made it safely out of the bog, and the ancient trails were behind them.

A stabbing pain was shooting through Alissia's hand when she jumped from the carriage, and she was just about to ask Bruna to check on Luke's wound when Grady began to scream wildly, his false reality having shattered the moment he stepped down from the carriage.

No longer living the perfect life, he was witnessing Alissia's death again. This time she was a teenager, and it was her father stabbing her with a knife. Grady was watching it happen from behind a window, and he was completely helpless, screaming for her to run.

Nothing she said or did would get his attention, and she could not pull him from his nightmare. The fact that everyone was listening to him describe certain details from her childhood did not help, and when Alissia saw the joy in Selona's eyes, a sudden fury came over her.

Just as she was within distance of knocking the smug smile from the creature's face, Luke grabbed Alissia around the waist with his left hand and pulled her back.

"That won't make things better," he said, at her ear.

She struggled in his grip for a moment, but even with his injured hand, she was no match for the skilled assassin.

"Please let me hit her. Please let me hit her," she begged.

He laughed and dragged her behind one of the covered wagons, giving them some privacy. With her back pressed against the wagon, he bent down. "Don't let her get to you."

The sound of Grady weeping loudly on the other side of the wagon brought tears to her eyes, and she had to force them back.

"She spent the entire day watching me with a grin on her face. I can't stand it!"

Luke placed a kiss on her forehead. "Just because she's smiling doesn't mean it's real. She's alone and away from her people, and she's probably scared right now."

Alissia scowled. "She doesn't look very scared. In fact, she seems to love it when Grady's in pain."

He smiled and stroked the side of her face before replacing his fingers with a tender kiss to her cheek. In a soft, reassuring voice, he said, "No, I think she only enjoys making you uncomfortable. You shouldn't let her get to you so much. That way she'll have less to smile about."

Alissia heard a growl, and she looked down to find Mia at their feet, staring up at the two of them. She chuckled when Luke backed away.

"I see she's recovered," he said.

A sudden idea came to her, and she bent down and picked up the tiny creature. In the old language, she said, "Can I heal Luke's hand?"

Mia shook her head fiercely.

"Why? I've already healed him before," argued Alissia.

Mia growled.

"I really can't tell if you like me or not, you know. You risk your life to follow me into the swamp, but all you do is growl at me. He's hurt badly, and I can feel his pain. I've healed him before, and I bet I can heal him again."

Mia growled, this time showing more teeth.

"I give up," Alissia said, in the modern language. She set Mia down. "She won't let me heal you."

"She probably has her reasons. We still don't know the consequences from the last time you healed me. What if you risked your own health when you did it? What if it took years off your own life?"

Alissia shrugged. "I don't care, and you know it."

He frowned and shook his head. "You're stubborn."

"I prefer to call it determined." As she went to walk around him, she added, "I've got to get back to Grady. He needs his wife."

Luke grabbed her by the arm. "Can you try to keep his hands and mouth off of you?"

"Are you jealous?"

"I know where your heart is, but it doesn't make it any easier when I see his hands all over you."

She smiled up at him and lifted her fingers to stroke his beard. "I'll try. But if it makes you feel any better, nothing strange happens when he kisses me. My temperature doesn't rise, and I don't lose control of my surroundings like I do when I'm with you."

He grimaced, pulling away from her touch. "So he can kiss you without killing you, but I can't. That's supposed to make me feel better?"

"That's not what I was getting at. I was trying to tell you he doesn't have a physical effect on me like you do."

"Great! So he can kiss you without being attacked by Mia. That makes me feel *much* better."

Her mouth curled into a playful grin. "Are you mad at Mia?"

Luke glanced down at the tiny creature, still watching them closely. Then he let out a resigned sigh, running his good hand through his hair. "I'm not angry with Mia. I'm just frustrated. That's all." He leaned down, his dark eyes searching hers. "You have no idea how much I miss your kiss." He looked away. "And part of me is worried I'll never be able to kiss you again."

Alissia put her arms around his waist, giving it a squeeze. With her face pressed against the burlap shirt he still wore, she said, "We'll have answers soon."

They held each other in silence for a moment before Grady let out another piercing scream and she pulled away. She took a few steps to leave before turning back around.

"You stink," she said, playfully.

He nodded. "I need your help with that. After you take care of Grady, I need for you to help me with a sponge bath."

Alissia nodded and walked away. As she stepped around the wagon, she met Selona's eyes, and she grinned smugly as she passed by the creature. She had only taken a few more steps when an unseen hand gripped tightly around her throat, cutting off her airflow.

Alissia scratched desperately at her throat as she struggled to breathe, and just as she thought she was about to pass out, the pressure lifted.

She fell to her knees and began to cough. A wild growling sound was coming from behind, and she turned around to find Mia standing in front of Selona. Black streaks covered the woman's face, beneath her skin.

Mia looked more threatening than Alissia had ever seen. Her sharp teeth were bared, her grey eyes were glowing, and all the fur on her body was standing up.

Luke was regaining his own breath, and fury slammed into her as she realized what Selona had done. Without even thinking, she jumped to her feet and ran past Mia, tackling the swamp creature to the ground. Normally she would have punched the woman, but her right hand was throbbing in pain, and she instinctively held it off to the side.

Instead, she grabbed a fistful of Selona's grimy hair with her left hand, pulling the creature's head up. With her face only inches away, Alissia snarled, in the ancient language, "If you ever try anything like that again, I will do more to you than has already been done to Luke and me." Her fist curled even tighter into the mass of hair. "And if you don't heal Grady when the time comes, I will throw you into the ocean and drown you with my own two hands. I will make it slow, and I will make it painful. Do you understand?"

When she did not get an answer, she yanked on the wad of hair and screamed wildly, "Do you?"

Selona nodded, and Alissia let go before standing. Her hands were shaking uncontrollably, and her chest was rapidly rising and falling along with her heavy breathing.

Except for Grady—still lost in his nightmare—everyone stared wide-eyed at Alissia and the two fearsome creatures. Mia gave Selona a low, threatening growl before she climbed up Alissia's body, scratching bare skin along the way, until she was sitting protectively on her ward's shoulder.

Alissia turned her eyes to Luke, now standing, and focused on her breathing, in an attempt to calm her anger. After a long moment of silence, Anika asked, "What's wrong with your hand?"

Alissia glanced down at her throbbing hand. "Nothing. Why?"

"You don't seem to be using it, and I thought you were hurt. That's all."

Ignoring the pain, Alissia lifted her right hand for everyone to see in the light of the fire and wiggled her fingers. "I'm fine," she said flatly.

She turned to Salvatore. "This is Mia. She's a pixet, and she's been with me since Pallen. I guess she's chosen to let herself be seen."

Salvatore gave a nod, and Alissia scanned the faces of everyone staring at her. "Can someone give Grady something to help him sleep tonight? I've got to help Luke get washed up."

Salvatore nodded. "We can give him something." He turned to Lita. "Get Alissia and Luke some water from the barrels."

Although Lita normally had something to say, the young woman nodded in silence and started walking toward one of the covered wagons. Alissia was all too aware of everyone's silence, and she quickly made herself busy by retrieving Luke's pack. She carried it to the back of the covered wagon she normally shared with Anika and Langley and set it down.

Luke walked over, leaned back against the wagon, and took her by the hand. As he pulled her to him, Mia jumped into the wagon.

They said nothing, and Alissia's heart rate soon settled back into a normal pace.

"Here's two buckets of water," Lita said as she and Carlo set them on the ground. "We haven't been around a water supply in days, and we're running low on bathing water. This should be enough to get the mud off though."

The young woman pulled two towels from around her neck and set them in the wagon. "Need anything else?"

Alissia shook her head, and Lita and Carlo both smiled before walking away. She pulled away from Luke and took a few steps back, into the privacy of the dark, and he followed.

"Can you take your shirt off, or do you need help?"

"I think I can get it," he answered.

After he removed the filthy shirt and shoes given to him by the swamp creatures, she brought the buckets into the dark and began to carefully scrub his battered body. She inspected the damage as she worked, grateful for her clear night vision.

She rubbed a soothing cream over his many insect bites and stings, and she gently put a salve on the cut above his eye.

Once finished, he walked to the side of the wagon and changed into his own clothing. Then he sat on the back of the wagon, and Alissia began to comb his hair.

"What?" she asked, noticing a strange look in his eyes.

Luke shook his head. "Nothing."

She finished with his hair and set the comb aside. "It's not nothing. What is it?"

He pulled her to him. "I was just thinking how this is the first time a woman has ever taken care of me."

"And?"

"And I like it, and I have a lot to look forward to with you."

She grinned, as a thought came to mind. "Luke?" she asked, her voice laced with sugar.

He squinted and studied her face for a moment. "No."

"But I haven't even asked the question yet," she pouted, rubbing her fingers along his short beard.

"No, but you have that look in your eyes."

Alissia lowered her hand and backed away, frowning. "What look?"

"The same look you give when you're trying to justify something I disagree with."

She briefly wondered if she should end the pretense, but then she smiled, stepped back up to him, and put her arms around his waist. She put her head on his chest and held him for a moment.

"Luke?"

"Yes, my little pixet?"

"Don't you think you need a good night's rest?" she enticed.

"Me or you?"

"Both of us. You know, one where we don't wake up all through the night in pain."

"I'm not going to fog my brain with strong pain tonics," he said matter-of-factly. "I have to stay alert at all times."

She pulled away and scowled up at him. "I'm not asking you to drink shroom juice. It hurts! It's distracting. It's making me cranky, and it hurts. It hurts! It hurts! It hurts!"

In a soothing voice, he said, "I believe I know how much it hurts, but do you really want my reflexes to be slow when we're surrounded by danger? I plan to take one of the watches tonight, and I need to be alert. Try to ignore the pain. You'll get used to it after a while."

"Ignore the pain?" Alissia asked incredulously. "It won't go away! And how am I supposed to get used to it? I wasn't raised in Sparta! I wasn't raised foraging for murdock root and... and..." She gave up and crossed her arms, looking up at him with a scowl. His laughter only worsened her mood.

Luke stared down at her for a moment, and then he pulled her throbbing hand up to his lips. After placing several kisses across the top of it, he said, "I'll get one of the others to put a fresh bandage on it, along with some numbing salve. That should help tonight."

He let go of her hand and implored, "Please understand that I can't take anything that will fog up my brain. I always have to be alert— even when I'm asleep. It's how I survive, and it's also how I choose to protect you."

Alissia's scowl softened, along with her heart. However, her pride did not follow. In a huffy voice, she said, "Fine. Just know that I hope

I can give birth one day, and I'll refuse anything for the pain—just so you can suffer."

He laughed. "And I believe you would, just to make me suffer."

Without warning, he grabbed her and pushed her up against the side of the covered wagon. Even with the throbbing in her hand, the look in his eyes sent a shiver throughout her entire body, as heat rushed to her head.

His fingertips trailed down her neck, and he lowered his lips to her ear and whispered, heatedly, "I will endure any pain it takes to have you as mine, Alissia, and I dream constantly of the day all this danger will be behind us. Then we can focus exclusively on making babies."

With that, he turned and left her standing there on shaky legs.

Chapter 11

It took Alissia a moment to pull herself together, and even when she joined everyone by the fire, she remained quiet. Although Anika, Langley, and Devon did not understand her threatening words to Selona, it bothered her that they had seen her lose control of her temper. And with the intense pain in her hand and Grady's constant ramblings about her abusive past, she could barely maintain the calm façade she hid behind.

Selona sat away from everyone else, and when Salvatore motioned toward a bowl of soup, she shook her head.

As Luke's wound was being cleaned, Alissia went to her covered wagon and struggled to put on fresh clothing. Once finished, she kept her head down as she made her way to the fire and tossed the skimpy clothing onto it.

She watched it burn for a moment before noticing Selona observing her with a taunting, smug grin. Alissia turned back to the fire, fighting to contain the rage that threatened to consume her.

It took a while for everyone to decide where to sleep. Selona's many bags, along with her plants, were arranged in the covered wagon Alissia usually shared with Langley and Anika. The married couple made the decision to move their belongings and sleep in Shade's wagon.

Although Alissia did not like giving the entire wagon to Selona—or giving the hideous creature a reason to believe she was scared—in the end, she decided to move out as well. Even her strong pride could not force her to sleep alone next to Selona and her mysterious gear, which seemed to be filled with many small living animals.

She arranged her blanket next to Luke's in Shade's crowded cage, and although he took the first watch alongside Carlo and was not around when she fell asleep, she tossed and turned all through the night next to him. She awoke in his arms around dawn.

After a quick kiss on her forehead, he stood, and she rolled over and moaned, her body feeling drained. The pain in her hand had kept her from entering a deep sleep throughout the night, and she wondered how Luke was even able stand.

Breakfast was quick, as everyone seemed eager to resume the journey. Since they were now on a public trail, Alissia and Selona had to stay hidden in the covered wagon. If guards stopped them, they could easily hide in the secret compartment beneath the floor of the wagon.

Anika was put in charge of taking care of Grady that morning, and he seemed content to stare blankly out in front of him.

Alissia spent the morning revitalizing the plants Selona brought along. She then healed and checked on the health of the many small animals. The two of them worked in silence, neither attempting nor wanting to make conversation.

The carriages stopped that afternoon for a quick picnic, which gave everyone a reason to stretch their legs. They were all gathered around the back of Carlo and Edda's wagon when Santo made the mistake of trying to interact with Selona.

The creature was sitting alone under a tree when Santo walked over with a small plate of food. He made it within a few feet of her before she abruptly reached out with her hand, and the black streaks began to show beneath the skin of her face. He immediately dropped the plate and began to tear at his throat.

Just as Alissia was about to intervene, Lita ran over and slapped Selona hard across the face. "He only wanted to give you some food!" she shouted, in the old language.

A look of surprise briefly filled Selona's face before she gave an eerie grin and reached both hands into the bag at her side. She then pulled out a large spider about the size of her hand. It was similar to a tarantula, with hairy legs, but it was black with bright orange stripes across its body.

Alissia had forced herself to touch and heal several of Selona's creepy animals all morning, and she recognized the spider as one of many traveling with her.

All eyes were on Selona as she pulled the legs of the spider above its body and pinched them together.

"What's she doing?" asked Anika feebly at Alissia's side.

Alissia shook her head, her eyes never leaving the helpless spider. "I don't know."

Selona stared into Alissia's eyes as she slowly lifted the small animal to her mouth.

"Please don't tell me she's going to..." Edda began.

"I think she's going to," said Bruna.

Selona licked her lips, dramatically, before opening her mouth wide. There was an unnerving crunching sound as the spider's head was ripped from its body. Juices began to drip down Selona's chin, and a sudden, high-pitched scream filled Alissia's head just before darkness overtook her.

"Alissia? Alissia, wake up!"

She opened her eyes to the sound of Anika's voice. Her friend was sitting at her side, shaking her shoulder. Salvatore and Langley were crouched down on the opposite side, and they were all staring down at her with worried expressions.

"Let me help you," Salvatore said, before gently pulling her into a sitting position.

Alissia looked around in confusion until she saw Luke sitting down on the grass with a dazed look on his face. They locked eyes.

"You fainted," said Luke, mentally.

"Did you?"

"Almost," he answered.

"The scream. Did you hear the scream?"

"A bit of it. Did you bond with that spider this morning?"

"I think so."

"Alissia!" Anika demanded. "Look at me! Are you well?"

She turned her attention from Luke and shook her head, blinking a few times. "I'm okay." She noticed Edda retching with Bruna holding back her hair. "Edda's sick."

"She'll be fine," Salvatore said. "Can you stand?"

Alissia nodded, and Langley and Salvatore helped her to her feet. Salvatore's eyes went to Luke and then back to her, but he said nothing.

She accepted a drink of water from Anika, and it was not long before the fog lifted from her mind and everyone began to prepare to leave. When she looked over at Selona, the creature was watching her with a satisfied grin, while using the last spider leg as a toothpick for her foul teeth.

In that moment, Alissia decided Selona knew what would happen to her when she ate the spider. She clenched her teeth, and her sharp nails dug into her palms, as she balled her hands into tight fists.

"You're not going to kill her."

"Stay out of my head, Luke," she mentally warned.

"I wasn't in your head. You were screaming into mine, and it's hard to ignore death threats. Don't let her get to you. Think logically, not emotionally."

Alissia turned her back on Selona and tried to calm herself, while forcing the moisture from her eyes. Her mental voice sounded strained and high-pitched as she vowed, *"She's not going to win!"*

"I didn't say to let her win. I just said not to let your anger get in the way. Don't give her the satisfaction of knowing she's bothering you."

She jumped when his arm unexpectedly reached around her waist, and he pulled her back against his chest. After a quick glance confirming she was being watched by Selona, she pasted a smile across her face and looked up at him.

"That's my girl."

"I'm still mad," she said, her smile not wavering.

His body shook with laughter. "I'm sure you are."

"Why can't I have cool powers like her and the mermaid people?"

"You don't think your healing powers are a good thing? Remember Fang?" He added mentally, *"Remember saving me?"*

"I wouldn't have to save anyone if I could defend them better in the first place."

He said cheerfully, "You never know. You may have more abilities than you're aware of."

"Yeah, but I can't cause pain, light a fire, put anyone to sleep, or do anything to physically defend myself."

His eyebrows rose. "And you've tried these things?"

"Of course," she answered. "Within the first few days of meeting you."

Luke laughed again. "Ah, but I do recall bird droppings on my head."

Alissia smiled mischievously. "Well, yeah, I had to have a little fun."

He leaned down and whispered, "I believe you enjoyed the physical defense lessons I gave you each night."

"Ouch!" Alissia pulled away as Mia scampered up her body. The tiny creature plopped down on Alissia's left shoulder and stared into Luke's face.

He said, "I think she's starting to like me."

"*Really*? And what makes you think that?"

"She hasn't bitten me in a while."

Alissia responded, "Maybe that has something to do with the fact that we haven't bathed in days. We don't exactly smell or taste our best."

Luke shook his head and grinned. "She likes me."

Salvatore walked over to them. "Alissia, I'd like for you to ride with me in the back of Romeo and Bruna's wagon, if you don't mind. Lita and Santo can drive Selona's wagon, and Lita can jump back there and help Selona into hiding if we meet any soldiers along the road." He turned to Luke. "Do you mind riding in the front with Romeo? That way you can join us if we need you."

"That's fine with me," Luke answered. He leaned down and gave Alissia a quick peck on her cheek, barely missing a swipe from Mia as he pulled away. He laughed, turning to Alissia. "Told you she likes me."

"She just tried to hit you."

"Ah, but she didn't hit me, and she didn't bite me either." He turned to walk away.

Shortly thereafter, Alissia and Salvatore were sitting across from each other in the comfortable leather beanbags. The smell in Romeo and Bruna's wagon was much more pleasant than the stench that now filled the wagon Selona had taken over.

Mia was purring loudly as Alissia petted the tiny fur ball in her lap. Unlike the wagons she had seen on television all her life, the covered wagons they traveled in gave a smooth ride and did not bounce all over the road. With the window flaps pulled back, a slight breeze entered the wagon, and Alissia could not help but feel relaxed.

She knew Salvatore would ask a lot of questions, but since meeting him, he had never tried to manipulate her to give him answers. He had always been straightforward, and she respected him for that. In fact, everyone in the group seemed to respect Salvatore. It just came easy.

He poured some hot, freshly steeped chet into a mug and held it out, and her hand left Mia to accept the soothing drink.

His eyes lingered on her hand for a moment. "I notice you haven't been using your dominant hand lately."

She blew on her drink before meeting his eyes. "And?"

"And I know you don't fully trust me, so I'll just tell you what I know."

He poured himself a drink and settled back into his beanbag.

"The Lamians live a long life, and although they don't trust us with much personal information, my people and ancestors have observed many things over time. Some of those observations have to do with their relationships. It seems that when one of them dies or gets sick, so does their mate."

Salvatore paused before continuing. "I can't help but notice you seem to be in just as much pain as Luke, and he nearly fainted with you today. I don't know how much you know about the Lamians and their ways, and I'm worried for you."

He asked, hesitantly, "Have you been intimate with Luke?"

Alissia nearly choked on the sip of chet in her mouth. She forced it down and looked up.

Before she could answer, he added, "I only ask because I don't know if you know the consequences that would bring. I mean, do you know? Is that something you've thought about?"

"What's a zeer?" she asked.

"A zeer is what the Lamians call their spouse. It's like a husband or wife. However, marriage is different within their culture."

Alissia tilted her head and looked questioningly at him. "How so?"

"They live to be over three hundred years old, and unlike humans, they don't rush into marriage. They usually don't even get married until they're in their fifties or sixties. My people have never witnessed a breakup between wed Lamians. It's for life. Like I said, when one dies, so does the other. However, it's usually at an old age. They don't seem to fall to diseases or sickness like we do, and their bodies heal after an accident."

"What else do you know about zeers?"

He held her gaze as he answered, "It's said that zeers can also mind speak to each other."

She nodded, casually. "Anything else?"

"My ancestors shared many stories of the torture the Lamians endured before going into hiding. They had a much closer relationship with them than we do now, as they not only traveled with them, but they also helped them to get started with their lives on the island."

He lifted his drink and blew on it before taking a long sip. Giving it an appreciative look, Salvatore swallowed before turning back to Alissia.

"During that time, my ancestors gained a lot of respect and love for them. They never witnessed them committing the atrocities we humans have grown accustomed to seeing. It's said they have beautiful souls and are gifted with the power to heal, not harm. They don't have the same desires we humans do, or at least, that's what my ancestors believed. And that's why they dedicated their lives and the lives of their descendants to the protection of the Lamians."

Salvatore stared into Alissia's eyes as he shook his head. "It was never about the money or wealth that came with the job."

She nodded in understanding, and he continued. "When a Lamian was tortured and killed, it destroyed entire families. Imagine a man being burned alive, yet his wife experienced that same torture and death while at home with her children. Although there was no visible fire, her children witnessed her agony and death."

Salvatore paused, and Alissia grimaced, envisioning the horrifying scene. "In the end, the Lamians that didn't believe in killing had to adjust. The slaughter was becoming too great, and some of the Lamians weren't strong enough to keep secrets. They gave in under the torture.

"That's when the Lamians decided they had to kill the connected zeer as soon as the torture began. However, they aren't killers. It's said that when a Lamian killed another of their kind, it pushed that Lamian into insanity, as they somehow connected with the Lamian they killed. The killer's zeer would also go insane, so one death meant two deaths and two mentally incompetent Lamians."

"Wow!" Alissia said.

Salvatore nodded and took a sip of his drink, and she stared down at her mug. After a while, she looked up. "I've never been intimate with Luke... other than kissing. The same with Grady, although... that was months ago. Something did happen, though."

She finished off her drink and set it down before continuing. "Luke... well, he almost died the night we fled the castle. I mean, he *really* almost died. Ian and his men tortured him severely. He was beaten, his league tattoo was completely sliced up with a knife, and then they stabbed him in his side."

A sudden wave of emotion came over her, and she looked down and pretended to be interested in petting Mia.

"What's wrong, Alissia?" came Luke's concerned voice within her head.

"I'm fine. Salvatore explained some things, and I'm telling him about what happened to you in the dungeon. It's time we try to get some answers."

The sound of movement coming from the front flap caught her attention, and it was not long before Luke clumsily made his way into the covered portion of the wagon. Stabbing pains shot through her hand throughout the entire process, and she was relieved when Salvatore helped him into a sitting position next to her.

They all stared at each other for a moment before the older man calmly asked, "Would you like to continue?"

She looked at Luke before turning back to Salvatore. "Yes, but could you tell Luke what you just told me?"

He nodded, and Alissia listened as he retold what he knew. He must have noticed her eyeing the chet, because while he was talking, he leaned down and picked up her mug and poured her another drink. Luke declined a drink offer, as he listened intently to all Salvatore had to say.

Once he was finished talking, they sat in silence for a brief moment before Luke asked, "So they die together?"

Salvatore nodded. "Yes, and Alissia here was just telling me how you nearly died the night you left the castle. However, except for the two of you sleeping all day, you seemed to be in good health when I saw you."

"He's in great health—or at least was until he was tortured again."

Salvatore responded, "I don't know much about your kind—I mean a human that's been changed by a Lamian. To my knowledge, that hasn't happened to any of my ancestors, yet they shared a friendship with the Lamians.

"I do know that before the Lamians went into hiding, some of their women were raped by human men, but nothing happened to the men. It didn't change them."

"That's what Ian was wanting," said Alissia.

Salvatore nodded. "I've also been told there have been marriages between humans and Lamians, and that's what started the killings. When they married, the humans experienced changes for the good. That's when the rapes began. Men wanted to be changed, and they believed if they were with a Lamian woman, they would go through those changes. It didn't work that way, though."

"So the Lamians weren't just burned and tortured for their secrets," Alissia said, "they were also raped in an attempt to be changed?"

"Yes, and with the Lamians having a slow reproduction process, their population greatly suffered. My ancestors believed if the Lamians had not gone into hiding, they would've been killed off."

He let that sink in for a moment. "So you're the only human I know of that the Lamians have trusted with their abilities in almost two thousand years. How you earned that honor, along with being chosen to journey back to their homeland, is truly a mystery. I can only imagine they chose you as a person of great character and integrity." He paused before adding, "And from what I've seen of you, they chose the right person to represent them."

"Oh, great! He thinks the Lamians chose me to represent them. He has no idea they made the mistake of saving my life and probably regret it by now," Alissia mentally said.

"Are you considering telling him the Lamians that changed you really live in this reality?"

"No, I think I'm ready to tell him everything but that. The biggest secret here is the location of the Lamians, and I'm not ready to give that up. As long as he and everyone else believe they're from my reality, that secret is safe, and I plan to keep it that way. I haven't felt their presence with me in over a week, and I wonder if I'm too far for them to watch me—or whatever it is they do when they see me at night."

Luke asked, *"Do you trust him?"*

"Do you?"

"He seems honorable."

"He already knows we're connected. He saw you almost faint when I did."

Alissia noticed Salvatore watching them with a knowing look, and she shrugged. "We can mind speak."

He nodded.

She added sarcastically, "And I feel every bit of the pain he feels in his hand, yet he refuses to take anything for it."

Salvatore's lip curled up, and he nodded again. To Luke, he said, "I understand."

"And we haven't been intimate," she added.

Luke's eyes widened.

"What? He asked," she said defensively. Turning her attention back to Salvatore, she explained everything that happened in the dungeon the night of their escape.

Once she had finished, he said, "You two have been through a lot." To Alissia, he added, "I just don't understand how you saved him without killing yourself or why he hasn't changed like you."

"Mia tells me it has to do with this," she said, showing him the star on her hand. "I can't really explain it, as I don't understand it myself. But, it helps me when I heal animals. It glows, and I think it gave me some extra power."

Salvatore leaned forward and examined the scar given to her by the unknown creature in the forest. When he leaned back, he asked, "And the Lamians gave you this, as extra protection?"

"No, not the Lamians. It's another mystery I'm hoping they can tell me about. I don't really know much about it."

He asked, "And your friend Mia, where did she come from?"

Alissia looked down at her tiny friend, sleeping peacefully in her lap. Then she looked up and shook her head. "I really can't say."

Salvatore looked disappointed as he responded, "So I haven't earned that much trust. I see."

Alissia said, "I'm sorry. I've been trusted with many secrets, and they're not mine to tell. I can only trust you with mine, and that has to do with what happened to Luke. I saved him somehow, but we have no idea what the consequences are. The creatures in the swamp tortured him because they were experimenting with our bond. The creatures that poisoned Grady and Luke don't affect me. The same goes for what Selona and her kind can do. She can't do that choking thing on me, but when she does it to Luke, it gets me too."

"I'm her weakness," Luke said.

"What?" Alissia asked in surprise.

He shrugged. "If I die, you die. You heal, but I don't. It's that simple."

She frowned at his way of thinking.

"Can I see your mark, Luke?" Salvatore asked.

Luke nodded and lifted his shirt to reveal the handprint on his chest. Salvatore leaned forward and studied it for a moment.

"So the power must have come through your hand," he said thoughtfully. He leaned back, and Luke lowered his shirt.

"I don't know," Alissia said. "We both passed out—I mean fainted. I woke up thinking he should be dead, but he wasn't. Then we had to rush to get out of the castle."

"And you've not noticed any changes?" Salvatore asked.

A hint of sadness seeped into her, and she knew it was coming from Luke, although his face gave away no hint of the emotion.

She said, "We can't kiss anymore."

Salvatore gave a confused look, and she explained how her body temperature rises and purple streaks cover her body whenever they share a kiss. She also told him Mia would not allow it, and she would bite the two of them if they got too close.

He turned to Luke and gave a sympathetic look. "It just gets worse, doesn't it?"

Luke shook his head. "You have no idea."

"Well, it sounds like the two of you have many questions to ask once we get to the island. Luke should definitely be allowed to meet with the Lamians as well. That's a plus. You won't be alone," Salvatore said, cheerfully.

Alissia nodded.

"What about Selona?" Luke asked.

Salvatore frowned thoughtfully. "I don't know. It sounds like they aren't a very pleasant people, and I can't take a threat to the island. Although, I guess she could be killed if the Lamians consider her a danger."

Alissia looked at Salvatore in surprise. Although she knew he was a protector of the Lamians and knew his way with weapons, she had never seen him as a killer. He had more of a fatherly personality, yet he had just mentioned killing someone as if it meant nothing.

Luke let out a small laugh. "Don't look so surprised. Just this afternoon, you were ready to do the job yourself, not to mention last night."

"It's not that I want her dead," Salvatore said. "However, we do what's best for the Lamians, and if she learns the location of the island, she won't be able to leave if she's a threat."

"What about me and Luke?" she asked. "If we're considered a threat, will we be killed?"

Salvatore looked out the back of the wagon for a moment. When his attention returned, he said reassuringly, "They won't consider either of you a threat. You were gifted with their abilities, and that should mean a lot to them. They also aren't killers. They don't think like that, and death is an unlikely extreme that would only be considered if given over to the human protectors. Even then, I have a say and can suggest alternatives."

"Will we ever be allowed to leave the island?" she asked.

His voice softened as he said, "I don't know. That's not my decision. I can tell you that the island is a beautiful place to live, and you wouldn't be in any danger. No worries. No danger. I think the two of you would be happy." Turning to Luke, he added, "Well, once the two of you get past the physical problem."

Alissia said, "They claim they used to trade with the Lamians, and Selona is bringing them something they greatly valued. It's one of their recipes using ingredients only found in their swamp. It's supposed to make the Lamian women more fertile."

Out of a sudden curiosity, she asked, "By the way, how many pregnancies does a Lamian woman usually have?"

Salvatore answered, "Four is the most I've heard of. Mostly only two or three."

A confused look came over her face, and she said, "But that sounds normal."

He shook his head. "Not when you consider that they live over three hundred years, and they don't even become fertile until after they're a hundred. You also have to remember that much of their population was killed off years ago, and they don't reproduce near as much as a human."

"Oh."

He looked at Mia and said, "Your pixet acts as your protector."

She stroked the length of Mia's back and smiled. "She does, except for when she's biting me or Luke."

Salvatore chuckled. "She knows the reason for that. They have other pixets on the island."

"They do?"

"Yes, they have a lot of exotic animals and creatures. That's where we got Shade, and we get many trained animals for trading purposes."

Romeo knocked on the front flaps of the wagon, and Salvatore stuck his head through the flaps. After a short conversation, he sat back down. "We're about to pass some wagons, but none of them appear to be military. You should get down and cover your head in case someone looks back."

Luke pulled a blanket from the corner and set it in his lap, and Alissia placed Mia in the beanbag and rotated it to keep her hidden. She lay down with her head in Luke's lap, and he covered her hair.

"What about Selona?" she asked.

Salvatore said, "Lita will take care of her. I just hope there's not going to be anyone at the spring when we get there."

"What spring?" she asked.

"We've underwent a stressful few days, and we're low on our water supply so I thought we'd stop at a natural spring for the night. If no one is there, we can stay for two nights and get some laundry done."

"Will that be safe?" Luke asked.

Salvatore shrugged his shoulders. "As long as no one is there. We won't know until we get there."

"We should avoid the spring and go to another water supply," said Luke.

"We could," Salvatore started. "And I understand as a member of the league, you would want to skip such frivolity, and under normal circumstances, I would as well. However, I'm under a bit of pressure to relieve some of the stress of late."

"What do you mean?" asked Alissia.

"We could refill our water somewhere else, but I've been asked to at least make the attempt to stop at the spring. It seems the two of you and Selona have a strong odor—especially Selona—and it's upsetting Edda. She's pregnant, and she's miserable."

Alissia's eyes widened, and she grinned broadly. "Edda's pregnant? How far along?"

Salvatore nodded. "About two months, and the poor woman was terrified her baby's life was in danger when you and Luke disappeared. She's been a mess, which has put stress on Carlo, and that has trickled down to everyone in my group."

He frowned and shook his head. Looking at Luke, he added, "It's amazing how one little female can be such a nuisance. We love her, but this pregnancy—along with Selona's presence—is beginning to put a strain on things."

"But y'all look so happy," Alissia said.

"And we are," he said reassuringly. "It's just that Edda is terrified of Selona—and justifiably so. She's scared the creature will harm her baby if she found out about the pregnancy. She didn't get any sleep last night after witnessing the invisible attack on the two of you."

His eyes stayed on Alissia as he added, "The smell is also making her exceedingly nauseous. Someone's going to have to bathe Selona when we get to the spring. Her stench will be a problem when we get to the port city. It draws too much attention, and that's the last thing we need."

Alissia watched Salvatore through narrow eyes as she asked slowly, "And you're thinking I'm that person?"

"That would be nice."

"Why not Lita?" she demanded.

He shook his head. "Lita doesn't have the patience and would wind up getting herself killed."

"And I have the patience?"

The older man studied her face for a moment before shaking his head. "No, I don't believe you do. However, her power has no control over you. If we keep Luke away from her, you'll be safe."

She frowned. "I know she stinks horribly, but is her smell that important?"

"Unfortunately, it is," Salvatore replied. "I'll sit down and introduce myself to her, and then I'll explain how we'll be entering a crowded city. If she wants to go unnoticed, she'll have to try to smell and look as humanly as possible."

"And what's so special about this spring?" Alissia asked.

Luke said, "The water comes from the ground. It's clear and much cleaner than other natural water supplies. It's completely different than a stream, river, or lake. And because they're more rare, many people will go out of their way to stop at a spring when traveling. It won't be as interesting as the underground one we went to at the castle, but you get an idea of the clear pool of water."

He looked at Salvatore. "I don't like the idea of Alissia being alone with Selona."

Although part of her liked the fact that he was worried for her, her pride was stronger, and she argued, "I can handle her."

"I didn't say you couldn't take care of yourself," said Luke. "I just said I don't like the idea of you being alone with her."

"How does not wanting me to be alone with Selona mean you think I can take care of myself?"

Luke let out a frustrated sigh. "I just don't like the idea of you being alone. That's all."

"Why?" she asked stubbornly.

"You don't always make the right decisions, and I worry about you. That's all."

Her face contorted into a scowl. "I don't always make the right decisions? Like when?"

He stared back at her as if the answer was obvious. "There have many. The last being Gafeen."

She rolled her eyes. *"Really?* We've talked about this. I thought you were dead, and there wasn't any hope for an escape. I was surrounded by swamp creatures of the dead, and I did what I had to do."

"You mean you attacked the largest and cruelest beast you could find." He turned to Salvatore and described Gafeen's appearance, ending with, "Her idea was to get him angry so he would kill her quickly. She attacked him first."

Salvatore stared down at her, his eyebrows raised.

She met his gaze with a smug look on her face. "In my defense, it would have been a great plan if it weren't for the fact that my body heals so quickly. Apparently, I can be beaten over and over again without dying." She lifted her hand and pointed into the air for emphasis. "It was a learning experience."

"And the mushrooms?" Luke accused.

She dropped her hand and glared up at him. "The best sleep I've had in days."

He turned to Salvatore and gave more details about that night. Once he was finished, she ignored the pain in her hand and crossed her arms, wishing she could sit up to face them. *"Really?"* she asked.

"Alissia, I love you, and you're a strong woman," Luke said firmly. "However, you don't always make the right choices when it comes to your own safety, and it makes my life stressful when I'm trying to keep you alive."

She looked back at him defiantly. "Well, I guess that would mean keeping yourself alive too, as it seems I can't live without you, and I mean that literally."

Salvatore's laughter filled the wagon, and she and Luke both turned to stare at him. When he finally stopped laughing, tears were in his eyes.

"Ah, young love. I remember those days. A feisty woman, and a man that has much to learn when it comes to feisty women." He grinned at Luke. "I wish you much luck with that, young man. You'll need it."

Chapter 12

It was late into the night when they arrived at the spring. Another group of carriages was already there, and except for going to the bathroom, Alissia and Selona had to remain hidden in the covered wagons.

Alissia slept in a corner of Romeo and Bruna's wagon, and although Luke refused to take something for the pain in his hand, Salvatore assured her that he would help with the care of the wound, applying more numbing cream throughout the day.

She opened her eyes the following morning at the sound of Shade's fierce roar and found herself alone in the wagon with all the flaps closed, leaving the interior dark as night. She rolled over and tried to go back to sleep, but the throbbing in her hand was too great.

After a while, she frowned in frustration and sat up. Mia opened her eyes and looked around before closing them again.

"*Luke, where is everyone?*" she mentally asked.

"*Stay hidden. We believe the other carriages will be leaving soon. It seems traveling with Shade has some benefits. Salvatore is letting him roam freely, and he's scaring the other travelers. They're packing their carriages at a rapid pace.*"

"*What time is it? What's everyone doing?*" she asked.

"*It's late morning. You're the last one to wake, but your breakfast is on a warming stone. I'll have Santo bring it to you. Everyone else has started on laundry and refilling our water barrels. Now that you're awake, Bruna can add some more numbing cream to my hand. She's been asking about it all morning, but I thought it would be best to wait until you were awake.*"

"*What about my clothes? I also need to do laundry.*"

"*I've already gotten them for you, along with mine,*" he answered. "*With my hand, I can't do laundry, and they're cleaning them for us.*"

"*How's Grady?*"

"*Anika says he recognized her for a short moment when he first woke up, but then he went back to having visions of you. We think he's reliving the night you left him in Pallen. He's now sitting by the fire pleading for you to listen to him. He's been doing that for a while now, and I must admit, I feel sorry for him at the moment.*"

Alissia closed her eyes, pushing back her own emotions as she let out a sigh. "*Why do all of his visions have to do with me? Doesn't he have anything else he's scared of or cares about?*"

"*I doubt it. He's lived the perfect life. He comes from a prestigious family in Allure. He's thrived in the Eldership ever since he was a child, and I doubt he ever really had a social life until he met you. His life has always consisted of work and training.*"

She frowned. "*So his life was perfect until he met me.*"

"*No, Alissia. I'm saying he's always been committed to his career within the Eldership. You also have to remember that his mind was already fixated on you at the time he was bitten. You had been missing, and he probably spent those two days filled with worry, thinking you were dead. Before that, he had to deal with losing you to me. And then there's what happened the night you left Pallen, the one he seems to be reliving at this moment."*

She put her head in her hand, groaning to herself. *"You're right. I ruined his life. No wonder he's so focused on me."*

"That's not what I'm saying! Here's Santo. I'll tell him to bring you and Mia some breakfast. Get ready for the pain. I'm about to have Bruna add some more numbing cream."

An hour later, Luke opened the back flaps of the carriage, and Alissia quickly grabbed her glasses at the bright sunlight.

"Ready for a day in the water?" he asked, in a surprisingly cheerful mood. As she hopped from the carriage, he said, "You and Selona need to go to the spring now, while no one's around. Although Shade seems to have scared everyone away, we don't know when or if there will be others arriving."

"Here's a bathing suit Selona can wear," said Edda, walking toward them.

"What about me?" Alissia asked.

"Mine and Bruna's will fall off you, but Bruna is getting a wrap you can tie around you to use as a small dress."

Salvatore joined them, and Alissia asked, "Did you talk to Selona?"

He nodded. "Yes, I don't believe she's happy about it, but she seems to understand she'll have to work with us to conceal her identity."

Mia hopped onto Alissia's shoulders, and Alissia looked up and asked, in the ancient language, "You want to go swimming?"

The tiny creature nodded, and Lita walked toward them with a basket full of wet clothing. The young woman stopped in front of them and set the basket down. She grinned. "I heard you're going to have a fun swim with your new friend."

Alissia gave a wry smile. "Yeah, Mia will be there to help, but I wish you could join us."

Lita shrugged. "I can help."

"I don't think that's a good idea," said Salvatore.

"She's not going to kill me." Lita turned to her father and put her hands on her hips.

"She's not the one I'm worried about," he responded.

She rolled her eyes and turned to Edda. "We'll need some gloves and a pair of scissors. I don't think those knots in her hair will ever come out. It's best we just chop it." She scrunched up her face. "There's no telling what's living in that mess."

Alissia grinned. Although Lita did not seem to have the best people skills, she was the perfect person to help with this chore.

Shortly thereafter, Alissia was standing at the edge of a clear pool of water, and she could easily understand why people went out of their way to visit the place. Her toes pushed their way into the white sand at the edge of the water, and she smiled as she took in her surroundings.

A variety of exotic tropical foliage surrounded the pool, and many large, wild purifying flowers floated along the surface. She could see their roots hanging from them.

The water was the perfect temperature, and she waded to a shady spot, eager to remove all the swamp muck from her hair and body. She pulled her sunglasses off and held them up while dunking her head into the water. When she came back up, she found Selona scowling at her, still standing at the edge of the water. Lita already had her gloves on and was ready to begin.

Alissia smiled and tried to sound friendly as she looked at Selona. "Come on in. The water's perfect."

The creature shook her head and crossed her arms.

"Is it because you can't swim? It's not that deep here."

"I can swim," Selona responded, in her creepy voice.

"Then what's the problem?" Alissia asked. "The water's clear and clean, and we have bubbly soap that smells like flowers." She motioned toward a group of tropical plants. "And look how beautiful it is here."

"I'm not a human," snapped Selona.

Lita said impatiently, "No, but if you want to stay hidden from humans, you'll make the attempt to wash that noticeably horrible stench off your body."

"You know nothing of what you ask of me," Selona hissed back, and for a moment—just a tiny one—Alissia felt somewhat sorry for the sad-looking creature.

Selona lifted her chin resolutely, and then she slowly made her way into the water. Instead of fighting, she said nothing as she scrubbed her body with the soap. Alissia thought she noticed tears in the creature's large, black eyes. However, it could have just been water.

Although she willingly bathed for them, Alissia and Lita could not talk Selona into using the mouth cleanser. The creature shook her head decisively and would not even consider it.

Lita was right about Selona's hair. Nothing could help with something neglected for so long. In the end, the creature sat on a grassy spot under a tree while Lita chopped away at her hair with scissors. Once finished, Selona's hair was short and—not surprisingly—completely uneven.

Selona's cooperative demeanor confused Alissia. Although she still looked evil, she suddenly looked defeated.

Through mind speaking, Luke constantly checked up on Alissia as they bathed. When she told him they were finished with Selona, everyone joined them at the pool. She instructed Shade and the dogs to alert them if another carriage arrived. However, they all hoped they would have the spring to themselves for the day, and she told Shade not to hide if another carriage did appear, hoping his threatening appearance would scare others away.

Alissia watched from the water as everyone put their towels, picnic baskets, and bathing supplies down in the shade of a tall, winding tree. Like Alissia, Devon had a rigged bathing suit, although everyone else wore normal ones.

After watching Edda for a moment, Alissia noticed the apprehension Salvatore had talked about. The woman apprehensively glanced at Selona often, and her husband stayed close by her side.

Salvatore brought Selona a blanket to sit on. However, she only seemed to be interested in studying the foliage in the surrounding area, and she began to pick, sniff, and even taste some of the foreign plants.

Anika led Grady to the edge of the water, and after he scanned his surroundings, his eyes fell on Alissia. A look of recognition came over him, and he smiled.

Wading up to him, she said, "Hey, Grady. Ready for a swim?"

"What are you wearing, Alissia?" He made his way toward her.

She looked down and laughed at her makeshift bathing suit. "Nobody had anything that would fit me."

"Ah," he said. He gave her a quick peck on the cheek and took her by the hand. "What do you think about this place?"

Alissia glanced over at Anika, and her friend raised her eyebrows and shrugged. She turned her attention back to Grady. "I think it's lovely, and the water's perfect. You want to swim some laps and get some exercise with me?"

He nodded, and after she buried her sunglasses in the folds of her outfit, the two of them started out. Although her hand was numb and achy, she ignored the pain and forced herself into a workout, as it had been days since she had gotten any exercise.

After a while, she swam over to a large rock in a shady corner of the spring and climbed onto it. She dug out her sunglasses and put them on while Grady jumped up next to her. He took her by the hand and then lay back to stare up at her.

In that moment, he seemed so happy, looking into her face. She knew he could easily start screaming and crying at any moment, and her heart ached for him. She pulled her hand from his and positioned herself onto her stomach.

She had no idea if he considered her his wife or girlfriend at the moment. All she cared about was that he was happy. For now, he was smiling, and in her opinion, he deserved to.

He closed his eyes contently, and she looked over her shoulder to find Luke sitting at the edge of the water. His shirt and hair was still dry. When their eyes met, she mentally asked, *"Do you need help bathing?"*

"Devon will help me. How's Grady?"

"He's happy, for now."

"That's good."

Alissia turned her attention back to Grady. She smiled to herself before lowering her face to his chest, and his arm went around her as she made herself comfortable. It was not long before the two of them fell into a peaceful sleep.

"Alissia. Alissia, we need to talk."

Without opening her eyes, Alissia frowned at the sound of Anika's whispered voice. "What?"

"We *need* to talk."

Alissia opened her eyes and slowly sat up, careful not to wake Grady. Anika's angry glare confused her, and she noticed Langley standing beside his wife, with a troubled look on his face.

"What?" Alissia whispered, suddenly fully awake.

Anika stepped back, expectantly, and Alissia lowered herself into the water and began to follow her friends away from everyone else. When they stopped, Anika turned around and crossed her arms. "Is there something you haven't told us?"

Confused, Alissia's eyes traveled from Anika to Langley. Suddenly, her heart fell from her chest, and she looked over Anika's shoulder to find Devon washing Luke's hair. To her surprise, Luke was not wearing a shirt, and the handprint that had been branded into his chest was on display.

Luke's eyes met hers. *"What's wrong?"* he mentally asked.

"What are you doing?"

"I'm bathing."

"Yeah, but I thought you were going to hide the handprint."

Luke responded, *"I don't see the need to anymore. We told Salvatore, and he's told everyone else. Devon already knows we encountered creatures in the bog, and he's seen Mia."*

"Yeah, but I haven't told Anika!" she snapped back.

"Are you talking to him?" Anika asked incredulously. She uncrossed her arms and shook her head, letting out a sarcastic laugh. "That explains it!"

"Explains what?" Alissia asked, trying to think of something to say.

"It explains why you laugh suddenly when staring at nothing, and you've been distracted lately, not hearing what I'm saying when I'm talking to you. It's because you and Luke can hear each other in your heads. Isn't it?"

Alissia glanced at Langley, only to find an expectant look on his face. "Anika, I'm sorry. We didn't know exactly what happened, and we decided not to tell anyone until we could get an idea. I mean..." she faltered, "it was sudden. Ian's men almost killed Luke the night we escaped the castle."

"That was four weeks ago!" Anika exclaimed, in a high-pitched voice. "When exactly were you planning to tell us?" She shook her head, and her face softened, revealing her hurt. "Langley, Grady, and I have risked our lives to help you. Then something this big happens, and you don't even tell us?"

Anika's eyes widened in sudden realization, and she glanced over her shoulder at the others. Turning back to Alissia, she asked, "Who knew? Did Salvatore and his people know?"

"Salvatore guessed it yesterday, and we told him what happened. There doesn't seem to be a reason to hide it anymore. Salvatore could tell I feel Luke's pain in my own hand, and that's why he's been getting Bruna to put more numbing cream on it."

A mixture of hurt and anger filled Anika's face, and she looked away, shaking her head.

"I'm sorry," Alissia said. She looked at Langley. "I was going to tell y'all. I was. We don't exactly know what happened, and at first we didn't know if Luke would start changing. Then it took a few days before we figured out we could speak to each other mentally. But there was so much other stuff going on at that time."

Anika turned back around, and Alissia looked into her eyes. "We didn't know if we could trust Salvatore and his people. I had to tell Grady I'm with Luke, and I've never had to do anything like that in my life." In a pleading voice, she added, "Anika, there was just *so* much going on."

A tear rolled down Anika's face. "Yet, you didn't trust me enough to talk to me. You had so much to think about, yet you smiled and acted normal around me." She wiped the tear away with the back of her hand. "I thought we were close. Langley and I even considered you like family, but I guess you didn't feel the same."

"It's not like that, Anika. I do consider you and Langley like family—honestly, even closer than my real family. And, I still love Grady, but everything is so confusing right now. It's complicated."

Anika turned and walked away. When Alissia looked at Langley, she couldn't read his face. "I'm sorry."

He nodded and turned to follow his wife.

Alissia watched the two of them swim for a moment, and then she turned back to Grady. He was still sleeping peacefully, so she decided to join Luke.

"I'll do that, Devon."

The young boy looked at Luke before handing her the wet rag. As he walked away, she lightly moved the rag over Luke's forehead and swollen eye. "Should I scrub your beard?"

"Devon took care of that when he washed my hair."

She nodded, examining his face and body for any dirt left behind. Once satisfied, she waded out of the water and picked up her towel. He followed, and when she noticed him trying to dry off with one hand, she wrapped her towel around her body and went to help him.

When she finished, he took her by the hand and led her to the blanket Devon had spread out for them. It was a short distance from the others, yet it was still near the edge of the water. They sat down and began to pull food from their basket.

"I'm sorry," he began. "I should have thought about Anika and Langley, and I see it's caused trouble."

Alissia studied her wrap filled with something similar to spicy hummus and sprouts. Some of Salvatore's ethnic food was hard for her to get used to, but she knew they were going out of their way for her vegetarian diet. She forced herself to take a bite.

"I didn't even think about it either," she said while chewing. "Things have just been too crazy the last few days with being kidnapped and dealing with Grady."

"What did she say to you?"

She told him how the conversation went, and then they finished their meal in silence, her mood lingering between them.

Luke set the basket aside and scooted closer. "What are you going to do about it?"

She shrugged. "What can I do? I've told them I'm sorry."

He nodded before Mia startled the two of them by leaping onto the blanket. The tiny creature began to plunder the basket, devouring everything edible.

Alissia looked out across the water and noticed Grady sitting on the same rock she had left him. He was watching Anika and Langley, with tears streaming down his face. After a long sigh, she said, "Do you think things will ever get better?"

"Of course." He chuckled lightly and took her hand. "Besides, it could be worse. We're alive, we're together, and you have some amazing, beautiful eyes."

"True, but you've almost been killed twice since meeting me. And I can't seem to stop getting kidnapped. I've ruined Grady's life, and now I've hurt Anika and Langley's feelings."

He turned his face toward the water and said, "I've been close to death many times before meeting you, and it's something I'm more than familiar with. Grady's life will go back to normal once he gets back to Allure, and he'll be distracted with trying to talk the Elders into preventing a war. Anika and Langley will forgive you. As for you continuously being kidnapped, think of all the adventures you've been on. You even got to meet me."

"So you finally admit that you kidnapped me?" She grinned.

Luke laughed. "No," he said, tapping his finger on her nose. "I admit to saving you from being kidnapped. I protected you—somewhat forcefully—but I protected you."

Alissia stared back at him blankly. "Luke, you tackled me, threw me on a horse, and then drugged me."

He gave a cocky grin. "And yet, you're still not grateful. Some women are just too hard to please."

Chapter *13*

They spent the next two weeks traveling hard. There was a lot of rain, which was heavy at times, but being so close to their destination, Salvatore refused to slow down.

They began to see more people on the roads, and Alissia and Selona had to remain hidden, even at night.

Grady had to be drugged quite often, as the dreary weather seemed to make his mood swings worse, and he had many flashbacks of Alissia crying beneath the tree. Although she was grateful no one asked questions, having her past continuously talked about greatly bothered her.

She continued to help Selona take care of her small plants and animals, and Alissia learned not to be near the creature when she ate one of her critters so that she could not feel the suffering the animal endured. It seemed to only have an effect on her if she watched the animal being eaten, her mind unintentionally entering into a mental bond.

When she was not helping Selona, Alissia spent most of her time reading in Romeo and Bruna's wagon, and she continued to sleep there. Anika stayed busy caring for Grady, while her husband Langley helped to drive the carriages.

The rain caused flooding on some of the roads, and the men had to work hard to keep from stopping. Alissia poured healing into the horses each night, fearing they were being overworked.

It was raining hard when the carriages finally stopped at the large city gates of Ellendale, the port city. However, the bad weather did not keep the guards from thoroughly searching the wagons, during which Alissia quietly endured sharing a cramped compartment with Mia and Luke. Grady had been given leo and was hidden in a separate wagon, with Selona being in another.

By the time the carriages stopped inside a large carriage house, it was late in the afternoon, and Alissia was miserable from spending so much time in such a small and noisy space. She and Luke were told to remain in the stall with their carriage, while Salvatore's group unharnessed the horses and led them away.

Unlike the last wooden barn they had stayed in, the walls of this one were made with a mixture of rocks and shells. Instead of having a large, open area, the carriage house had passageways with many stalls along each side. Simple sconces made with glow stones were situated along the walls, and although the ceiling of the stall was clear like most others in this reality, it could be turned into an open skylight to let fresh air in. A crank was built into the wall, a thin chain attached to it.

When she turned to Luke, she found him smiling at her, and she gave him a questioning look.

He took her by the hand and pulled her into his body. By now, his injured hand no longer needed to be wrapped, and he was able to use it to pull a loose tendril of hair behind her ear.

"Have I told you lately how much I adore you?" he asked.

Alissia slipped her arms around his waist and smiled up at him. "No, you've been too busy."

"Hmm... we'll soon be sailing to a beautiful tropical island together."

"Yeah," she started, "but we'll be meeting more creatures that possibly hate us, and from our luck, you'll somehow be tortured. We'll have to talk or fight our way out of it, only to have me kidnapped once we escape."

His body shook with soft laughter. "You've lost the faith, Pixet."

"I prefer to call myself a realist, and I'm beginning to think we'll never have a normal life."

He leaned down and placed a series of tender kisses along her neck, and by the time his lips made it to her ear, her knees were weak.

"Who said we were made to be normal when we can be so much more?" he murmured softly, his warm breath caressing her neck.

In a flash, his body pulled away, and they both stared down at the tiny amount of blood trickling along his arm. Mia had scampered up Alissia's body and was now glaring at Luke from her position on Alissia's shoulder.

"Mia!" Alissia scolded. "He wasn't kissing me, and his hand is just now healing. Will you stop?"

"Did you feel it?" Luke asked, grabbing a cloth from the wagon and wiping the blood.

Alissia pulled Mia from her shoulder and set her on the ground. "No, it's not bad enough for me to feel it."

"Good," he said, putting the rag back down. "You won't try to make me take pain tonics or mushroom juice."

"Really?" she asked, sarcastically.

He dodged Alissia's swipe at him before grabbing her around the waist and pulling her back to him.

"Tell your nanny I don't intend to break any rules. You're more than worth the wait."

Mia looked as if she was ready to pounce.

Alissia scowled down at her. "He's not going to kiss me. Leave him alone. We haven't had time to talk in days."

The tiny creature hopped back into the wagon, pulled a blanket to the edge, and plopped down, her eyes resting on her two wards.

Alissia shook her head and turned her attention back to Luke. "I guess that's the best we can get."

Luke grinned. "I'll take it." He led her to the wall, where he leaned back and pulled her against him.

She slipped her arms around him and rested the side of her face against his chest. The sound of his heartbeat was soothing, along with his fingers slowly trailing up and down her back.

At that moment, she didn't care about all the unanswered questions and danger surrounding them. She had Luke, and that was all she needed. She gave an affectionate squeeze as she realized she wasn't scared of her emotions toward him. For the first time in her life, she knew what true love was, and she was ready to fully embrace it.

They silently held each other, completely at peace, until the sound of footsteps caused them to turn their heads toward the opening of the stall.

"You two ready?" asked Lita.

Alissia pulled away from Luke and walked over to the wagon. She held out her arms, and Mia jumped into them.

"Who owns this place?" she asked.

"Someone we trade with," Lita answered. "They know about Shade and have closed off a portion of this building for us. As long as you stay where I show you, you'll be hidden until we can find a way onto the ship."

"How hard will it be to get on the ship?" Alissia asked.

"Father will know more tonight. He won't be around tonight or most of tomorrow. He needs to find out which of our ships are in the port and how high the security is here. That'll determine a lot."

"What do you mean?"

"Well, Father sent a message to our leaders when we first arrived in Pallen. He told them he planned to bring you to this port, but we still don't know which ship they sent for you. That means we don't know which crew we'll be with. We also don't know if the guards are searching for you in this city."

Alissia looked at Luke. "Are we still in the Eldership's territory?"

"Yes, and I believe they'll be searching for you, which will make it difficult to get aboard a ship."

Alissia wrapped the blanket around Mia to conceal her body and frowned. "Can't anything be easy?"

"And where's the adventure in that?" Luke responded.

She rolled her eyes and shook her head. "I believe I've had enough adventure to last a lifetime."

He laughed as they followed Lita into the passageway.

Although glowing sconces were arranged along the walls, white bella flowers also covered them. The floors were made of large stones, leaving enough space for a moss-like grass to grow along the edges of the wall. The sound of rain and people's voices bounced off the clear ceiling and stone floors, and it reminded Alissia of being in an alley of an old city.

Lita led them to a room filled with bunk beds lined against the walls. A long bench table was in the middle of the room, and a door in the bedroom led into a small bathroom.

Just as with the rest of the carriage house, the ceiling could be opened to let fresh air in, and white bella flowers and glow stones were used for the lighting.

Lita immediately closed the thin curtains of the few windows in the room. She then turned her attention back to Luke and Alissia. "Don't leave this room. I'll be back with the others, but this is where you'll be staying until we leave the city. The fellows will bring your bags soon, and your food will be brought to you this evening."

After she left, Mia hopped down and began to investigate their surroundings, and Alissia went to the bathroom. It did not take long before Lita came back with Selona, Devon, and Anika.

"Are you okay?" Alissia asked, looking at Anika.

Her friend shook her head slightly. "I've got a fever, and I'm not feeling well." She made her way toward one of the lower beds. "I just need some rest. I'll be fine."

Alissia turned to Lita. "Where's Langley and Grady?"

"Grady's still asleep from the leo, so Langley's staying with him. Santo, Romeo, and Carlo plan to keep watch to make sure no one accidently ventures this way, so they'll be safe."

"Where's Bruna and Edda?" asked Alissia.

Lita glanced at Selona and answered, "They'll be staying in a nearby hotel."

"Oh," Alissia replied knowingly.

"I'm going to go help my brother," Lita said. "We'll have your bags shortly." She looked at Anika, now resting on a bed, and added, "I'll get you some tonic for your fever too."

As she went to walk out, she turned around abruptly. Looking at Selona, she said in the ancient language, "Don't leave this room."

Selona nodded and made her way to one of the beds along the opposite wall as Anika.

Luke strode to the bathroom, and Alissia decided on one of the lower bunks along the back wall. As soon as she sat down, she realized how tired she truly was. The sound of rain pouring on the roof suddenly seemed soothing, and she began to remove her boots, turning them in her usual way to conceal her knives. By the time Luke walked back into the room, she had made herself comfortable on the bed.

He gave Devon a light punch on the shoulder, shaking his head at the boy's failed attempt at a block. "You're soaked." Motioning at the pack over the boy's shoulder, he added, "You should get washed up and get some rest. You've worked hard these past few weeks."

The boy's face brightened from Luke's subtle compliment, and he made his way to the bathroom.

Alissia slid over as Luke sat down on the bed and began to remove his boots.

"What are you doing?" she asked.

"About to take a nap with you."

"I thought that wasn't proper for this reality," she said, playfully.

He flopped down beside her and put his arm around her waist. Then he closed his eyes. "No, this is not proper. In fact, you're now a harlot. But, no worries. You're my little harlot."

"Really, Luke? Must you?" He grinned, his eyes remaining closed, and Mia hopped onto the bed and pushed her way between them.

Luke opened his eyes. "Your nanny has saved you from an act of harlotry, my love. Now I can go to sleep without fearing you'll attack me for my body."

Alissia rolled her eyes and flopped onto her other side, leaving him with her back to stare at.

Chapter 14

"What do you think you're doing? Get your hands off her!"

Alissia opened her eyes and rolled over, just in time to see Luke hit the floor. Grady was holding Luke's shirt with one hand, as his other one slammed into the side of Luke's face.

The amount of rage coming from Grady scared Alissia. He looked completely out of control.

"Grady, it's nothing." Langley tried to pull him back.

He shoved Langley away and went to hit Luke again. However, this time Luke caught his fist and held it.

"You need to calm down," Luke said in a firm voice. "We're trying to hide, remember? And you need to stop making so much commotion." He glanced at Alissia. "You want to protect her. Am I right?"

Grady said nothing, his breathing heavy.

Alissia slid to the edge of the bed, causing Mia to jump to the floor. She reached out her hand and tugged gently on Grady's pants, and when she got his attention, she patted the bed.

"Come here," she said. "Where have you been? I fell asleep waiting for you." He stared uncertainly into her eyes for a moment, and she pleaded, "Please, Grady."

He turned his attention back to Luke and said, through clenched teeth, "Stay away from her. We've had this conversation before. You don't know her, and you're not good for her."

Luke nodded. "I'm sorry. My mistake."

Grady's body relaxed, and he pulled back his fist and let go of Luke's shirt.

"Come here," Alissia said, sitting up and turning so that her feet were on the floor. When she caught a glimpse of Selona smiling, she had to force her anger aside.

He sat down beside her, and she lifted her hand to rub her fingers in his beard. "You're getting scruffy," she teased, but his eyes never left Luke, now standing.

She frowned and pulled her hand away. "Anika's sick," she said. "I believe she has a fever." When he looked across the room, Anika waved, and Alissia said, "I'm worried for her."

Grady took her hand and placed a kiss on it before setting it down on his leg. "I'm sure she'll get better. She just needs some rest." He began to rub his thumb along her palm, stirring sad emotions and memories within her.

For a moment, she was at a loss for words, not knowing how much he remembered about their present situation. She was scared something would prompt certain memories or cause him to lose control.

"How are you feeling?" she asked.

"I have a headache."

She knew that could be a side effect of the leo, but she asked, "Do you want to lie down?" He shook his head, and she struggled for something else to say until Lita and Santo entered the room. They were pushing a cart packed with food and chet, and Alissia pulled her hand from Grady and stood. "Let's eat."

*****

The next two days went by slowly for Alissia. Anika's fever kept her in bed, and Alissia tried to help Langley take care of her. They had not had a chance to talk much since the day at the spring, and Alissia could tell their friendship had shifted.

As if being stuck in the same room with Selona and her strange ways wasn't enough, Alissia had to take care of Grady and his unpredictable mood swings. Luke did not go near her, and he spent most of his time working out and training Devon. The young boy was good at using his fist, and Alissia could tell Luke enjoyed spending time with him.

She savored the simple things of sleeping in a bed, waking on her own time, and going through long yoga sequences.

They did not see Salvatore until he joined them for breakfast on the third morning. Luckily for her, Grady awoke in one of his silent moods, staring out in front of him and completely void of expression. He stayed in bed, and this allowed Alissia to be a part of the group discussion over a hot breakfast.

Salvatore sat at the end of the table, and he ate quickly before pushing his plate aside and looking up at everyone.

"Everything is in order," he said. "However, we just have one problem. Romeo, Carlo, and their wives, along with Shade, will be the ones escorting Grady, Langley, and Anika back to Allure. I have the proper documentation for them to board one of our trade ships under false names." He looked at Langley. "From here, you'll be traveling to Hausling, and then you can go the rest of the way by carriage. Hopefully, that will help to avoid most of the rebels and guards."

"Rebels?" asked Alissia.

He nodded. "It seems since we left Pallen, the talk of war has begun to spread. I'm sure the Elders in Allure are aware of things by now, and there is a definite threat of a war if they don't get this under control." He glanced at Grady. "I believe he needs to get back to Allure to help with the situation."

Langley nodded, and Salvatore continued, "Our problem is with our latest creature. I believe her plans are to heal him once she's on the island, but he doesn't need to go with us. She'll need to heal him so they can go their separate ways."

Dread filled Alissia, knowing how adamant Selona was about not healing Grady until she was with the Lamians. It was her only guarantee at safety.

"If we can talk her into healing him, everything else should be easy," Salvatore said. Looking at Alissia, he added, "Although, maybe not so much fun."

She swallowed her latest sip of chet and frowned. "What does that mean?" she asked, knowing she would not like the answer.

He smiled and looked at Luke, sitting beside him. "It seems there may be some night swimming with dolphins for you three."

Luke grinned. "I'm guessing you couldn't get proper documentation for us."

"Not even going to attempt that one," responded Salvatore.

Alissia shook her head adamantly. "We can hide in a carriage or somewhere with Shade," she said. "We can sneak onto a boat."

Luke responded, "The security at the docks is much different than dealing with guards."

Salvatore nodded. "We can't get away with much, and everything will be documented. They're on high alert. Guards are posted at each boat, and even the sailors have to show proper documentation just to board their own ship after a night out for ale."

He took a sip of his chet. "I've thought this through, and the easiest solution here is for the three of you to enter the ship by water, on the other side. No one will see you, and we'll set sail early the next morning."

Alissia shook her head again. "No! No! And no! The last time y'all said it was an easy thing, I got kidnapped by a bunch of freaky creatures that nearly killed Luke and me. I don't even know if the dolphins y'all have here are the same as in my reality, and how do I know there's not any merpeople in the water?" She looked at Luke. "Remember the merpeople? They aren't very nice."

"Even if there are merpeople, they wouldn't live this close to a port city filled with humans," Luke stated.

She crossed her arms and scowled back at him. "And how can you be so sure?"

"Let's just ask Selona," said Salvatore. He looked at the creature, currently sitting alone at the far end of the table. She was chewing on one of her foreign meals, with slime oozing from her mouth. Alissia flinched, fearing it was one of the animals she had bonded with.

Although Carlo and Romeo were at the table with them, Edda and Bruna remained in the city. The two women had not made an appearance since their arrival, and Alissia guessed Edda was completely done with Selona.

When Selona noticed everyone staring at her, a guarded look came over her face as she finished chewing her food. Then she licked the slime from her chin, while studying the faces of everyone at the table.

In the ancient language, Salvatore said, "Selona, we're trying to plan a way to board the ship unnoticed, and we need to know if there are merpeople living in the ocean. Will there be a danger if you, Alissia, and Luke enter the water to get onto the boat?"

Her black eyes scanned each of the human faces before answering, "No merpeople near a human city. We can enter the water."

Salvatore smiled. "Thank you, my dear." He turned to Alissia. "It seems you have nothing to worry about."

Alissia shot Selona a dirty look. "And how do we know we can trust her?"

Luke chuckled. "We don't trust her, but we do believe her. Besides, if anything's in the water, I'm sure there'll be plenty of scarletons nearby you can control, if needed."

She frowned. "I don't even know what a scarleton is."

"Maybe it's best you don't know," Luke said with a grin.

Salvatore laughed. "It's a solid plan. Now we just need to get her to release Grady from his affliction."

Alissia shook her head. "Good luck with that. He's her only guarantee to get to the island. Cure him, and she has nothing else to hold over us."

"Then we just have to give her something else," replied Salvatore. He looked back at Selona, now watching everyone curiously. "Selona, we have a problem. We need to get to the island. However, as a guardian to the Medicians, I have orders I must follow, and I can't take unnecessary humans with us."

He paused, letting his words sink in. "My son and daughter are not a problem. However, Carlo and Romeo need to escort Langley, Anika, and Grady back to their homes. They don't know the location of the island, and since they're not an interest to the Medicians, I'm not allowed to let them near it. They cannot go with us."

Selona shook her head. "I will not cure him until I'm with the Medicians."

"I understand your situation," Salvatore responded. "And I propose we make a tradeoff. Is there a way you could cure Grady and sicken me?"

For a moment, it looked as if Selona considered his words, but then she answered, "I don't have a felium with me."

"No, you don't, but is there something else you can do? I only ask this of you because there's no other way, Selona. I have my own orders to follow, and I cannot allow extra humans to board the ship. My ancestors have protected the Medicians for almost two thousand years, and we have to keep our secrets hidden. That is how it's always been done."

Selona's face curled up in thought, and after a moment of silence, she turned to Santo. "I can sicken him."

"Me? Why not her?" Santo pointed to his sister sitting directly across from him.

Lita's cloth napkin nailed him in the face. "She chose you. Be the man, Brother."

"I would rather you choose me, Selona," said Salvatore.

The creature shook her head. "I choose your son, and that is my decision."

Salvatore let out a breath. "What do you have in mind for him?"

"I can give him something to sicken him. I carry the venom with me."

Alissia said in the modern language, "Am I the only one that sees a problem with that? Why is she carrying the venom around?"

"She's scared," answered Carlo. "She doesn't trust us."

Salvatore turned to Santo. "Son? What are your thoughts?"

Santo shrugged. "There's no other way."

"Tomorrow night then," said Salvatore. In the ancient language, he continued with, "We leave tomorrow night. Our ship is already docked. Lita, Santo, and I will board the boat, and Selona, Alissia, and Luke will have to swim to get to the boat. Each of you will then have to climb the ladder to get on board."

He glanced at Mia, still filling her mouth with food while standing in the chair next to Alissia. "Although I'm thinking Mia could easily get on the boat by herself, she'll probably want to stay with you."

Alissia nodded, and Salvatore turned to Langley. "You, Anika, and Grady will board the other boat tomorrow afternoon. As for Devon, I need to discuss things with Luke before that decision is made."

The young boy shifted uneasily in his seat, and Alissia wondered what he was thinking.

To Selona, Salvatore asked, "When do you need to administer the venom to Santo and the cure to Grady? How long before they work?"

"The venom will work shortly after given. However, the cure is more gradual. He'll feel drained for a few days but will soon be at a full recovery."

"How about memories?" Alissia asked. "Will he remember everything from these past few weeks?"

"It's different with each of the humans we've studied."

Alissia said in the modern language, "Notice how she said humans and studied in the same sentence?"

Salvatore nodded and then turned to Selona. "Since Grady will be boarding the boat tomorrow afternoon, when do you need to administer the cure for him? He'll need to be able to stay out of trouble, and he can't be screaming Alissia's name, especially while everyone seems to be searching for her."

"I can do it tonight, but I'll only give the cure after I've administered the venom."

Salvatore nodded in agreement. "I understand. I'll need to get Santo onto the boat tonight then." To Santo, he said, "You need to be packed and ready."

His son frowned but nodded.

Alissia touched Salvatore's arm and asked in a low voice, "Won't he also be screaming?"

His eyes seemed sad and distant as he answered, "Yes, but it won't be your name he'll be screaming."

Salvatore abruptly pushed his chair back and stood. "Everyone needs to take inventory of their bags and purge anything not needed. Lita and I will do some quick shopping this morning and will be sure to get everyone some new clothing for this part of the journey."

Turning to Lita, he said, "You need to write down everyone's sizes, and we need to get started. We have a busy day ahead of us."

Alissia stood up. "Could I have a moment alone with you?"

Salvatore nodded and made his way toward the bathroom, and she rushed to grab her pack before joining him.

"What's troubling you?" he asked, closing the door behind them.

She set her pack on the floor and kneeled down beside it. Chewing on her bottom lip, she began to go through her clothing and the pockets of the large bag before she pulled out a tightly wadded shirt and set it down in front of her.

"Um... I kind of need a favor and have something to show you," she said hesitantly. She unrolled the shirt to reveal her stash of jewels and looked up at him.

It took a moment for the shock to leave Salvatore's face before he asked, "From the castle?"

She nodded. "But I didn't steal them. All of it was given to me, and even Luke says no one will be angry about it. They were all a gift."

"It's a good thing you showed me, because I'll have to get them aboard the ship. I'll collect them when I come back this afternoon, and we'll finalize all the packing then. They'll be waiting for you on the boat."

Alissia lifted the engagement ring Ian gave her. "Can you do me another favor?" she asked. "Is there a way I could get money for this, and you could give it to Anika, Grady, and Langley after they've left? I don't want to be the one to give it to them."

Salvatore smiled. "I think I understand. Although I won't risk selling it here—in Eldership territory—I can personally buy it from you and then resell it overseas, where it won't be recognized. I can put it in a gift package and pass it to Carlo to give to your friends—at the right moment."

"You can do that? You have that much money that quick?"

"I'm in the trade business. Remember?" He laughed. "I may not flaunt money around like most of my relatives, but I assure you that I have more money at my disposal than even them. It's one of the benefits of being on the inside and knowing things."

As he took the ring from her, she asked, "Is it worth a lot?"

He nodded. "This is an extremely pricey ring."

Alissia recognized the question on his face, and she said, "It's the engagement ring from Ian."

"I see." He put it in his pocket. "I'll make a withdrawal and have it ready for your friends. Is there a certain time you would have Carlo give it to them?"

As she began to roll the shirt back up, she said, "I don't know. I guess shortly after Grady's back to normal." Tears began to threaten, and she kept her eyes down as she put the shirt back into her pack. Once she reclaimed control of her emotions, she looked up and tried to appear unbothered.

"Oh, and there's my knives as well."

She pulled a knife from one of her boots. "How will I get these on the boat?"

"You and Lita have a lot in common," he said, laughing. "You'll be swimming in a suit tonight, but we'll see to it that your knives board the ship safely." He put his hand on the doorknob. "It seems Lita will have no problem shopping for you, as you two share similar tastes in clothing."

Alissia scrunched up her face and shook her head. "I don't think so."

"Oh, yes. That child has more daggers hidden on her body than you would think." He winked and added, "Got that from her mother too."

She could not help but smile at his adoration for his late wife. From all she had learned, the woman had been a challenge, but he had loved her dearly. That was evident each time she was mentioned, even by Salvatore's children. Alissia wished she could have met the woman, as she sounded intriguing—although a lot like Lita.

"Any other surprises I need to know about? Another creature? Have you hidden another man around here?"

Alissia laughed and shook her head. "I'm done. I promise."

"Good." He turned the handle, and before he stepped out, he added, "It's hard keeping up with you and Lita. The two of you are giving me grey hairs."

Chapter 15

Salvatore and his group returned that evening with food and many shopping bags, and surprisingly, Edda and Bruna were with them. They had spent the entire day buying new clothing for everyone.

Grady, Langley, and Anika were traveling as wealthy traders, and Salvatore felt they needed to dress the part as they got on and off the boat at the ports. He also bought them new traveling clothes for their time on the boat and during their carriage ride to Allure.

"Here." Lita approached Alissia with her hands full of bags, setting them on the bed. "It will be cool on the boat the first bit of travel, but it will soon get warmer. That's why you'll find a variety of clothes. Tomorrow night you can just wear your cloak over your swimsuit."

"Thanks," Alissia said.

Lita gave an awkward smile and walked away, and Alissia began to pull the clothes from the bags. Half of them consisted of leggings and long-sleeved poet's shirts, while the other consisted of sarong wrap skirts with thin matching shirts. There were also a few brightly colored sarongs, a sleeping gown, jacket, pair of sandals, two pair of extra dark and durable sunglasses, some intimate items, toiletries, and a wooden buckle to use with the sarongs. Together, it was an assorted mix of pirate and island clothing.

"I helped to pick out the sarongs. I hope you like them."

Alissia grinned and turned toward the familiar voice. "I do. Thank you. I was wondering if I would see you again."

Edda said, "I wouldn't go without saying goodbye. I've just been uncomfortable around our new company."

"I understand."

Bruna joined them. "We tried to save you from Lita's choice in clothing. Do you like the sarongs?"

Alissia laughed and nodded. "Yes, thanks."

"Are you nervous?" Bruna asked.

"About what?"

"Meeting the Medicians."

Alissia frowned. "Do y'all know them by Medicians or Lamians?"

"Our ancestors always called them Medicians out of respect," answered Bruna.

"So I should definitely get used to that word," Alissia replied.

Bruna nodded. "Humans have always called them Lamians out of fear. It's amazing how they could fear them yet also abuse them to get what they want."

"We're destructive by nature," Edda stated.

Alissia noticed everyone else standing around Grady's bed, where he had spent most of the day. There were signs of a struggle, and she rushed toward him.

"I won't drink it," Grady said firmly, pushing the mug in Anika's hand away.

Although the fever had lifted that morning, Alissia could tell Anika still did not feel well.

"Please, Grady. It will help you," Anika pleaded.

Alissia stepped beside her and put her hand on his shoulder. "Grady, you really need to drink it," she persuaded. "It's important."

He stared uncertainly into her eyes for a moment, and then he surprised her by taking the drink from Anika's hand and turning it up to his mouth. A surge of emotion caught in Alissia's throat, knowing he would do anything for her.

Once finished with the drink, he held it out, and Anika took it. Alissia squeezed his shoulder and smiled. "Thank you," she said. "Now you should try to get some rest so the medicine can help."

"I don't feel sick."

"I know. But you are, and you need to get better."

He allowed her to help him get comfortable on the bed as the others walked away. Then she sat down beside him to make small talk. After a while, she noticed the room had become quiet, and she turned to find Santo sitting at the table. He was staring up at his sister, who was standing beside him, and tears were in his eyes.

"Mamma?" he asked, in a heart-wrenching tone.

Lita looked at her father, and Salvatore frowned worriedly. "We need to get you to the boat, Santo."

Santo slowly turned his face from Lita to look at his father. He said something in his natural language, and although Alissia could not follow the conversation, she could clearly see the pain coming from Salvatore and his two children.

Tears began to flow freely down Santo's face, and out of respect, Alissia turned her attention back to Grady.

She gently rubbed her fingers along his forehead, and he closed his eyes. A smile came to his face, and she began to ponder how they would soon be going their separate ways. She wondered if she would ever see him again, although she knew it was for the best if she didn't.

He needed to return to Allure and take his place at the Eldership, and he needed to forget about her.

"Excuse me, Alissia, but I would like to show you something before I deliver Santo to the boat."

Alissia pushed her melancholy thoughts aside, and she masked her face with an instinctive smile before turning to Salvatore.

"Sure." She looked down at Grady. "I'll be back to check on you. Try to get some rest."

She stood and followed Salvatore to a large leather trunk—nearly as tall as her—someone had placed beside her bed.

"It's a wardrobe trunk," Salvatore said, opening it. "I got it for your birthday. Now you have a place of your own to store your belongings, and it has a key to keep everything safe."

Alissia ran her fingers along the side of the trunk, taking in its fine leather. Then she opened one of the handcrafted drawers.

Salvatore said tenderly, "I understand you've not had a place to call your own since coming to this reality, and although a lot is uncertain about your future, hopefully you can use this to build a new life."

"Thank you. It's beautiful." She smiled up at him.

He surprised her by pulling her into his broad body, and she put her arms around him and squeezed back.

He was a good man—with his children and with others—and Alissia could not help but wish her own father had been like him.

When they pulled away, he said, "You should sort through your belongings and put them in the trunk."

The left side of the trunk held a group of hangers, while the right side consisted of various-sized drawers. Salvatore squatted down and opened the bottom drawer, and after pulling a knife from his belt, she watched as he carefully put the tip of the knife along one of the natural cuts in the bottom edge of the drawer. He pulled it back, revealing a hidden compartment set beneath the drawer.

"This is for your jewelry and anything else you want to keep hidden." He stood back up and pulled a silver chain from his pocket.

Two small keys dangled from it. "You can wear this around your neck beneath your clothing. You have an extra key. Would you like for me to keep it, or do you want to give it to Luke?"

She thought of the ring Luke wore on the chain around his neck, and she answered, "I'll give it to Luke. He already has a place for it."

He nodded and glanced worriedly at Santo, now beginning to get restless and loud with Lita. "I'll see you again tomorrow. I must now get Santo to the ship."

She watched as Salvatore and most of his people walked out of the room, leaving Carlo and Romeo to guard the halls. The two men finished their conversation with Luke before leaving the room as well.

Alissia noticed the happiness in Luke's face when he turned his attention to Devon. The young boy was sitting on his bunk looking at his new clothing. There was something about his facial expression that tugged at her heart, and she wondered if anyone had ever taken the time to go shopping for him.

After glancing at Grady to make sure he was asleep, Alissia walked over to Luke and took him by the hand. He turned his eyes from Devon and smiled down at her.

"What will happen to him?" she asked in a low voice.

"You mean Devon?"

She nodded.

"He's going on the ship with us." Her eyes widened in surprise. "I've spoken to Salvatore, and we agree the boy knows too much already. It's best to keep him close and with us."

"But what about when we get to the island? Salvatore said we can't take extra people."

"He can't leave the ship, but from what I've been told, he'll be safe on the boat."

"You trust Salvatore?" She raised her eyebrows. Although she felt in her heart that Salvatore was an honest man, she had not expected Luke to trust anyone.

He grinned. "I believe Devon is safe with him, and I believe Salvatore is good for the boy."

"That means you trust him."

He laughed and led her toward her new trunk, and she grinned, knowing he was avoiding admitting his feelings.

Luke inspected the wardrobe trunk, and he accepted the extra key before helping her to clasp the chain around her neck. He then left her to finish packing.

The rest of the evening went uneventful. Grady did not wake up, and Anika and Langley seemed busy with their packing. Alissia smiled to herself as she watched Anika inspect her new clothing, and although she wanted to playfully tease her friend, something held her back.

Since the day at the river, Anika had seemed distant, and Alissia had never pursued a relationship in her entire life. She told herself to give Anika the space she wanted, even if it meant the end of their friendship.

Although the thought of losing Anika and Langley as friends caused a deep sadness within her, she told herself that is how things were in life. People came, and people went. No one ever stayed.

Not only had she learned that lesson as a young child but also as a paralegal. She had witnessed much heartbreak of others. Friendships were destroyed every day. Marriages usually ended in divorce. She had even witnessed mothers that had given up their career and life to stay at home and raise their children, only to have them grow up to hate her. No relationship was sacred, and love could be cruel.

Those thoughts continued, and even when Luke told her he could feel her sadness within his own body, she pasted a smile onto her face and told him she would be better soon. She knew he wanted to pursue the conversation, but he reluctantly gave her the space she wanted.

However, Alissia was still awake hours later. To reinforce the wall building around her heart, she opened the door to her childhood memories—her ultimate reminder of why she needed no one.

Her mind could be cruel, and there were plenty of memories to remind her of what loving someone could do to a person. She always got hurt when she opened her heart, and she accepted a life of solitude long ago. Her time with Anika and Langley had just been a small gift, but it was over now.

Thoughts of Luke came to mind, and a tear rolled down her face, landing on her pillow. One day he would leave too. Maybe not physically because of their bond, but she was certain his love for her would drift or come to an end one day.

When Luke sat down on her bed, she closed her eyes. She knew he could not tell what she was thinking. That only happened when her heart was beating rapidly, and she was out of control. However, it bothered her that he could feel her pain and see past her façade. She wanted to be alone, and as he slid beneath the covers, she wondered where Mia was for the night.

He said nothing, and he began to rub his fingers soothingly in her hair. At first she resented his touch. Eventually, though, it began to ease her pain, and the memories stopped flowing. Her mind settled, and she fell asleep.

When she awoke the next morning to the sound of talking within the room, she rolled over. Luke was in his bed, still asleep, and she wondered what time he had left her.

She watched him sleep for a moment before turning her attention toward the middle of the room. Grady was sitting at the table with Anika and Langley, and he was watching her with a pained expression on his face.

He turned to Langley and said something in a low voice before standing. As he walked over to Alissia, she sat up and leaned her back against the wall.

"May I join you?" he asked.

She nodded. "How do you feel?"

He sat down and made himself comfortable beside her. Then he let out a shaky breath. "Much better, from what I've been told."

"What do you remember?"

"Bits and pieces. Some good. Some bad. But mostly bad." He took her hand and placed it in his lap. They sat in silence for a moment. "I hear we're going our separate ways today."

Alissia nodded, not knowing what to say. She wondered if he would fight against it.

He looked down at their hands and said softly, "I'll miss you, Alissia."

She struggled for the right words, but nothing worthy of the moment came to mind. "I'll miss you too." After more silence between them, she stammered, "Grady... I never wanted to hurt you or the others. Please believe me."

He squeezed her hand. "I know. I don't think less of you. You made your decision, and I'm not the one. I can't say I'm happy about it, but I can't force myself on you either."

"Are you mad at me?"

"No." Grady turned his face to stare out in front of him. "I still remember some of the visions, and I must say losing you to Luke is much better than losing you to death. It still hurts, but at least I know you'll be happy. It's what I've always wanted for you." He turned back to look into her eyes before adding, "From the very first time I saw you beneath the tree, I only wanted to see you happy."

Her eyes filled with moisture, and Alissia turned away, forcing back her tears.

His thumb began to rub along the inside of her palm. "Do you think you'll still try to meet the Lamians that saved you? The ones in the mountains?"

With her emotions back under control, she turned back to face him. "Yeah, I definitely want to meet whoever saved me."

"Then promise me one thing."

"What?"

"That you'll try to get a message to Anika and Langley to tell them where you are. Maybe try to see them again." He added softly, "See me."

She nodded. "I'll try."

"We'll worry about you."

"I know."

"We care about you, Alissia—all of us. You know how I feel, and Anika and Langley love you too."

She nodded, not knowing how to respond. After a while, she asked, "What are your plans? Are you going to be accepted back at the Eldership?"

"Yes, and there'll be much to keep me busy when I return."

"Do you think there'll be a war?"

Wrinkles lined his forehead as he briefly pondered her question. "I believe the Elders will listen to reason."

A bit of relief came to her knowing he would soon have his life back. He was a man accustomed to law and order, not traveling all over the land in hiding. She knew his hair was now the longest it had ever been, not to mention the scraggly beard covering the lower portion of his face. It was not right for her to demand so much from him or her friends. They needed to go home.

"What are you thinking?"

His question pulled her from her thoughts. "I'm sorry. I was just thinking about y'all's journey home." She dared not say anything else. She knew how he would respond if she asked if he was eager to see his family or Allure again. He would rather be with her, and he was not going home willingly—even if it was where he truly belonged.

The sound of Selona rummaging through one of the boxes beneath her bed drew both of their attention, and when Alissia noticed her pull out a squirming amphibian, she quickly looked down.

"Don't watch," she said.

Grady groaned, and she looked up to find his face full of disgust. She began to envision what he was seeing, and a nauseous feeling came over her.

"Stop! Turn away," she said, playfully.

He looked at her, shaking his head in disbelief. "She's beastly."

Alissia laughed. "You have no idea. She's actually better than some of the others of her kind."

He turned his gaze back to Selona and shuddered, and Alissia laughed even harder. She was grateful for the distraction when Salvatore and Lita entered the room with two rolling carts of fresh food and chet.

After a quick stop at the bathroom, she was soon sitting across from Anika and Langley for breakfast. Grady was situated to the right of her, while Lita sat to the left.

She listened as Salvatore explained how Grady, Langley, and Anika would be boarding the trade ship. He called off various names of cities, and then he talked about their carriage ride to Allure.

As he spoke, Alissia imagined her friends' journey home. Although she was happy for them and envisioned Anika's excited face when she finally returned to her cottage, a conflicting sadness lingered.

After breakfast, she sat at the table and watched as Anika helped Grady prepare for their journey, and she noticed he acted sluggish and had a hard time concentrating on the tasks before him.

She smiled when he came out of the bathroom dressed for the day. Although he was wearing a new suit with a matching hat, he still looked much different than his usual self. Not only was the suit not his typical style, but he also still had his beard, although it was now freshly trimmed.

He strolled over and took her by the hand. Lifting it to his lips, he bowed and said formally, "Hello, Lady Alissia. My name is Benton Wells. It is a pleasure to meet you."

She laughed, and he let go of her hand to sit down beside her. The two of them looked over at Anika and Langley sitting on their bed with Mia sprawled out between them. The tiny fur ball was receiving her daily spoiling from the two of them—although at this moment, they were overindulging her.

Alissia shook her head and rolled her eyes. "She's going to miss them."

"Does she know we're separating?" Grady asked.

She nodded. "I explained everything to her yesterday."

A silence fell between them, and Alissia continued to watch her friends. Although the room was filled with conversation, she could still hear Mia's purring. After a short while, she turned to find Grady watching her, and she realized she had not told him everything.

Remembering how hurt Anika had been, she abruptly stood. "Hold on. We need to talk, but I want it to be in private."

She strode to where Salvatore was helping Selona prepare her belongings for transportation. Alissia had no idea how he was going to explain all the strange plants and animals when he loaded them onto the ship.

When he looked up and noticed her, she asked, "Is there a place other than the bathroom that I can talk to Grady?"

He glanced over at Grady and nodded. "You can use the storage room nearby. Follow me."

She motioned to Grady, and the two of them followed Salvatore to a storage room not far away.

"No one's supposed to be in this part of the carriage house, so you shouldn't be bothered. Just don't go anywhere else." Without waiting for a response, he turned and left.

Alissia looked around the room at the wooden crates and bags lining the walls, and then she walked over to a crate and sat down. She patted the spot next to her, and as Grady sat down, she pulled up her feet and turned to face him.

"Where are you?" came Luke's mental voice.

"I'm saying goodbye to Grady. I'm fine. Just give us a moment."

When he did not respond, she turned her attention back to Grady. "There's something I need to tell you." She began to chew on her bottom lip as she considered her words.

Grady gave a reassuring smile. "You can tell me anything."

She nodded and let out a small breath. "Something happened the night we escaped the castle. Luke was almost killed. He was beaten and stabbed, and I didn't think he would survive. So I cried, and I said goodbye to him. Then I kissed him. Only... something happened when I kissed him."

Alissia briefly stared at the faint blood splatter, still on her boot. Then she held Grady's eyes as she said, "I blacked out, and when I woke up, Luke was healed. Now my handprint is branded into his chest where his league tattoo once was."

His smile faltered, and he began to stare off to the side in deep thought. She continued, "It took us a few days before we realized we can mentally speak to each other. Not only that, but we share each other's physical pain. From what Salvatore and the creatures have told me about the Lamians, we also believe we'll die together." He looked at her in confusion, and she quickly clarified, "I'll die if he dies, and he'll die if I die."

Grady nodded in understanding, and she went on. "We don't know why he isn't changing, and strange things are happening. We're physically connected—for life."

He closed his eyes and looked down. After a moment of silence between them, he turned back to her. "Do you love him?"

"I do," she said with a nod. "I'm sorry, Grady. I just want you to know the truth."

Alissia took his hand between hers. "I love you, and I want you to be happy. Luke loves me, and I'm happy. You need to forget about me and find someone that can give you the love you deserve."

A tear broke free and trickled down her face, and her voice filled with emotion. "You're an amazing man, and you showed me what love is. You opened the door to my heart, and I thank you for that. Thank you for loving me."

He pulled her into his arms, and she returned his embrace. They held each other in silence for a long moment, their bodies trembling with emotion.

"So this is truly the end?" he finally asked.

She closed her eyes, trying to regain control of herself. "Yes."

"I'll miss you, Alissia."

"And I'll miss you."

He pulled away and wiped the tears from his face. "Will you still try to visit Anika when you go to the mountains?"

"I will."

"I'll worry." He tried to smile.

She nodded and dabbed at her eyes, forcing her tears to stop. "I know, but I'll be fine. I'll soon meet the Lamians and will know what's going on with my body. Everything will be okay." She gave an encouraging smile. "You need to focus on this war when you get home. Maybe they'll make you an Elder, and you can fix everything."

Grady shook his head. "Not yet. I'm still too young for that position."

Alissia frowned and said, with concern, "Have I ruined the chances of you becoming an Elder? I mean, you didn't turn me into the Eldership. Will that be a problem?"

"Your story of trying to find your people will help. I'll think of some other things too. They may not be happy with me, but they'll need all the supporters they can get now that they realize the people are dividing against them."

"You going to keep the beard?" she teased.

He grinned and rubbed his face. "It's not for me."

"Salvatore says it's almost time for them to leave," Luke mentally said.

"We're coming."

To Grady, she said, "I think it's almost time for you to go." She scooted down from the crate, and he stood.

They walked back to their quarters in silence. When they entered the room, Anika was hugging Devon, and when she released him, Langley shook his hand. Alissia and Grady joined them, and Anika gave Alissia a big hug. Alissia put her arms around her friend and squeezed back.

When they pulled away, Anika said, "We'll miss you."

"I'll miss y'all."

Langley pulled her into his arms for a bear hug, lifting her from the ground, and she laughed. After setting her down, he said tenderly, "Be safe."

"You too."

He grinned. "Maybe you'll be purple the next time we see you."

"Oh, yeah." She looked at the three of them. "I'll try to send a message or something."

Anika nodded. "That'll be great."

"Is everyone ready?" Salvatore asked, walking up to them.

The three of them nodded and went to grab their belongings. Then Grady pulled her in for one last embrace. Langley smiled and waved before walking out of the room, and Anika followed, glancing back over her shoulder to give a quick smile.

Grady was the last to walk out, and once in the passageway, he stopped and turned back around. He stared into Alissia's eyes for a short moment before his lips tightened, and after a curt nod, he turned and walked away.

Chapter 16

As soon as they disappeared, something within Alissia said she would never see them again.

"How are you feeling?"

She instinctively smiled up at Luke and answered, "I'm fine."

"We have some time before it's our turn to leave. Want me to throw you around the room in the name of self-defense lessons?"

She shook her head and gave a small laugh, knowing he was trying to distract her from her melancholy mood. "No, I think I'm going to do some yoga."

He grinned. "Then I shall do yoga with you." He turned to Devon. "In fact, Devon wants to try yoga as well."

The young boy nodded in agreement. He would do anything Luke required of him.

"You don't have to do yoga," she said to Devon.

He glanced at Luke. "I'll do yoga."

"Fine then. But I'm not going to go easy."

Luke turned to Devon. "She's talking to you."

Alissia frowned and shook her head. She considered reminding Luke of the time he was not able to complete one of her moves, but in the end, she began to get ready.

She started out slow and easy before running through a complicated series of moves. Although she did not let Devon's failed attempts slow her down or stop her, she smiled when Luke helped him.

The two of them did not make it to the end of her routine and were in the middle of a self-defense lesson when she finished. She sat down at the table with a warm cup of chet and watched as Luke showed Devon some new fighting techniques.

Watching him with the young boy warmed her heart. Before seeing him interact with Devon, she would never have guessed him to be so good with children. She smiled to herself as she took a sip of her drink. Although she knew so much about him from the bond, he was still full of surprises.

Her mind soon drifted to how he would act with their children one day, and when she realized what she was thinking, she scolded herself. At the moment, she did not even know if the two of them would ever be able to kiss or be intimate with each other. The last thing she needed to do was start dreaming of something that could never be.

A tinge of longing seeped in as she stared at the muscles along his bare torso. What if they could never go beyond holding each other *forever*?

His eyes met hers, and he winked, giving her a roguish grin. Realizing there was a chance he could feel her sudden desire, she pretended to ignore him and lifted her mug to her lips, taking a long sip. Although her skin tone never flushed, her eyes could easily betray her hunger for him.

It was dark by the time Salvatore and Lita returned. As the small group ate at the long table, Salvatore told how Grady, Langley, and Anika boarded the ship without any problems. He reassured Alissia that nothing would go awry on her friends' journey back to Allure. They would soon be home and safely away from the corrupted portion of the Eldership.

Alissia smiled and nodded all throughout the conversation, ignoring the dull sadness that pulled at her. She reminded herself that her friends were better off without her, and Anika and Langley knew it. She imagined the two of them were happy to finally get away from all of the drama and danger surrounding her.

Once everyone finished eating, Lita and Salvatore delivered the dirty dishes to the kitchen. When they returned, they were carrying a bundle. Salvatore set it on the table and removed three wetsuits before giving them to Selona, Alissia, and Luke.

"The water will be cold, and this will help to keep you warm," Salvatore said in the old language. For Selona and Luke's benefit, the conversation had switched between the two languages all throughout their meal.

Alissia examined her strange suit, and it did not take long before she realized it was made from the skin of an animal. She guessed it to be aquatic, as it was silver, shiny, and had a rubbery feel to it. The material was somewhat thick, with a layer of blubber for insulation. She lifted it to her nose and took a whiff, surprised to find a tropical, fruity scent coming from it.

"Cantorna oil is rubbed into the hide to keep it from hardening," said Luke.

She looked up and noticed him watching her with a smile. She smiled back before her eyes went to Selona to find the creature intently examining the seams of her suit.

Salvatore sat down at the table. "Your luggage has been loaded onto the ship, and I'll bring the rest of your clothing when I board tonight." He glanced between Alissia and Selona. "I hope the two of you don't get seasick. The ship we'll be traveling on is smaller than most, yet it's built for speed. It moves fast along the waves."

"I should be fine," Alissia said. "I've been deep sea fishing more than once and have never gotten sick."

Selona replied, as if offended, "My people do not get sick over water."

Salvatore nodded before turning to Luke. "We should leave soon while there are still other carriages along the roads. We'll take the three of you to Seller's Bay, and you'll need to wait until the early morning hours before arriving at the ship. That way most people will be asleep. The fact that harbor guards are posted at each boat will help us. I imagine with the extra security, fewer sailors are on watch aboard each ship."

He pulled out a small map and set it on the table, using his fingers to mark each spot. "Here's Seller's Bay, and here's the harbor. Our ship will be the sixth one from that direction. It's a three-masted garlier." Noticing Alissia's confused expression, he said, "No worries. It will be smaller than most of the trade ships in the harbor."

Salvatore paused and focused his attention on Alissia. "I know you've never told me, but I've assumed you can see in the dark. Am I right?" He grinned when she nodded.

"Great! That'll help you to find the right ship tonight, as it should be the only one with sheets tied along the side of it." He pulled out a piece of paper from his front pocket and unfolded it. "Here's what the flag looks like, and we'll add glow stones at each window along that side too. The name of the ship is *Fetunia*, and we'll have someone blowing a scotter whistle—that's a high-pitched whistle humans can't hear but the dolphins can. You can tell the dolphins to travel toward the sound once they get to the harbor. A rope ladder will be hanging down, and you'll need to climb aboard the ship. We'll be there to help you."

He looked from Alissia to Luke. "Any questions?"

Alissia ignored a vision of a merman dragging her to the bottom of the ocean and pasted a smile onto her face. "Can't think of any," she answered light-heartedly.

While Luke asked detailed questions about timing and location, she stared down at the strange suit in her hands and began to mentally reassure herself everything would be fine.

Shortly thereafter, Lita, Devon, and Salvatore left to check the passageway for people, and she went to the bathroom and wiggled her way into the tight-fitting suit. She then pulled her hair into a quick braid that hung down her back.

Her adrenaline picked up as soon as she sat down in the enclosed carriage. Devon sat up front with Salvatore, while Lita sat in the covered portion with the swimmers.

She could sense Luke's excitement over their plans, and she hoped he was not aware of the dread she felt. As the carriage made its way through the city's winding streets, she pretended to occupy herself with showering affection on Mia.

After a while, she looked up. "What'll we do if there aren't any dolphins when we get there?"

Lita responded, "That won't be a problem. This bay is filled with them."

Alissia nodded, although she doubted the certainty of finding dolphins in a certain area of the ocean.

Luke said, "From what you've told me of your reality, I believe we have more numbers when it comes to living things."

"More numbers and more variety," Alissia agreed. She withdrew into her thoughts again, imagining the ocean filled with strange, massive creatures.

The carriage came to a stop, and the door swung open.

"Hurry," said Salvatore. "Get to the water and stay hidden." As Alissia stepped out of the carriage, he grabbed her by the arm. Looking hard into her eyes, he said, with certainty, "I'll see you again, my dear. Soon."

She nodded and forced a smile onto her face, and Luke took her by the hand. He began to lead her down a narrow walking trail. Large palm trees surrounded the path, and she was surprised they were not covered in bella ivy. The only light around them came from the moon.

Mia and Selona followed quietly from behind, and although the scurrying sounds of animals distracted Alissia, she kept her attention on the path in front of her. It was a short while before it ended, and they were standing on a secluded beach.

The sound of a woman's laughter caught their attention, and Luke abruptly pulled her back into the trees. With her night vision Alissia could see two young couples sitting on a blanket.

"It's a double date," Alissia said, mentally. *"Two men and two women."*

"We'll need to find another spot away from the path. They should be gone before it's time for us to leave."

Alissia led the others away, and after a while, they found a spot beneath some palm trees near the sand dunes. They could no longer hear the conversation and laughter coming from the couples, and Alissia could barely see them in the distance.

Luke sat beside her, and Mia plopped down in the sand between Alissia's legs. Selona made herself comfortable a short distance away.

As Alissia buried her toes in the sand, she frowned, wishing the suit did not cover her feet. Then she plunged her hands into the cool sand and savored the feel of it on her skin.

After a while of contented silence between them, Luke asked, "What are you thinking?"

She smiled and closed her eyes for a moment, taking in the fresh, salty breeze on her face. Then she looked out at the water. "Any time I'm on the beach at night, it takes me back to when I was a little girl." She paused. "Before my father began to hit me... we were happy. We used to go beach seining all through the night with my distant relatives. The men would drag these massive nets along the bottom of the ocean, and all the children would follow the adults along the beach.

My sister, cousins, and I would run along after them with our flash-lights, and when the net was pulled out of the water, I'd get so excited to see what was in them.

"We'd spend almost the entire night doing this, and then we'd go home and get some sleep. The following evening we'd have this massive seafood dinner outside with my relatives."

Luke put his arm around her, and she lifted her hand to hold his. They sat like that for a long moment, enjoying the distinct smells and sounds of the ocean together, as a couple. After a while, Luke grinned and asked, teasingly, "So you love seafood?"

She closed her eyes and groaned before responding, "I'll miss shrimp now that my diet has changed. I think that's the only type of meat I'll truly miss."

His body shook with mild laughter, and she asked, "What about you? How much time have you spent around the ocean?"

"Not much. There's no beach where I'm from, and I was an adult when I visited a port city for the first time. My childhood memories are limited to the orphanage and Eldership school walls."

Alissia nodded, remembering his memories she had relived while saving his life. His childhood consisted of the orphanage and the Eldership school—nothing more. There were no vacations with a family, or even a family.

She looked out at the water. "Sitting on a beach like this has always calmed me. It's peaceful."

"Then we should try to settle near an ocean one day."

Alissia let out a sarcastic laugh. "Like we have a choice where my future will be."

His free hand came up, and he turned her face toward his. Staring into her eyes, he said, "Wherever it is, I'll be there as well."

She smiled, trying to ignore the sensations his touch and intense gaze stirred within her. "Ever since I've been in this reality, all I've done is run."

Luke gave a reassuring smile. "This is temporary." He kissed her tenderly on the cheek, causing her temperature to rise even more. In a whispered voice, he added, "This is a temporary battle, and one day it will be over." His mouth went to her ear, and she closed her eyes, his touch intoxicating. "One day all of this will be behind us."

A low, menacing growl threw Alissia back into reality, and he swiftly pulled away.

Without a word, she turned back to gaze out at the water. Ignoring her own rules about never hoping for things beyond her reach, she smiled and began to dream of the day she and Luke would be free from danger—and free to be together.

Chapter 17

"Are you ready?" Luke asked.

Alissia braced herself for the next wave and watched it roll past the lower portion of her body. She smiled and nodded, as Mia's grip tightened around her neck.

"There's no danger in this," Luke said, too confident for her liking.

She took a deep breath and nodded again. "I got this."

He frowned. "There's no merpeople here. You'll be fine."

Alissia forced her body deeper into the water and said tensely, "Just because you know what I'm feeling right now doesn't mean I want to talk about it, Luke. Let's just get this over with."

"I'm just trying to calm you."

"I *am* calm!" she snapped. "Stay out of my head."

With the water up to her shoulders, she closed her eyes and reached out with her mind. Lita was right about the dolphins. The water was filled with aquatic life, which caused her heart to beat even faster.

Her fear lessened when three dolphins swam over to them. Their shiny skin looked pink in the moonlight, and their heads were much rounder than the ones she was used to seeing in her reality.

Eager to get out of the water, Alissia did not get distracted from the task at hand, and she mentally conveyed to the dolphins what she expected from them. Luke told her which direction the harbor was located, and it was not long before she was holding onto the fin of a dolphin while gliding through the water.

Although she struggled to maintain her hold with Mia clinging to her neck, she did not complain about the speed, especially since she instructed the dolphins to do their job quickly.

It took all of her focus to keep her and Mia's face above the water, as it was not easy or pleasant with Mia's sharp nails digging into her skin.

They slowed down once they made their way into the harbor, and as they neared the boats, Alissia located the one with bed sheets flapping at its side. While guiding the dolphins toward the ship, she realized they could hear the high-pitched whistle, as the animals went straight to the rope ladder.

Mia grabbed the ladder and swiftly began to climb up it, and relief filled Alissia as soon as she pulled herself out of the water. Once at the top of the ladder, Salvatore reached down and lifted her over the edge of the boat, setting her down beside him. She shivered as a breeze glided over her body, and Lita wrapped a towel around her.

As Salvatore helped Selona onto the ship, Lita tugged at Alissia's towel, and Alissia followed her down a set of stairs, only to stop midway at the second level of the ship.

Stepping away from the stairs, she found herself at the end of a narrow corridor. Lita opened a nearby door to reveal a small bathroom. She pointed at a crate hanging from the wall.

"Hurry and rinse off the salt water. Your clothes are over there." Without waiting for a response, Lita dashed back up the stairs.

It took a while for Alissia to wiggle out of the skintight wet suit, and it was a workout all in itself. Once finished, she quickly washed in a bath resembling a small hot tub. It was built off the ground, and a cover was placed next to it.

Looking around the room, she noticed everything was securely attached to the walls or ceiling, and she guessed the cover was used to keep the water from sloshing out of the tub when not in use. The only lighting in the room came from glow stones set in small cages attached to the walls.

Her knives were also there, and she hid them on her body as she dressed. When she opened the door, Lita was waiting for her. "Follow me."

Alissia followed the young woman down the dimly lit, narrow corridor. Closed doors were situated along each side, and they stopped at the very last one. Lita knocked, and Salvatore soon opened the door, inviting them into an elegant living area.

In one corner of the room, a thick, moss-colored curtain was pulled back to reveal a large bed carved into the wall. Built-in drawers were beneath it, and a sizeable wardrobe closet was constructed along the other wall. A closed door was beside it.

The opposite corner of the room consisted of a long, rectangular table made from the same thick, dark, and elaborately carved wood as the bed. Solid bench seats were carved into the wall and came up from the floor on the opposite side.

A matching desk was directly across from the door they entered, and elegant sconces holding glow stones were situated along each wall.

The décor was in olive and gold tones, and with the elaborate furniture, the room exuded wealth and power.

"Not what you were expecting?" Lita asked.

Without answering, Alissia followed Lita and her father to the table, where an unknown man was sitting with his back against the wall. Luke and Selona were situated on the opposite side, with their backs to Alissia, and they were also dressed in fresh clothing.

The man stood, and Alissia put her hand on Luke's shoulder before stepping over the bench and sitting down. Salvatore sat down beside the man, and Lita scooted in next to her father before the man sat down across from Alissia.

He was tall and lean, and he looked to be older than Salvatore, although his grey hair still retained some brown. It was pulled back in a braid, ending slightly below his shoulders. He wore a formal olive-colored buccaneer coat, with a white button-up shirt. Ruffles from his shirt flowed out of the top portion of his coat. A gold sash was tied around his waist, and Alissia wondered if there was something symbolic in the matching colors adorning him and the room.

Like Salvatore, he looked as if he spent a lot of time in the sun, and she noticed tribal tattoos peaking out from his coat and traveling down his hands. His posture was straight and formal, and similar to the furniture in the room, his presence was dominating and suggested power.

Salvatore said, "Alissia, this is Captain Blackwell. He'll be taking us to the island."

The man gave a curt nod, while his penetrating hazel eyes seemed to size her up. To ease her nerves, she grabbed Luke's hand beneath the table.

"He's never seen anyone like you before," Luke mentally said.

Alissia heard the door open and close again before a female's voice cheerfully said, "Here we are. Some fresh chet from the kitchen."

She came up behind Alissia and set a tray down on the table, and Alissia looked up to find a woman similar to Salvatore's age. She was stocky, and her blonde and grey hair was set in a disheveled bun on top of her head.

Everyone silently watched as the woman rushed through pouring cups of chet and passed them around the table. Then she plopped down beside Alissia and gave a friendly smile.

"Hello, dear," she said, in the same thick and foreign accent as Salvatore and his people. "You must be Alissia. I'm Debina, the captain's wife." She turned to her husband. "Have I missed anything?"

Captain Blackwell frowned and shook his head, turning his attention to Luke. "You're a member of the league?"

"I was," Luke answered.

The captain turned to Alissia. "And you're not from this reality?"

"No."

Not taking his eyes from her, he said, "Salvatore is an old friend of mine, and he's explained the situation in great detail. We'll be traveling directly to the island, without stopping. Although my men are aware of your presence aboard this ship, I ask that you refrain from trying to socialize with them. You'll either eat here with my wife or in the dining area after meal hours. As for being on deck, you're limited to the women's area. If we reach a storm, you need to go to your living quarters and stay there.

"The men aboard this ship know their place. However, they will be curious about you. If any of them reach out to you or act inappropriately, you need to direct your concerns to me or Mr. Killingsworth, my first officer."

He looked at Luke. "I'm the law on this ship. If you have a problem with any of my men, I'll deal with it appropriately. Aboard this ship, you have no authority. Do we have an understanding?"

Luke smiled politely. "I'll respect your rules and your ways, and I don't foresee a problem."

The captain gave a nod and turned back to Alissia. "I was told you have a pixet with you. Where's your creature now?"

Alissia shrugged. "I don't know. She usually stays hidden, even from me. She's extremely private."

"Just make sure she doesn't try to scare my men."

"I'm pretty certain that won't be a problem," Alissia responded.

The captain turned to Selona and said firmly, in the ancient language, "There'll be no tricks or problems from you. If you try to harm any of my men, you'll be thrown overboard. You are—"

Luke's voice within her head drowned out the rest of Captain Blackwell's words. *"I can't tell if he's threatened by us, or if he's merely establishing his authority over us."*

"He's stuffy and rude," Alissia thought back.

"That comes with his position. Don't be so quick to judge. If you notice, his wife doesn't seem to fear him. Salvatore and Lita also look at ease. There's a difference between fear and respect. A true leader aspires for respect, and it's too soon to recognize what type of leader this captain is."

"Hmm... Formal, bossy, arrogant, stuffy..."

Luke squeezed her hand beneath the table as she tried to think of more adjectives. His mental voice sounded amused as he said, *"I believe you used those same words to describe me at one time."*

"And I was right too," she shot back.

"Someone has a problem with authority."

Before she could respond, the captain's wife placed her hand on Alissia's shoulder. "Are you ready to be shown to your room?" Glancing at Lita, she added, "The two of you will be sharing. You'll have to excuse the accommodations, as we have a newlywed couple onboard. We've also given Santo and Salvatore our other better arrangements."

Alissia smiled politely. "I'm sure it will be fine."

She took a sip of the warm drink in front of her and was instantly surprised by its unique flavor. Unlike all the other chet she had tasted since coming to this reality, it was slightly red in color and left a thick, somewhat buttery aftertaste in her mouth. She thought she recognized the soothing flavor of ginger.

Looking at Debina, she said, "This is delicious. What am I drinking?"

The woman grinned, sending creases along her face. Unlike her husband, she appeared open and unguarded. "I'm glad you like it. Unlike most chet, this one isn't made from leaves. It's made from a root, and many herbs and spices are added to it for extra flavor."

Lita said, "I haven't had this in years."

"Ah, you know my love for chet, my dear," Debina said. Turning to Alissia, she added, "One of the benefits of being a captain's wife is that I get to purchase things from all over the world, and I get fresh supplies of exotic chet and other foods most people never get the joy of tasting."

"Mother always loved your gifts."

Debina turned to Lita. "Your mother was a beautiful woman, and I see so much of her in you, Lita." Her eyes went to Salvatore. "We've greatly missed you."

She stood and looked from Lita to Alissia. "You two ready?"

They both took a few more sips of their chet before standing. As they walked toward the door, Alissia asked, "What about Selona? Where will she sleep?"

The captain answered, "She'll remain under guard at all times, and her accommodations are less desirable."

Alissia nodded and followed Debina and Lita out of the room. The older woman briskly strode along the narrow walkway, and Alissia's short legs worked fast to keep up.

"Here you go, girls." Debina stopped at a door. Without pausing, she opened it and stepped through.

There were two wooden beds located at opposite sides of the room. Drawers were built in beneath each of them, and a nightstand was carved into the wall beside each bed. A closet and some cabinets were carved into the wall between the nightstands. A small window with a thin curtain was over each nightstand, and a long mirror was attached to the wall beside the door. Alissia's new wardrobe trunk was strapped to the wall at the end of one of the beds.

"Do you remember this room?" Debina asked, smiling at Lita.

Lita nodded, looking around the room.

"Duff is eager to see you. Maybe you can help him with his responsibilities—that is, if you remember your way around a ship."

"Haven't forgotten a thing." Lita grinned.

Debina reached over and pulled Lita in for a hug. Squeezing tightly, she said, "I'm so glad you're here."

Alissia watched in disbelief as Lita put her arms around Debina and wholeheartedly returned the hug. She had never seen the young woman show that much affection—not even to her own father.

When they pulled away, Debina turned to Alissia. "I hope this is suitable. It was once our boys' room, but now it's just an extra bedroom. The bathing room is at the end of the hall.

"You should probably get some rest." She motioned toward the bed meant for Alissia. "The crew will be waking soon, and we'll be sailing out shortly thereafter. You need to stay hidden below deck until we get out of the harbor."

She walked over to one of the cabinets and showed Alissia how to open it, as everything seemed to be locked in place. It was filled with a variety of books, and the one next to it was filled with board games and cards.

"We'll leave your breakfast on a warming stone," Debina said, walking toward the door. "I imagine after tonight's swim in the ocean, you'll want to sleep in."

"Thank you," said Alissia. As Debina opened the door, Alissia added, "Oh, I didn't know what to do with the wet suit, so I just left it in the bathing room."

"I'll take care of it, dear. You're a guest on this ship. Now get some rest, and I'll see you later today."

After she left and closed the door, Alissia grinned mischievously and turned to Lita. "So who's Duff?"

Lita sat down on her bed and began to remove her boots. "Just an old friend."

"Uh... huh. And how old is this old friend?" Alissia asked, sitting down on her own bed and removing her boots.

"He's just a friend—nothing more." Lita frowned and made herself comfortable under the covers of her bed. Then she stared up at the ceiling. "Just someone I've known since I was little. He's their youngest son."

"And is he cute?" Alissia questioned, crawling into her bedding.

There was no need to cover the glow stones in the room. Daylight was beginning to show through the curtains.

Lita rolled over. "I haven't seen him in years, and he's just an old friend—rather annoying at that, him and his older brothers. Now let's get some sleep. Santo kept me busy last night, and I'm exhausted."

Alissia stared at Lita's back for a moment, remembering how craftily Debina had mentioned her son. It seemed the captain's wife was really fond of Lita, which surprised Alissia.

The young woman didn't seem to make friends easily, at least, not from what Alissia had witnessed since meeting her in Pallen. She seemed more of a loner—not exactly a people person. Sometimes Alissia wondered if Lita even liked people. Although, Alissia could easily relate to that.

Chapter 18

Alissia opened her eyes to find the ship moving. The swaying motion was heavy, and there were creaking sounds coming from the walls and ceiling. She could also hear the sound of footsteps coming from above.

Lita closed one of the cabinets nearest her bed. Her hair was wet, and she was wearing fresh clothing.

"Ready to eat breakfast?"

Alissia blinked a few times before forcing her body from the bed. "What time is it?"

"Nearly time for lunch. We slept late."

She unlocked her wardrobe trunk, and after selecting a pair of dark sunglasses, she turned around to find Lita opening one of the windows over a nightstand. She then began to gather the glow stones on her side of the room.

"What are you doing?"

"Putting our stones out to charge. There's a place for them attached to the ship." Lita reached through the window and then did the same to the glow stones on the other side of the room. Once finished and the windows were closed, Lita turned and said, "Ready?"

"Let me do something with my hair."

"Hurry. I'm hungry."

Alissia looked in the mirror. Her hair was a wild mess of curls, and she quickly pulled it into a ponytail.

She had a hard time following Lita to the kitchen, as the rocking of the ship was more than she had expected.

As soon as they entered the dining area, she caught a whiff of the food, and she immediately walked back into the corridor and leaned against the wall.

"What's wrong?" Lita asked, following her out.

"I can't go in there. It smells like meat, and I'll get sick."

Lita frowned. "They're cooking lunch. I hate to be the one to tell you, but the men on this ship are going to eat meat."

"Have I asked them not to?" Alissia countered.

"I'll tell Debina. Wait here."

Lita returned a short moment later with a basket. Debina bustled behind her, carrying two covered drinks.

"Sorry, dear. We're cooking now. The two of you can eat in my room, or you can go above deck. It's not too windy, and it's safe enough now. I would join you, but I'm needed in the kitchen."

After passing the drinks to Alissia, she looked at Lita. "Do you re-member where everything is?"

"We'll be fine."

Alissia followed Lita toward the stairs. They stopped and watched as a young sailor made his way up from the lowest level of the ship.

His eyes went to Alissia, and he gave a curt nod as he continued up the stairs.

Once above deck, they went to the back corner of the ship, where padded seats lined the high walls. The two women sat down, and Lita set the basket between them before she began to rummage for food.

They both ate quickly without speaking. Then Lita placed their empty cups in the basket and set it down at her feet. Alissia brought her legs up and rested her chin on her knees. She closed her eyes, and as she took in the salty smell of the ocean, loose strands of hair tickled her cheeks while dancing in the breeze. She smiled, feeling full and content.

The sound of men's voices could be heard over the waves, and without opening her eyes, Alissia asked, "Do you know everyone on the boat?"

"No."

"Where's Santo?"

"Father thinks it's best for him to stay below."

Lita stood, and Alissia opened her eyes and watched as the young woman picked up the basket.

"I should go check on him and see if I'm needed."

"Do you need help?" Alissia asked.

"No, there's nothing you can do." Lita's eyes looked distant as she added, "Sometimes my presence comforts him, but sometimes it only makes things worse."

"Why's that?"

Lita frowned. "He sometimes gets me confused with Mother, and it either comforts him or distresses him even more."

A young man walked over to them, and Alissia immediately guessed him to be the son Debina had talked about. Although he was tall and lean like his father, he greatly resembled his mother. He had her blue eyes and blonde hair, and like her, his face expressed an unguarded kindness. However, there was also a hint of mischief.

His hair fell down in loose waves to his shoulders, and he wore a cream-colored poet's shirt that hung over his dark pants. With his sleeves rolled up and his top buttons undone, Alissia caught a glimpse of tribal tattoos and firm muscles on tanned skin.

He barely glanced her way before turning his full attention to Lita. "Finally awake? I see you've grown soft."

Lita's eyes narrowed. "I see you're still delusional, and I can still take you when it comes to a bow and arrow and a crossbow."

"Ah, but not with a sword." Duff took a few steps until he was standing directly in front of her. "I can still take you down."

Lita stepped around him. "And how many times have you had to use your sword in the past few years? Your life is pretty comfy compared to traveling on land. I imagine you've grown soft."

He laughed heartily and began to follow her. Neither of them looked back at Alissia as they strolled away. She shook her head and grinned, staring at their backs.

"Oh, no. There's totally nothing going to happen between those two. No chemistry there," she said, laughing to herself.

The women's area was somewhat secluded in the back corner of the ship. However, she soon began to notice many of the sailors staring at her, and it was not long before she walked back to her room to retrieve her toiletry bag. She then went to the washroom to freshen up. Afterwards, she went back to her room and sat on her bed.

"Where are you?" she mentally called out.

Luke answered, *"I'm helping on deck."*

"You know how to sail?"

"No, but I plan to learn. Devon needs to learn as well. He's never been on a boat until now, and you should see how excited he is. Never pass up an opportunity to acquire a new skill. You never know when you might need it."

She frowned. *"I can't leave the women's area. Remember?"*

"There's a reason for that. Captain Blackwell has to maintain order on his ship, and he doesn't want you to distract his men. From what I've seen, he's greatly respected by everyone. He's not so bad."

Groaning out loud, she flopped backwards onto the bed and sprawled out. *"You love structure and order, don't you?"*

She heard his mental laughter before he responded, *"And you love random chaos. You really don't like authority, do you?"*

"And what do we have in common?"

Mia unexpectedly pounced onto Alissia's stomach, and she cried out in alarm. Luke's urgent voice immediately filled her head. *"What's wrong? Are you hurt?"*

Alissia scowled up at the big grey eyes staring down at her. *"Nothing. Mia just jumped on me. I'm fine."*

"Well, I'm about to dine with Salvatore and the captain. We'll talk this evening."

"Okay. Have fun," she said, lifting the tiny fur ball from her body. She set Mia on the bed and rolled onto her side.

"You know, for a cute little critter, I think you enjoy biting and scaring me." She began to pet Mia along her back. "Are you hungry?"

Mia shook her head.

"You've already eaten?"

She nodded.

"Don't steal any of their food or anything. The captain's strict, and we'll get into trouble."

Mia nodded before closing her eyes, and Alissia continued to stroke the creature's body until she realized her small friend was asleep. She then rolled onto her back and closed her own eyes.

Although the swaying of the ship was relaxing, she was wide awake, and her eyes soon popped open. She let out a frustrated sigh, realizing the only place she could go was the women's area, the bathroom, and the small bedroom.

Everyone on the ship had a job to do, except for her and Selona, and she wished Edda and Bruna had taught her how to knit.

Thoughts of Anika came to mind, but then she remembered that their close relationship was over. Even if she did see Anika again, it would never be the same between them.

Loud voices came from outside the door, and she listened as a group of men passed by on their way from the dining area. Their laughter filled the corridor.

After a long moment of complete boredom, she stood and began to rummage through the cabinets. She found a large stash of books and chose one that promised an adventure with mermaids—the sweet and beautiful kind, not anything like the ones that had almost killed her.

Thanks to books, her knowledge of this reality was growing. Fiction taught her about the culture of the people, and it greatly broadened her vocabulary. She hoped the book in her hand would describe some of the sea animals she did not know about.

Alissia waited for the voices to clear out of the hall before she opened the door to the bedroom and slipped out. Once at the women's area, she sat on her knees and looked over the side of the boat. She watched the ship glide through the water for a long moment before she closed her eyes and reached out with her mind.

She found the ocean to be filled with aquatic life, and it slightly overwhelmed her. Although fish were easier to control than insects, her presence did not excite them, and their thoughts were limited in many ways.

"Ah, there you are. How are you today?"

Alissia turned around to find Salvatore standing behind her. He was balancing two large mugs in his hands. Before she could respond, he sat down. She grinned and lowered onto the bench, tucking her feet under her.

"Debina sent this from the kitchen."

She accepted the drink and set the lid beside her before taking a sip, savoring the warm chet with a subtle tropical flavor.

"Lita told me the smell in the kitchen made you sick earlier today." She nodded, and he continued, "Well, there won't be meat at every meal. There's a limited supply, and the people from the island don't eat much meat."

"The sailors are from the island?"

He nodded. "I guess I can tell you more about where I come from." He took a sip of his drink, and a smile lit up his face. "Mmm… that woman does have an assortment of chet."

Salvatore leaned back. "Every sailor on this ship is from the island. In fact, the men on this boat are considered elite, because they were each chosen for this ship. You see, unlike our trade ships, this one is much smaller. It's one of only a few that can dock near the Medicians' living area. The trade ships we use are much bigger and have a larger crew.

"I believe I informed you when we first met that not everyone involved in this business actually knows the truth of what we do. That even goes for the people that live on the same island as the Medicians. Many of them don't even know they exist."

He seemed amused by Alissia's confused expression, and he took another sip of his drink, letting his words sink in. Then his eyes became distant. "It's a large island, and you'll love it there. It's filled with life—in the water and on land. There are beautiful waterfalls and mountains. It's like paradise."

"How long has it been since you've been there?"

The distant look in his eyes faded, only to be replaced by a hint of sadness. "Many years. I left there shortly after the passing of my wife, and I've kept myself busy by traveling to foreign lands."

"Oh," she said, not knowing how to respond.

Salvatore took a sip of his drink and then smiled at her. "You remind me of her in many ways."

"Me? I thought Lita did."

"You and Lita have a lot in common, my dear."

"Like what?"

"You're both stubborn, not the trusting kind, have a thing for keeping people at a distance, don't like asking for help, and you both would die fighting for what you believe in. You have high morals—a sense of right or wrong. You're both also softies on the inside, but I think you'd die to keep that a secret."

Alissia took a long sip of her drink. Then she smiled coolly. "Nope, I have a lot of friends, and everyone knows I'm a softy."

He chuckled, and to her relief, he changed the subject. "It's a large island. The Medicians have their place, and we have ours. Very few of the humans know the truth behind the arrangement. Most of the people believe the other side of the island is used for mining, as that is what the island is known for. When our trade ships dock on the loading side of the island, there are strict rules they have to abide by. The sailors aren't even allowed off the boats.

"The other harbor is in the port city of the island, where everyone lives. Massive rocks surround the island itself, so boats can't just land wherever they like. We also have many military ships that sail along the border. It's completely protected under the façade of it being a mining island. We have our own government, and there are many regulations to protect the true secrets of the island—even from our own people."

Alissia raised her eyebrows. "How do you keep a secret from that many people?"

"It's really not that hard. People believe we protect the mines when we're actually protecting the Medicians. The size of the island, along with the natural land formations, also helps."

She took a long sip of her drink, envisioning an island filled with cliffs and surrounded by massive rocks along its border. "And where do the Medicians live?"

"They live in the area near the trade port, yet not close enough to be seen by the ships. Very few boats are allowed to dock directly at the Medicians' living area. Captain Blackwell will have to maneuver around many rocks, but he's very skilled and has done it before."

Alissia scanned the deck. "And these men? They know the truth?"

"Yes, these men are not just sailors. They're among the select that know the truth of what we do, and they also know the consequences of breaking that oath."

"And what is that?"

He looked hard into her eyes. "Death. They've sworn to protect our ancestors' secrets and to protect the Medicians with their lives."

Alissia frowned. "I love how you now call them Medicians. I almost got killed for calling them Lamians. Someone should have told me their true name."

He shrugged. "You were calling them Lamians when I met you, so I went along with it."

They sipped their drinks in silence for a moment. "How are you feeling now that Anika, Langley, and Grady are no longer around?"

She stared into her mug. "It's for the best."

"I understand that, but I also know they're the only other people you know in this reality. You've shared a lot with them."

Alissia looked up and shrugged, his watchful eyes making her uncomfortable. "I knew it wasn't forever. They have their lives, and I have mine."

He nodded thoughtfully, and she distracted herself by taking another sip of her drink.

"You're still young, Alissia, and many people will come and go throughout your lifetime. Nothing ever stays the same. The biggest challenge in this world is to continue to believe in and look for the good when you're surrounded by the bad."

Salvatore took her by the hand and gave it a squeeze. "Don't let anything harden your heart. You're very blessed to have Luke in your life. I can see his love for you, and I can also see your love for him."

A look of sadness came over his face. "You remind me a lot of my wife, and although I loved her dearly, she didn't always make it easy for me."

He smiled weakly. "I know she loved me, and I was greatly blessed to receive her love. Yet, there were times when she didn't want to be loved. The walls around her heart were thick, and no matter how much I cared for her, sometimes I couldn't reach her. She would keep me at a distance, and it pained me greatly during those times. I'd watch her retreat into herself, and I couldn't get to her."

Alissia stared down at the mug in her lap, and he released her hand. "I guess I just want things to be easier for you and Luke. Don't make it too hard for the poor boy."

She looked up and asked hesitantly, "How did she die?"

"It was an accident." Turning to stare out in front of him, he added, "There was a shipwreck somewhere in the ocean, and the wreckage and debris began to wash up on our shore.

"The ship came from a distant land, and many people were intrigued with the strange and rare things being found. Latina and her sister were both excited to see if they could find anything too. While I was at work, they took the children to the beach for a fun scavenger hunt."

Salvatore paused in thought for a moment. Then he turned his eyes to her. "She succeeded in finding a crate filled with some beautiful shells. When she picked up one of them, a gandoly stuck its tentacle out and stung her."

"What's a gandoly?"

"It's a small sea creature we had never heard of before Latina's death. It's not from this part of the world. They're highly venomous, and she was dead within an hour."

"Did anyone else get stung?"

He shook his head. "No, she was the only one. The people on the beach secured the crate, and Latina was rushed to the clinic, but there was nothing to be done. Our doctors were dealing with something they had never seen before."

They sipped their drinks in silence again before Alissia turned to him.

"Salvatore?"

"Yes?"

"There's something we've never really talked about." She paused, chewing on her bottom lip as she contemplated how much to tell him. "What if Luke and I want to leave the island after we get there? You've mentioned how heavily guarded it is. What's the plan for us?"

"Well," he started, "I don't truly know. I won't be the one making those decisions. I believe you and Luke will be safe, and you'll be accepted. But I really can't promise they'll consider letting you leave. You caused a great stir among my people by being seen. Now everyone seems to be talking about you, and that means they know about the Medicians. They're searching and reading legends about the Lamians, and that's not a good thing."

He gave a reassuring smile and patted her on the shoulder.

"You'll be safe. I'll explain how you've done everything in your power to protect the Medicians. You've kept their secrets—even from me." He paused. "I'll represent you the best I can, but it would help if you tell me the truth about your circumstances."

Alissia rubbed her thumb along the rim of the empty mug in her lap, recalling some of Grady's words during his irrational rants. Salvatore learned a lot about her in those moments—more than she wanted him to. Yet, he had never asked questions.

"I am from another reality." She stared up at the large sail towering in front of them, taking in the soothing breeze and then turned to meet his gaze. "When I was pulled into this reality, I almost died. The Medicians found me and saved my life. However, they were interrupted at the end of the process, and they ran away. I never got to meet them, and I didn't know anything about them. Grady and I spent weeks in the Pallen library looking through the historical section, and when I went to the ball, I had no idea how much damage that would cause."

"So you've never met them?"

"No, but they've been watching me—or at least they were." At his confused expression, she added, "In the beginning, I could tell they somehow visited me during my sleep. I would wake up each morning feeling as though I had been watched.

"And when Luke started taking me to the North, they even spoke to me one night during my sleep. I was told not to tell him anything or use any of the gifts they gave me. Eventually, I got too far from them, and I didn't feel their presence anymore. However, when I got closer to them again, I could feel them."

"Can you feel them now?" he asked.

"No, I'm too far away. I don't think they can see me."

He stared up at the sail and considered her words for a moment. "How about Mia? How did you find her?"

"She came to me while I was at the castle. She ate the note that came with her. It only said they couldn't help me. Mia was supposed to do that."

Alissia snickered. "I was a little mad about that too. I didn't see how Mia was supposed to help, but then I saw what she did to one of the men back at the castle."

He nodded. "So she protected you?"

She looked back down at the mug in her lap. "I killed Ian, but Mia helped us to get out of the room that was guarded by three of his men."

Salvatore put his hand on her shoulder and gave it a gentle squeeze. "I understand you've had a lot to deal with since coming to this reality. You've had to adjust to a lot of things. I promise you I'll inform my people of your loyalty during your circumstances."

She looked up hopefully. "Does that mean they'll let Luke and me leave to go back to the Medicians that saved my life? I want to meet them."

"I'll see what I can do. However, I can't make that promise. It's a high risk and not my decision." Although he smiled, she could see his worry.

She nodded, and he let go of her shoulder. "So how did you get pulled into this reality?"

Alissia frowned and shook her head. "That's another story all in itself. Someone set it up ten years ago, wanting to go to my reality. He thought my body would make the window bigger so that he could pass through."

"Did it?"

"Nope, my body squeezed through, nearly killing me with it." He winced, and she nodded. "Exactly, but what's done is done."

"Do you know who did it?"

"I do, and I even met him. He apologized."

"And you forgive him?"

She let out a thoughtful sigh, staring out in front of her. "I was angry with him for a long while, but yeah, I forgive him. I don't even think about him anymore." She smiled and turned to look at him. "I kind of like this reality," she added, sheepishly.

"Ah, true love." Salvatore grinned.

She laughed at the sparkle in his eyes.

Changing the subject, she asked, "So, how am I supposed to help while I'm on this ship?"

"You can relax. You're traveling as a guest."

Alissia shook her head. "Everyone has something to do but me—even Devon."

"True. You can probably help Debina and Tabitha in the kitchen when they aren't preparing meat. I'll also need you to occasionally help with the dogs if they begin to get seasick."

"Who's Tabitha?"

"You'll probably meet her this evening. She and one of the sailors were recently wed, and since she's the daughter of another captain, she's already visited the private port and knows certain things. That's why she's allowed onboard. Most wives are not."

"So there are perks to being a captain's daughter?"

"Perks, along with curses," he answered. "Although most children raised at sea grow to love this lifestyle, a few choose land when they become adults."

"And that's a problem?"

"Rarely, but there's an old story of a captain's daughter that fell in love and married a shopkeeper. She told him of the Medicians, and it was not long before they were both relocated to a private, guarded area on the island."

"You mean a prison?"

"I was told they lived happily ever after in guarded seclusion." Salvatore grinned. "That could be pleasurable or immense torment—depending on the couple."

Alissia laughed as an unknown man joined them. He looked to be in his early thirties and had light brown hair pulled back into a short ponytail. Unlike the other sailors, he wore a coat somewhat similar to the captain's.

He bowed slightly. "Hello, Alissia Roswell. I am Evan Killingsworth, the first officer of this ship. If you should have a problem while on-board, you can bring it to the attention of the captain or myself."

Alissia smiled politely. "Thank you."

Salvatore stood and took the empty mug from her hand. "I need to go check on Santo."

"How is he?" she asked.

"He's having a good day—at least, he's not screaming or crying."

She nodded understandingly. "Let me know if I can do anything to help."

"There's really nothing you can do." Motioning toward Evan he added, "Although, there is something I do need you to do. You can get Mr. Killingsworth to show you where Selona is, and you can try to help her with her plants. I believe she's out of her living animals and is now forced to eat our food. She's not happy about it, and I believe she's also unhappy with her accommodations."

Alissia groaned. "So you need me to go talk to the she-devil?"

"Unfortunately, I do."

She reached for the book at her side and stood. Salvatore began to walk away, and then he turned around.

"Oh, and Alissia, don't forget she has the cure for Santo. Under no circumstances are you to throw her overboard."

Chapter 19

Evan led Alissia to the lowest level of the ship, where glow stones dimly lit the narrow corridor, and a musky odor filled the air.

Selona glowered from behind the bars of the holding cell she was in. Although she was wearing a simple dress Salvatore had bought for her, the creature still looked greatly disturbing to Alissia. In fact, she looked even more menacing than usual.

She was sitting on a small cot in the corner of the dark cell, with her back against the wall. Her pale skin looked ghostly in the prison setting, along with her large, unnatural eyes.

The creature grinned leeringly at Alissia, and fresh blood oozed from between the gaps of her sharp teeth. The bright red liquid covered her chin and streaked down the front of her neck, staining the top of her dress.

"Want a bite?" Selona jeered, holding out the body of a half-eaten rat.

Alissia gagged and turned her eyes to Evan to find a disgusted look on his face.

"What are you doing?" she asked, keeping her eyes on the collar of the first mate's jacket.

"I got hungry."

"And I heard they've been feeding you," Alissia shot back.

"Yessss," Selona hissed. "But I want fresh meat. Want a taste? I'll share."

Alissia's grip on the book in her hand tightened, and she clenched her teeth. "I came here to help you with your plants, but I'm not coming near you when you're acting like this. You're not even trying to act sociable."

The body of the rat slammed against the bars directly in front of Alissia, splattering blood onto her clothing and face.

"I'm not a human!" Selona screamed.

Alissia turned to meet the creature's eyes. "No, you're definitely not!" she fumed. "You're worse, and I won't help you while you're acting like this."

She spun around and walked back toward the stairs, not meeting the eyes of the two guards standing at the end of the corridor. She could hear Evan's boots following her.

Memories of Gafeen's torture filled her mind as she marched up the stairs, and a flash of anger came over her. When she stopped at the bathroom door on the same floor of her room, she turned to Evan and forced calmness into her voice. "Thank you for taking me to see her."

He responded with a polite nod. "If you should need anything else, please don't hesitate to ask." He smiled. "At least she'll help to purge our ship of rodents."

Alissia forced a smile, and then she opened the bathroom door and stepped inside. Once alone, she stared down at her shaky hands and took a deep breath.

Luke's voice entered her head. *"I see you visited Selona."*

"I'll tell you about it later. I'm not in the mood."

She spent the rest of the afternoon curled up on a seat in the women's area above deck, and the book did its job of offering her a temporary escape from reality.

Later she joined Debina, Captain Blackwell, Duff, Salvatore, Lita, and Luke in the captain's suite for dinner. Other than mentioning what happened with Selona, she remained quiet and was content to listen and watch the others.

Luke sat beside her, and now that Grady was no longer with them, he openly showed affection to her in subtle ways. Before sitting down, he gave her a quick kiss on the cheek, and his eyes often went to her throughout the meal.

His face was freshly tanned and was no longer hidden behind a beard. After a day at sea, his black hair had a tousled, windblown look to it.

She enjoyed his passion to learn new things, and she smiled as she noticed the twinkle in his eyes as he discussed various nautical techniques with the captain. Captain Blackwell seemed just as eager to teach as Luke was to learn.

Although Debina politely kept Alissia in the conversation, the woman's attention seemed to be devoted to Duff and Lita. During the meal, she told stories of their amusing childhood schemes, and Alissia learned that although Lita and Duff did not spend a lot of time together as children, they were inseparable every time they saw each other.

She noticed how Duff looked at Lita, and she wondered if her friend was truly blind to his obvious interest in her.

Salvatore ate quickly and left early so that he could get back to Santo. However, he seemed interested in the young couple as well. As he ate his meal, his eyes stayed on them, and Alissia wondered what he thought of Duff with his daughter.

After dinner, they made their way to the women's area on deck, and Alissia was soon snuggled up to Luke with a blanket over her body and his arm around her. It was dark, and laughter was in the air, although mostly Debina's.

Alissia could not believe how opposite the captain and his wife were. While he was stern and somber, she was happy and lively. Duff took after his mother, as a smile seemed to come naturally for him.

"You're quiet tonight. Anything wrong?" Luke asked softly.

She shook her head and smiled. "Just watching everyone."

"You're usually planning something when quiet, but I guess I'll believe you tonight."

"Where's Devon?"

"He's with the sailors getting some rest. He worked hard today."

A young woman in her early twenties sat down beside Debina. She had silky, dark brown hair that fell to her shoulders, and she was not much taller than Alissia.

"Where's Griffon?" Debina asked.

"It's his bath schedule," the woman answered. She turned curious eyes to Alissia and smiled.

Debina said, "Alissia, this is Tabitha. She's our latest addition to the crew and works in the kitchen. She also just married one of our sailors."

"It's nice to meet you," Alissia said.

"I'm sorry the smell of our cooking made you sick," Tabitha said. "We don't prepare meat at every meal, and we'll keep the windows open to help air out the kitchen. Hopefully, you can join us sometime."

"I'd love to be able to help y'all… I mean, you all, in the kitchen."

Tabitha said, "The meals are planned out, and I could let you know when we aren't cooking meat, if you would like."

Alissia nodded. "Yes, I would definitely like that."

"You're a guest and really don't have to do anything," Debina said.

"Thanks, but I would like to be able to contribute."

While she had spent most of her day resting and reading, she had seen men scrubbing the deck, oiling the wood along the ship, and doing various other chores. Everyone seemed to have a job to do, except for her, Santo, and Selona.

Even young Devon had made himself useful, and Alissia did not have the personality to just sit and watch others do things for her. She needed to keep busy. That was just who she was.

"I heard you're from another reality," Tabitha said.

"I am. Would you like for me to tell you about it?"

Tabitha and Debina both grinned and nodded. By now, Alissia was used to telling others about the ways of her old life. She knew which details would fascinate those around her, and she got the expected reactions as she described the big cities in her reality. They could barely fathom the idea of an underground subway or bulldozers destroying forests.

Even the captain seemed intrigued by her words, and when Tabitha's husband walked up and asked if she was ready for bed, she shook her head. He also sat down and began to listen.

She talked for a long time, and Captain Blackwell was the first to stand. He looked down at his wife and said, "It's getting late, and morning comes early."

Debina reluctantly agreed. "We'd love to hear more. Do you mind sharing with us again?"

"I'd love to," Alissia answered. "There's a huge difference in where I come from, and there's a lot to tell."

Griffon turned to Tabitha. "Ready, Peacock?" She nodded, and he stood and helped her to her feet. Then she turned and said goodnight to everyone.

Like the captain and Debina, Tabitha and Griffon seemed to be opposites. She smiled a lot and appeared to love the company of people, whereas he seemed shy and somewhat awkward. He was much taller than his short wife and wore glasses.

As the young couple strolled away, Debina grinned and said, excitedly, "Aren't they the cutest pair? So in love. He even calls her Peacock." She stood and looked down at Lita. "You should help Duff with his duties tomorrow—just like old times, although more advanced skills. He could teach you."

Turning to the captain, she asked, "You don't mind her working alongside Duff, do you?"

He looked at Lita. "When you're not busy with Santo, Duff could use your help."

Lita nodded, and as the captain and Debina walked away, Luke stood and held out his hand.

"I'll walk you to your room. We should get some rest." He pulled Alissia to her feet, and after putting the blanket away in the storage area beneath her seat, she followed him.

At her door, he slowly trailed his fingertips along the side of her face and down her neck. Then he placed a gentle kiss on her lips. "Goodnight, Pixet."

"Where are you sleeping?"

"In the bunkroom with the other men."

He grazed her forehead with his lips before turning and walking toward the stairs, and she stared longingly at his back for a brief moment. As she closed the door to her room, she realized it had been a while since the two of them had been separated. She was used to being with him, and it bothered her a little as to how much she craved his presence.

Alissia collected her gown and bag of toiletries before heading to the washroom. As she prepared for bed, memories of how Luke had openly shown affection toward her that evening brought a smile to her face. A warm feeling filled her as she remembered the first time he had claimed her as his in a cabin outside of Pallen.

Now that they did not have to hide their feelings for each other, they could finally be themselves in front of others.

They were an official couple. She was his, and he was hers. Although that thought brought a tinge of fear with it, it also filled her with excitement.

Chapter 20

The next two weeks went by slowly for Alissia. Although she did get to help in the kitchen with the meatless meals, she spent most of her time reading.

She only saw Luke in the evenings, as he spent his days working alongside the crew. When Devon wasn't doing chores, he was learning how to tie a new kind of knot, and he seemed to enjoy the company of the sailors. She even noticed the captain giving him a lesson one afternoon.

Lita was either taking care of Santo or working with Duff. The two of them spent a lot of time together, but Lita would never admit to being more than friends.

Alissia continued to visit Selona, and she helped to take care of the creature's plants, moving some of them into the sunlight on deck.

She also helped to take care of Salvatore's two dogs, as they did not enjoy being confined to their quarters on the ship.

Through Luke, she learned the sailors onboard were highly educated, and they spoke a variety of languages. They were trained in combat, and Luke was very impressed with the regime they adhered to.

Like the Eldership, there was much structure and order, and each of the men believed in their sense of duty. They were protectors of the island and the Medicians, and they each vowed to keep the secrets of their ancestors. However, Luke informed her that the word ancestor was used broadly, as people often left the island, and many sailors married women from other lands. Although the majority of the sailors claimed they were of the same bloodline of the people that originally protected the Medicians, many could not make that claim.

One afternoon the waves were much higher than usual, and she was told the ship was moving toward a storm. Devon helped her to move the plants below deck, where they were secured in the corner of Selona's holding cell.

All of the crew worked fast to secure everything onboard, and Alissia helped to put things away in the dining area. However, the ship's heavy swaying soon made it difficult for her to walk, and Debina told her she should go to her room to wait out the storm.

At the door to her room, she paused. The boat was creaking much louder than usual, men were booming out orders above deck, water was slamming into the ship, there was an occasional rumbling coming from the sky, and she could hear Santo frantically screaming in a foreign language.

The ship abruptly lurched to one side, and her grip on the door handle was not enough to keep her from hitting the floor. As she began to tumble along the corridor, a young sailor made his way toward her. He helped her stand and then walked her back to her room.

"You may want to stay in your room until this storm passes. Things will be rough," he said, opening her door. After she walked through, she turned, and he added reassuringly, "Don't worry. We've been through worse, and the ship will hold."

Before she could ask him if he was sure about that, he closed the door. She frowned, studying the creaking walls around her. Although she had been on boats during her lifetime, it had never been anything like this.

Alissia grabbed her pillow and sat down in the corner of the room, near the end of her bed and beside her trunk of clothing.

"Luke, where are you?" she mentally asked.

He seemed distracted as he answered, *"I'm helping. You need to stay below deck."*

"Where's Devon?"

"He's helping too."

"He's too young to be up there. He could get hurt."

Luke snapped, *"You try telling him that! The boy's been taking care of himself his entire life, and he won't like it if you try to hold him back."*

She frowned, beginning to feel defensive. *"He may just want someone to care enough to look out for him."*

"And that's what I'm doing! I'm making sure he learns enough skills so he'll have a decent future. I can't talk right now."

She scowled and mumbled a few words about his attitude. With nothing to distract her mind from the terrible storm, fear soon began to creep in. She knew Luke would be able to feel her anxiety if she did not get it under control, so she immediately decided to focus on her anger, letting it be the dominant emotion.

Devon was not even a teenager, yet he was working alongside grown men in a dangerous situation. Yes, the boy needed to learn skills, but he also needed to be shown that he was loved and cared for. Someone needed to worry about his safety.

The more she thought about it, the angrier she got. By the time Lita stepped into the room, Alissia was certain she had a justifiable reason to be mad.

She watched her friend in silence for a moment before saying, "I thought you'd be with your dad and Santo."

"He's been given something to put him to sleep during the storm, and Father wants me to keep you company."

As Lita struggled against the swaying of the ship, Alissia thought she noticed fear on her friend's face, but she knew better than to mention it.

A knock came at the door, and Alissia scooted closer to the end of her bed so she could see around her wardrobe trunk. Lita opened the door to reveal Duff standing there, shirtless and soaking wet.

Alissia smiled when she noticed her friend checking out his lean and muscled torso. He ran his hand through his dripping hair. "I came to make sure you're all right."

"I'm fine. I've traveled through many storms," Lita replied matter-of-factly.

He grinned. "Remember the time you hid—"

"I'm not a child anymore," she interrupted.

Duff shook his head. "I know, and I know you can more than take care of yourself. I just wanted to see your face... maybe... to settle my own nerves."

Lita's face softened, leaving her looking somewhat awkward, especially since she was struggling to stand against the rocking of the ship.

"Well, I guess I should get back to work."

As he turned to leave, Lita blurted out, "Be safe. Don't fall overboard."

With that, Duff unexpectedly turned back around and entered the room. He grabbed Lita and planted his mouth over hers.

The kiss was passionate, and Alissia stared in shock, wondering if Duff even knew she was in the room. He abruptly pulled away, and without a word, he walked out, closing the door behind him.

Lita's fingers came up to her lips, and the young woman looked completely stunned. The ship abruptly leaned to one side, and she tumbled toward her bed and fell onto it.

"Still say y'all are just friends?" Lita glared at her, and Alissia continued, "Oh, don't tell me you didn't see it coming. I knew since the first time I met him. He didn't even notice I was there, and I'm pretty much a freak in this reality." With a knowing smile, she added, "And don't tell me you don't like him—not after what I just saw in that kiss. The guy is ripped, and you know it. And he only has eyes for you. His mother even adores you. What more could you ask for?"

With a scowl, Lita replied, "I'm not talking about it."

"There's nothing to talk about. He likes you. You like him. That's pretty much how things start out."

"I'm not spending the rest of my life on a boat!"

"Ah, now I see," Alissia said. "You don't like his lifestyle."

"He's spent his entire life on this ship, and I've spent most of my life traveling by horses."

"Have you mentioned this to him?"

"I don't want to talk about it."

Lita tried to make herself comfortable in the bed before she fell to the floor. Throwing her hands up in exasperation, she asked, "See why I hate boats?"

The two women spent the rest of the day struggling with the heavy rocking of the ship. Although they did get some sleep during the night, they both woke often, and Lita frequently grumbled to herself in frustration.

Alissia climbed onto her bed when she awoke early the next morning, and she was surprised to find Mia curled up into a ball in the middle of her bed. The tiny fur ball slightly opened her eyes and closed them again when Alissia gently scooped her up and placed her at the head of the bed.

Lita was in her own bed, staring up at the ceiling as if in deep thought. Alissia flopped onto her side and watched her friend for a moment. Realizing the storm had lessened greatly, she snuggled into her pillow and wondered if she should let herself fall back to sleep. The sound of the steady rain pounding on the deck above her was greatly soothing.

"I could never ask him to leave the ocean," Lita said softly, still staring at the ceiling.

Alissia's body tensed, as she and Lita had never confided in each other. She considered her words before responding.

"Well, you may not have to. Both Luke and Grady willingly wanted to give up their lives and lifestyles for me, and I never asked them to. In fact, I always disagreed with Grady giving up his position in the Eldership for me."

Lita let out a sigh and rolled over to face her.

"What I've learned," Alissia continued, "is that sometimes love overrides everything else." She gave a sad smile, not meeting Lita's eyes. "Grady is now going back to his life and the Eldership, but there's no doubt in my mind that he's hurting right now. He truly loved me."

After a pause, she continued. "Then there's Luke. He's lost everything and can't go back to his former life, but I know he's the happiest he's been in his entire life. In fact, I lost everything and can never go back home, but Luke has given me something I've never had. I'm happy just being with him." She frowned. "Although, I'm mad at him right now. He's annoying, but I still love him."

Alissia asked softly, "Do you really like him?"

Lita looked worried as she nodded.

"Then let it be," Alissia said. "You don't need to think of those things right now. The two of you haven't seen each other in years. It's obvious he really likes you, and you like him. For some people, that's rare. I mean, I'm twenty-nine, and I've never had a relationship or liked anyone until I met Grady and then Luke. I don't fall easily. I would just let him know you don't want to spend the rest of your life on a boat. Be honest with him from the start."

Lita nodded, and some of the worry left her face.

Then Alissia grinned roguishly. "Besides, after seeing the two of you kiss last night, you don't stand much of a chance." She sat up. "And I should know. You think I wanted to fall in love with Luke?" Shaking her head, she said emphatically, "That man was the most annoying and infuriating kidnapper, and the last thing I wanted to do was fall in love with him."

Chapter 21

It was almost noon by the time Alissia strolled into the kitchen to find Debina and Tabitha sitting at one of the tables. Both women had their backs against the wall and their feet were propped up. Their eyes were barely open.

"Need help?" Alissia sat at the end of the table.

Without lifting it from the wall, Debina shook her head. "No, there's not much we can do in the kitchen with these waves slamming into us. Tabitha and I have set out plenty of food for the men." She pointed toward the serving area in the kitchen. "Go and fill you a plate, dear. There's plenty to choose from."

Alissia did as she was told and was soon back at the table with a hummus and sprout sandwich and an assortment of nuts and dried fruits. She had one of those rare moments where she resented being a vegetarian, as she was not very fond of the bean mixture and would much rather be able to eat some of the cured meats on her sandwich.

Lita entered the kitchen and prepared a plate before sitting down at the table. She did not seem to notice Alissia eyeballing her towering sandwich, as she struggled to fit it into her mouth.

Alissia frowned before forcing herself to take a bite of her own sandwich. After swallowing her food, she said, "Y'all look exhausted."

Tabitha nodded. "We made the mistake of sitting down and getting relaxed."

"Too relaxed," added Debina.

"Did y'all get much sleep last night?"

Debina lifted her head and opened her eyes. "There was an accident. Poor Devon broke his arm."

"What?" Alissia asked, nearly choking on her sandwich.

"Oh, he's fine, dear," Debina reassured. "These things happen. Duff was about his age when something similar happened to him, although he almost fell overboard."

"Where is he? I should go check on him," Alissia said.

Tabitha lifted her head from the wall and warned, "Trust me. You don't want to go down there. He's in the bunkroom, and after last night, I imagine the men are barely dressed and are asleep. You would cause a stir, not to mention it smells like sweaty men down there."

Debina laughed and nodded. Looking at Alissia, she said, "There are some places on this ship I even avoid."

"Where's Luke?" Alissia asked.

"I imagine he's with the boy," Debina answered. "He never left his side the entire time the doctor was splinting the arm."

"When you say he broke his arm," Alissia began, "was his bone sticking out? Was it bad?"

"I've seen a lot worse. It's a small break," answered Tabitha.

Debina nodded. "It should heal fine, and he's getting a lot of support from the men. Everyone likes Devon. He's a great young man—hardworking and eager to learn."

Tabitha added, "Griffon says the men are teaching him our language, and he's a natural—absorbing the words like a sponge."

Alissia frowned in frustration. "Luke should've made him go below."

"He wouldn't have listened," Lita said, shaking her head.

"He would've listened to Luke," Alissia countered. "He does everything Luke tells him to do."

"Yes," Lita began, "but it's because Luke respects him and doesn't treat him like a child. He's been taking care of himself too long for that, and he won't respond to anyone that tries to baby him now."

"I didn't say to baby him, but Luke should've been more stern with him."

Lita shook her head, but it was Debina that said, "I understand your fear, but Devon was securely tied to the ship and was never in danger of falling overboard. He greatly wants to be accepted by the men, and each of them was looking out for him. My boys were doing the same thing at his age, and it's not so uncommon for a boy of his age to help out in a storm. If it had been severe, he wouldn't have been allowed on deck."

"You mean last night's storm wasn't severe?" Alissia asked, wide-eyed.

Tabitha laughed, shaking her head. "I've been in much worse. Last night's storm was a bother and caused a lot of extra work, but the ship isn't damaged, and we didn't lose anyone."

Alissia stuffed a large bite of her sandwich into her mouth and glanced at Lita. Now she understood why her friend refused to live on a boat.

"Devon is sleeping now," said Debina, "as many of the men are at the moment. Once the rain stops, there'll be a lot to do."

Tabitha stood. "I believe I'm going to join Griffon for a nap." She looked at Debina. "I'll be back in time to help prepare dinner."

"If these waves settle down, we can cook," Debina said, standing. "Well, ladies," she added, looking from Lita to Alissia, "it's rare that

I don't have to spend a day in the kitchen, and I believe I'm going to take advantage of it."

As she and Tabitha made their way toward the door, Lita called out, "Have you seen Father?"

Debina stopped and turned around. "He came in late this morning to get him and Santo some breakfast, but I imagine he's resting now. There's not much you can do with the rain still going."

*****

Alissia and Lita spent a quiet day in their room. While Alissia read a book with Mia snuggled up to her, Lita made bracelets to sell.

Although the rain stopped late in the afternoon, the swaying of the ship was still stronger than usual. At one point, the corridor filled with voices and laughter as a large group of men made their way to the dining area. Alissia was tempted to open the door to see if Luke was among them, but then she reminded herself that she was mad at him.

Lita's eyes went to the door often, but Alissia decided against mentioning Duff.

A short time after the noise died down in the corridor, someone knocked on the door. Alissia looked expectantly at Lita, and she thought she detected fear in the girl's eyes for the first time since meeting her. They stared at each other for a brief moment before Alissia said, "You know it's for you."

The knock came again, and Lita called out, "Wait a moment."

She fumbled out of her bed and paused at the mirror. Squaring her shoulders, she reached for the handle and opened the door. She then turned to Alissia to reveal Luke standing in the doorway. A covered dish was in his hands.

"What do you want?" Alissia asked with a slight edge in her voice.

He smiled. "I thought you'd be hungry, and I brought you some food."

"You can give it to Lita."

When Lita tried to take the plate from his hands, it did not budge. His smile never faltered. "No, I was hoping to see you for a moment. I know it's too windy above deck, but maybe you could join me in the dining area. It's mostly empty, and there's a spot in the corner."

"I'm reading." Alissia lifted the book in her hand. "You can give it to Lita."

Lita grinned. "Yes, you can give it to me."

The smile left his face, and he looked at Lita with narrowed eyes. "I'm not giving it to you," he said firmly. Turning back to Alissia, he smiled. "You're not angry with me, are you?"

"Nope, I'm not mad," she answered. "Just feel like reading. That's all."

He dropped his cheery façade and frowned. "You're angry. I can feel it."

"I'm not mad, Luke. I prefer to say I'm just not in the mood for you right now."

"You've heard about Devon's arm?"

Although her eyes turned to daggers, she kept a controlled voice. "Yep, I heard about what happened to Devon's arm."

"The doctor says it'll heal."

Duff walked up, and Luke stepped aside so the two of them could share the doorway. The younger man looked as if his hair had just been combed, and unlike the work clothes he usually wore, he had on a deep blue poet's shirt and dark pants. He looked fresh and clean, and Alissia noticed Lita's hand self-consciously go to her braid.

As usual, Duff merely glanced over at Alissia with a polite smile before turning his full attention to Lita. "Have you already eaten?"

Lita shook her head.

"Want to join me then? There's a great spot in the corner, and the dining area is almost empty."

"So I've heard," Lita said, smiling at Luke. "Yes, we can eat together." To Luke, she said, "Shall I take that to Alissia now? You know the captain's strict rules about men being in a woman's room. If you're not related or married, it just doesn't happen."

Alissia felt Luke's anger shoot through her, but the look on his face remained calm. He turned to Alissia. "Will you join me?"

She looked down at her book. "I'm reading."

With that, he turned and walked toward the dining area. Lita walked out and shut the door behind her.

Alissia let out a long sigh, realizing she did not really know why she was mad at Luke. She understood why he allowed Devon to help with the storm. He had trusted the boy with her life when it was time for her to escape from the castle in Pallen. Devon had proven himself capable of many things beyond his youth.

Then she remembered how Luke had talked to her the night before, but she also knew he had been busy and distracted with the storm.

All the reasons for being angry with him suddenly seemed trivial. However, her pride refused to let it go at that moment.

"I'll be nice tomorrow," she said, opening her book. She then spent the next hour hungry but not daring to leave her room.

Chapter 22

Alissia and Luke's spat did not last long, and things were soon back to normal between them. The next three weeks went by slowly, and she easily agreed with Lita about not wanting to live at sea. Although she enjoyed reading on deck, living on a small ship surrounded by men was not her idea of a great life.

Space was limited, and because the captain did not want her too close to his men, it did not take long for her to begin to feel isolated and alone. She greatly enjoyed the days she could help Tabitha and Debina in the kitchen, but she still found herself with a lot of time on her hands with nothing to do.

Even with a broken arm, Devon continued to work alongside the sailors, and Alissia noticed how the men interacted with the boy.

They seemed patient, and they genuinely seemed to enjoy his company. Not only was he learning how to be a sailor, but he was also beginning to speak some of their natural language.

He was thriving on the ship, and Captain Blackwell pulled Luke aside one day to ask about the care of the boy. Since no one truly knew if Luke and Alissia would be allowed to leave the island once there, Devon's future was also uncertain. No one believed he would be allowed to join them with the Medicians.

Salvatore and Luke had already privately agreed that Salvatore would be the one caring for the boy if something were to happen to Luke. However, the captain and his wife wanted him with them. In the end, Luke agreed to sit down with Devon and explain that he and Alissia may not be allowed to return from the island. He would then tell him of his options, and Devon would get to choose who he would live with.

Lita and Duff continued to grow close as time went by, and Alissia began to notice subtle changes in her young friend. She began to wear her hair unbraided more often, her natural honey-colored highlights hanging loosely down her back.

She began to look at herself in the mirror and take more time in getting dressed, even occasionally wearing a touch of makeup. When she and Alissia talked, Lita often seem distracted.

The biggest change, however, was in her face. She smiled and laughed often, which she had rarely done before.

Since she shared a room with Lita, Alissia was repeatedly an unwilling witness to the couple's secret displays of affection. She was grateful for the captain's strict rules about men not entering a woman's room. However, that did not stop Duff, and he continuously slipped into the room for a goodnight kiss.

At first, Alissia would awkwardly pretend she was asleep or keep her head turned in the opposite direction, but that got old after a while. She then began to narrate their kiss, judge the kiss, hold a conversation with herself, and do various obnoxious things in the hope of discouraging the young couple from their displays of affection in front of her.

Her attempts, however, were always futile, and the couple never acknowledged her presence.

Alissia was finishing her breakfast in the captain's suite one morning when a loud bell began to ring on deck. Debina was making her bed, and she looked up excitedly. "We've reached the island. Come."

She followed the captain's wife to the top deck, and instead of going to the women's area, Debina led her to the front of the ship, where Salvatore turned and greeted her with a smile. "Ready to see land?"

"You have no idea," she answered. "I don't think I like sailing very much."

She looked up as Luke's arms came around her from behind. He was staring intently out in front of him. "How long before we get there?" she asked, turning back to Salvatore.

"Not too long. Captain Blackwell and I will be the only ones allowed off the ship at first. I'll have to explain our presence before you, Luke, and Selona will be allowed onto shore. Get ready for a lot of talking."

He turned and added firmly, "You'll need to tell them everything, Alissia. Don't keep anything from them, and start from the beginning."

She nodded. "Think they'll let us leave?"

"I don't know, but I promise I'll support you in your efforts." He looked up at Luke. "Have you had your talk with Devon?"

"Not yet. I'll get it done this morning."

"You understand that you may not be seeing him again?" Salvatore asked.

Luke nodded, and Alissia could feel his sadness seeping into her.

"Like I've told Alissia, I'll do everything I can to sway them into allowing you to leave the island, but I don't know if they'll consider it."

The three of them stared out into the distance for a moment before Alissia broke the silence. "I should get dressed."

"And packed," Luke added.

Salvatore said, "You'll probably want to watch as the captain takes the ship into the harbor. It's quite impressive."

"Then I'll hurry," Alissia said, pulling herself from Luke's arms.

As she strode to her room, a mix of emotions began to swell inside of her—some hers, some Luke's. Her jitters grew even stronger as she bathed and packed.

"Get it together," she said, staring at her reflection in the mirror by her bedroom door.

The weather was much warmer now that they were closer to the equator, and she chose to wear one of the sarongs Edda and Bruna had picked out for her. Her hair was in a simple braid down her back, and she applied a touch of makeup in hopes of boosting her confidence.

Alissia took a few deep breaths, telling herself she would be fine. She and Luke would finally get some answers. As for thoughts of not ever being able to leave the island, those were contemplations she refused to allow her mind to entertain.

"You should come up. You don't want to miss this," Luke mentally said.

"I'm coming." She took one last apprehensive look at herself in the mirror before walking out of the room.

The deck was filled with men, and most of them were eerily quiet, looking out over the railing. As she walked toward the front of the boat, she noticed the massive rocks on each side of the ship, and fear began to set in.

Luke turned around and smiled reassuringly as she joined him and Salvatore. She stepped in front of him and looked over the edge of the ship into the clear, blue water. He put his arms around her from behind and bent down to her ear.

"We'll be fine," he whispered.

"I'm not worried," she whispered back, turning her head toward him.

He raised his eyebrows knowingly, and she frowned.

"Stay out of my head," she mentally said.

"I wasn't in your head. I can feel the fear coming from your body."

She scowled up at him for a moment before turning her attention back to the front of the boat.

"Only a skilled captain and crew can steer through these rocks," Salvatore said in a low voice.

Alissia could feel the tension in the air as members of the crew called out to the captain in a foreign language. When they finally made their way around the last rock, the crew celebrated with shouts of joy and laughter.

The ship entered a private cove surrounded by lush, green mountains. One of the mountains had an extensive waterfall flowing down into the ocean. A long pier extended from the shore, with a much smaller boat attached to it.

Salvatore put his hand on Alissia's shoulder and gave it a slight squeeze. "Nervous?"

"A little."

"How about you?" he said, removing his hand and turning his attention to Luke.

"She needs answers," Luke replied.

Salvatore nodded. "And so do you." He patted Luke on the back and walked away.

The two of them silently stared out at the island for a long moment.

"It's beautiful," Alissia said.

"Still want to leave?"

"Maybe after a short vacation." She let out a sigh, taking in the paradise around them.

He shook with laughter as he squeezed her tightly and kissed the top of her head.

"Ever seen anything like this?" she asked.

"Never."

"Neither have I," she said.

Tabitha strolled over to stand beside them. She stared at the distant waterfall for a moment before turning to Alissia. "Well, I guess I should go finish cooking."

"Need any help?" Alissia asked.

"No, I don't want you to get anything on your dress. You look nice. Are you nervous?"

"A little. Have you ever met them?"

Tabitha shook her head. "No, and I doubt I ever will."

Debina came up to stand next to Tabitha. "There'll be a riot if we don't get their food out," she said. Looking at Alissia, she added, "You look lovely, dear. What do you think of the island?"

"It's beyond beautiful," Alissia answered. "Is it like this on the other side of the island too?"

Debina nodded. "Our side of the island is much easier to get to and has fewer mountains, but it's just as beautiful. In fact, I've never seen a place more spectacular than this island, and I've been to many great cities along the sea." She gave a broad smile. "I'm sure you'll love it here." Turning to Tabitha, she asked, "Ready to set the food out?"

The two women walked away, leaving Luke and Alissia to themselves.

"Did you speak to Devon?" she asked.

"I did."

"And what did he say?"

"He's chosen to stay with Captain Blackwell if I don't return."

Alissia looked up at him in surprise. "I thought he really liked Salvatore."

"He does, but he loves sailing, and this crew has been good to him. In my opinion, he made the right decision."

"I'm just surprised." She turned her head back around and rested it on Luke's chest. "Salvatore has been great with him, and I haven't seen him spend much time with the captain."

Luke chuckled. "You mean you're surprised Devon chose a life of rules and structure. Some people actually thrive from that lifestyle."

"Well, I find it quite stifling—the rules and living on this ship. I can't wait to feel the sand between my toes. Hopefully, we can spend a month here getting answers and relaxing. Then we can go to the mountains and meet the ones who saved my life."

"What if they don't let you leave?" he asked somberly. "Salvatore seems to believe that's a great possibility, as your presence in Pallen has upset his people and threatened to expose the Medicians."

"What about Selona?" she asked. "She's here to open trade with her people and the Medicians. If they consider that, they'll let me leave."

"Yes, but Salvatore doesn't believe they'd risk exposing themselves after all these years of hiding. If they did, they'd use his people to do the trading. He seems sure that the Medicians will never leave this island—not even one of them. They're highly secretive and have the perfect relationship with his people as their guardians."

Alissia frowned, staring out at the island. "You don't think we'll be able to leave, do you?"

He let out a long breath. "I believe that's a strong possibility."

Chapter 23

Alissia accepted Salvatore's hand before stepping off of the plank and onto the pier. Although Captain Blackwell was dressed in his formal clothing, Salvatore still looked his casual self. The first few buttons of his shirt were undone, and his sleeves were rolled up. His relaxed confidence was reassuring, along with his warm smile.

The captain gave a curt nod and said his goodbye, even shaking Luke's hand, while assuring him that Devon would be well taken care of.

The young boy watched them from the ship, and she smiled and waved one last time. Debina put her arm around him and pulled him reassuringly into her side.

Alissia carried Mia as she and Luke followed Salvatore and Selona down the long pier. Her wardrobe trunk, along with the others' belongings, was being carried by some of the crewmembers walking behind them.

When Salvatore and Captain Blackwell returned from the island earlier that day, Salvatore informed her and Luke that they would be taken into the Medician's living area to meet with them.

She noticed Salvatore's excitement as he spoke of meeting with the Medicians. He said it had been many years since any of his ancestors had visited the living area of the creatures, and this was a rare and great occasion.

As they walked along the pier, Alissia's anxiety grew, and she gazed out into water. It was clear, with mild, peaceful waves moving along the surface.

After reaching the end of the pier, they walked toward the edge of the beach, where tall palm trees lined the clearing. Three carts with small donkey-like animals attached to them were waiting at the beginning of a trail.

The crewmen placed all of their belongings into the first cart, as it was just a wagon. The other two were small carriages, with bench seats.

Once the crewmen were a short distance away, four small creatures stepped onto the trail from among the trees, and Luke took Alissia's hand as her heart began to pound with excitement.

The creatures seemed just as intrigued with Alissia as she was of them, as they openly stared at her and Selona for a moment.

They were short and slim, about four feet tall, and their hair varied in shades of purple. Their skin was pale and shimmered much more than Alissia's.

The two men were dressed in sandals, light-colored loose pants that ended shortly below their knees, and loose shirts in the same thin and shimmery material.

The women's sundresses were made of the same material and ended slightly below their knees. They wore sandals and simple jewelry, and all four of them wore extremely dark sunglasses.

The creatures appeared fragile and somewhat angelic, and she could not help but think they could never stand a chance in a physical fight against a human.

Although their bodies were child-like, their faces showed signs of aging and looked similar to someone in their fifties, but Alissia knew better than to try and guess their ages.

One of the women stepped forward and bowed slightly. In a soft, somewhat high-pitched voice, she said, "My name is Kawena, and we're here to escort you to the ancients. They're eager to meet you, so we must not delay."

She walked over to the second carriage and motioned for Alissia and Luke to get in. Once they were seated, with Mia sitting attentively in Alissia's lap, Kawena and one of the men sat down in the seat across from them. The other two Medicians joined Salvatore and Selona in the last carriage.

The carriages lurched forward without any help of reigns or physical guidance. After a short, awkward silence, Kawena's companion said, "I'm Haku."

Alissia gave a polite smile, and motioning with her hand, she responded, "I'm Alissia. This is Luke, and this is Mia."

Kawena and Haku studied Luke for a moment. "Is he your zeer?" Kawena asked, confusion showing on her face.

"I don't really know exactly what that means, but we're not married," Alissia answered. "Oh, and he doesn't speak your language."

The two Medicians nodded, and the awkward silence returned. Alissia peered into the trees along the trail, taking in her tropical surroundings.

Abundant life surrounded them. The birds and small creatures were brightly colored and made a lot of chatter.

"It's beautiful here," Alissia said.

"We take great care in tending to the island," replied Haku.

The plants along the trail did not look randomly placed. They were arranged and looked as if a gardener had planted them, and they were large and healthy.

Kawena asked, "Do you possess the ability to care for plants?"

"I do, and I can heal animals as well."

"Oh," started Kawena, not hiding her surprise, "we've never seen anyone like you before, as it's forbidden for us to connect ourselves with a human. The ancients will have many questions for you, and I must admit to my own curiosity."

"I also have a lot of questions," Alissia said. "Especially when it comes to me and Luke. I don't understand what's happened between us."

Kawena and Haku looked at each other for a moment, and Alissia got a feeling they were sharing a mental conversation. Then Haku cleared his throat while turning his eyes back to her. "Have the two of you physically connected with each other?"

Alissia shook her head. "No, I mean, we used to be able to kiss but not anymore." At their confused expressions, she said, "But I did save his life. He nearly died, and I healed him."

Disbelief immediately replaced their confused looks, and Kawena said, "I don't see how that's possible. That would have killed you. You must've thought he was near death, but he had a lot of life still in him."

Alissia shook her head and turned to Luke. In his language, she said, "Show them your scar." He lifted his shirt, and her fingers touched the branded handprint on his chest. "When I did this, he was almost dead. I fainted, and when I woke up, all of his wounds were healed."

The couple studied the print for a moment and then turned to look at each other. Luke lowered his shirt, and Alissia sensed they were holding another private, mental conversation.

When they turned back around, Mia grunted and pointed at the star imprint on Alissia's hand. She then began to manipulate her tiny fingers in a way resembling sign language, and the two Medicians watched intently.

"She can speak?" Luke mentally asked.

"I don't understand any of it," Alissia thought back at him.

When Mia lowered her hands, Kawena and Haku stared at Alissia with wide eyes.

"You've been blessed," Kawena said. "I've only read about this in the scrolls. The guardians have only made their presence known a few times in our history."

"What do you mean by guardians?" asked Alissia.

Haku answered, "From what's recorded in the scrolls, our ancestors believed our people are the only ones to have ever seen a guardian. None of the other higher races know of them, and we know very little about them."

Kawena added, "They've only shown themselves to a few of our ancestors, but each appearance was out of necessity."

"What do you mean?"

"Each appearance came at a great time of need for our people," Kawena said. "They would appear to only one, and they'd mark them with a blessing. Each blessing was different for each person, but it was always with a gift they'd need in the future."

Haku added, "Which means the guardians believed you needed the gift of healing for some reason. Somehow that gift would save our people."

Sensing their apprehension, Alissia said, "Maybe they gave it to me so that I could save Luke."

Kawena shook her head. "The guardians only appeared at great times of need for our entire people as a whole—never to help just one person. That's why we consider them our guardians."

Alissia said, "Well, if I hadn't of saved Luke, I would never have been able to escape from a bad situation. Saving him saved me."

Haku frowned worriedly but said, "Maybe you're right."

At that moment, they entered the living area of the Medicians, and Alissia instantly became captivated by the unique village.

Large, tall trees with many thick, winding branches provided a heavy shade for the community. Although there were thatched huts strategically built on the ground, the trees were filled with tree houses of various kinds. Each house had a porch with hanging chairs, where women sat in small groups weaving baskets, cutting vegetables, and doing other various chores with their hands.

A network of swinging rope bridges filled the air above them, providing even more shade to the ground below. The sound of children's laughter, music, and animals produced a soothing and pleasant feel.

Brightly colored, exotic plants and flowers were abundant, and colorful bella flowers winded along the rope railings of the swinging bridges.

Small people seemed to be everywhere, but unlike a busy city, they were smiling, waving, and talking to those around them. Tiny children walked around carrying animals resembling monkeys, birds, lizards, snakes, and many other strange-looking, exotic animals. There were pixets too, and many of them sat watching the children play.

Some of the Medicians noticed the humans in the carts, and they stopped what they were doing and stared curiously.

"Is this similar to where our relatives live?" Kawena asked.

Alissia snapped out of her moment of awe and wonder, dread settling in. "Uh... well... I really don't know. I've really never met the Medicians that saved my life and changed me."

The look of shock on both of the Medicians faces was exactly what Alissia expected, and she felt herself swallowing nervously. After a moment, she continued with, "I don't really know anything about my body anymore. I don't understand what's happening between Luke and me. My blood is now purple, along with my hair and eyes. All I know is that the Medicians saved my life. As to how or why, I don't know."

Haku replied, "You have much to tell the ancients."

Alissia nodded in agreement.

"As for the physical changes you're experiencing," he started, "we can explain some of that, although not everything. You've gone through a procedure that's forbidden by my people. Since hearing of your existence, the ancients have been searching the scrolls for details of the outcome.

"My father is one of the ancients, and Kawena and I are to one day take his place as a keeper of the scrolls. We maintain and preserve them, along with adding our own historical events to them."

He took Kawena's hand in his before continuing, "It would take two Medicians to save you from death, and they would've had to pour a lot of their own energy into you. It would also have to be a couple, a man and his zeer, and their sacrifice was great. They're now linked to you, and that link can never be broken."

Kawena added, "They must've thought highly of you to give you that honor."

"They replaced your dying energy with their own," said Haku.

"How come I woke up knowing the ancient language, but I didn't know certain words, like zeer or jade?" Alissia asked.

"Those aren't from the ancient language and are more in depth with our culture," Haku answered. "I don't know the exact answer to your question, as I don't really understand how the healing bond works."

"What about the abilities I now have?" asked Alissia.

Haku said, "Our blood now flows through your body, pumps into your heart, and supplies your life force. It gives your skin, hair, and everything in your body the nutrients it needs. Your human energy is no longer there."

"So I'm no longer a human?"

"Physically, no," Haku said. "However, you still have the mind of a human, which is slightly different than ours. We don't seem to react in ways that humans do, or at least from what we've read about them in the scrolls. We really don't know any humans, as we don't have much contact with our human protectors."

Kawena said, "Our people never decide war, and we've never murdered anyone."

"So there's no crime among your people?" Alissia asked.

"There are many disputes that are taken before the ancients, but murder is never one of them," Haku answered. "If we take the life of another with our own hands, it would mentally destroy us. We weren't created for death. We're healers."

"I've had to kill someone out of defense since the changes. Does that mean something will happen to me?"

"I don't believe so," Haku replied. "You still have the mind of a human. The scrolls said you wouldn't be drawn to healing, as we are."

"What do you mean by that?"

Kawena answered, "We feel the needs of the plants and animals around us." She motioned to some trees. "They thrive, because we take care of them. This entire island is filled with life, because we put our energy into it. It's what we do."

"So if I'm no longer a human, what does that mean about Luke? He still bleeds human blood, but we're connected. We can mind speak, and we can feel each other's pain. However, we can't kiss each other."

"Do you love him?" Kawena inquired.

"I do."

Haku asked, "Enough to be with him for the rest of your life?"

"Yes."

The two Medicians smiled, and Haku said, "Then it's a blessing. If you had connected with someone you do not love, it could easily destroy you."

"What do you mean?"

"Haku is my zeer," Kawena said. "Our people do not rush into such choices. Once we bond, it's for life. The two of us our connected now, and one day, we'll die together."

"Yes, but why didn't Luke physically change?" asked Alissia.

Haku answered, "The bond's not complete. When you healed him, how did you do it? What were you thinking at the time?"

Alissia's mind went back to that horrible night in the dungeon, and emotions began to swirl within her. She forced calmness into her voice. "He was dying, and he wanted his last memory to be of me holding him. I decided his last memory should be of me kissing him, so I leaned down and kissed him."

"With your hand on his chest?" Haku asked.

She nodded. "He had a large wound there, and I guess part of me wanted to stop the bleeding. I really don't know. I just did it."

"And what exactly were you thinking when you kissed him?" Haku asked. "Were you trying to heal him?"

"No, I had no idea I *could* heal him. I just wanted him to know that I loved him."

"So you poured your love into him," Kawena stated, looking at Haku.

"Yes."

Kawena turned back to Alissia and said, "You unknowingly triggered the zeer bond between the two of you."

"You didn't heal Luke with a healing bond, Alissia," Haku added. "You did something much different."

"And much stronger," Kawena replied.

"Why can't the two of you kiss?" Haku asked.

"For two reasons. One being, Mia will attack us if we do, and the other is that my blood starts glowing beneath my skin. My body temperature rises, and I think I'll lose control."

Mia began to speak with her hands again, and Alissia silently watched. Her curiosity grew when the two Medicians laughed. After a moment, they both turned their attention back to her.

"You're very blessed, Alissia," Kawena said. "You've been healed at a great cost. The guardians have blessed you, and you've been given the loyalty of a pixet. Each of these things is extremely rare, even to my own people."

Haku said, "The reason Mia will not allow the two of you to finish the bond is because it will physically change him, and that's not a wise thing to do around humans. If he changes, others will know what you've done, and that reveals too much of our ways to the humans. It could not be allowed until you were safe among our people and away from the eyes of humans."

"So I won't kill him if we kiss?"

Mia growled, and Haku laughed. "No, but Mia may decide otherwise."

The carts stopped, and each of them stepped out of the carriage. They were standing at the bottom of a large mountain covered in greenery. A wide entrance was carved into the mountain, with intricately detailed beams at each side.

Unlike the carefree village of the Medicians, the entrance conveyed ancient power. It reminded her of pictures she had seen of historical temples in foreign countries. It was massive, stone, and filled with detailed carvings.

"We should hurry," Kawena said. "They're waiting."

Leaving their belongings with the carts, the visitors followed the group of Medicians into the cave. They walked through a wide tunnel with elegant carvings covering the ceiling and walls. Glow stones situated into the walls of the tunnel gave off a dim amount of light.

"Have you learned anything?" Luke mentally asked.

"Only that I'm stuck with you for the rest of my life, but we already knew that," she teased.

"Did you ask them why we can't kiss?"

"Is that your biggest concern? Out of all the questions I have, you think that's the first one I'd ask?"

He answered, *"We have many questions, but since we both don't fear you're dying, it's a bit of a mystery why I can't kiss the woman I love."*

"Lucky for you, then, that I asked."

"And?"

"They said we can never do anything like that, and if I want, I can turn you into a mindless slave. They can teach me how to do it." When he did not respond, she added, *"I'm joking. I'm not going to turn you*

into my slave any time soon, and the reason Mia won't let us kiss is that it will change you."

The corridor rounded and came to an abrupt end, and Alissia's eyes widened, as she and the others stopped walking.

"You're the worst interpreter ever," Luke mentally said, stopping beside her.

"I'll do better," she answered, too distracted by her surroundings to tease him more.

They were standing in a large, circular room with many openings and doors along the walls. Obelisk crystals, about eight feet tall, were strategically arranged around the room. Each of the statues illuminated from within, their white glow shimmering brightly to light the open area.

Intricately carved stone benches were situated around the room, many of them being used by Medicians, and it reminded Alissia of an oversized lobby.

Above each opening or door were more detailed carvings, and all of the mountainous stone had a waxy sheen to it.

Luke took her by the hand, and she allowed him to pull her along as she continued to examine the well-designed cave.

The sound of Luke and Salvatore's boots along the stone floor seemed out of place, especially compared to the light and graceful steps of the Medicians in their sandals. It caught the attention of those sitting in the room, and Alissia tried to appear uninterested in the many eyes turned her way.

As they neared one of the doors, it opened, and an older Medician man stepped out. As soon as he noticed them, he turned back around and announced their arrival. He then left the door open as he turned to leave, staring at Alissia as he passed. She was reminded of everyone's reaction to her in the castle of Pallen, and it bothered her somewhat in knowing she would always cause that reaction wherever she went.

The four guides stopped outside the door, and Haku turned. "This is where we must leave you. We'll have your things delivered to your rooms."

"You're not coming with us?" Alissia asked, suddenly feeling as if she were about to step in front of a firing squad.

Kawena gave a reassuring smile. "No, you must speak to the ancients now. It's not our place, but we'll see you again soon to show you to your rooms."

Alissia nodded, while trying to push back her fear. When Luke squeezed her hand, she forced a smile onto her face and looked up at him. *"It's nothing,"* she mentally said.

She pulled back her shoulders and lifted her head, feigning confidence. Then she stepped toward the open door, reminding herself that fear would never get her anywhere.

Chapter 24

Unlike the oversized lobby, the room had a low ceiling, and Luke, Salvatore, and Selona could easily reach up and touch it with the tips of their fingers. Eleven elderly Medician men sat along one side of the room. They each wore a navy-colored robe made in the same shimmery material that Kawena and Haku wore. The men were seated at a long stone table, with many scrolls and papers strewn across it.

They were not wearing glasses, and their purple eyes seemed to glow brighter than hers. Unlike the many shades of purple hair she had seen in the village, the only colors left in the ancients were pale lavender to nearly white.

Large glow stones lining the built-in shelving along the walls lit the room. One of the men pointed to the five seats situated in the middle of the room, and Alissia let go of Luke's hand and took the middle one, setting Mia on her lap. Luke sat down on her right side, and Salvatore took the seat to the left of her. Selona sat down next to him.

The men seemed more intrigued with Selona, as they all stared at her for a moment before one of them said, "We weren't expecting so many guests. What do we owe the honor of your presence before us?"

Alissia stared in disbelief as an unnatural smile filled Selona's face. In a pleasant, yet still creepy voice, she said, "I'm Selona, a healer of my people, and I bring you a gift, the one my ancestors often shared with yours. I come with great news. However, it's a matter that needs to be discussed in private."

Many of the men nodded, and one stood. "Then I shall have someone see you to your rooms. Let us first deal with the expected matter, and then we'll meet with you."

After escorting her into the lobby, he returned and went back to his seat. "I assume you're Salvatore, one of our great protectors." He turned his eyes to Luke. "And who is this?"

Alissia tried to sound confident as she replied, "He doesn't speak your language, and he's here because of a zeer bond we accidently triggered but have yet to finish."

The ancient sat back in his chair. "Then why don't you tell us everything? How did you come to be, and how fare our relatives?"

Alissia nodded. She introduced herself, and then she started from the beginning—the very moment she was pulled into this reality.

She talked slowly, trying to remember every detail they would need to know. Although they listened quietly, each of them occasionally wrote something down. At one point, one of the men poured her a drink. She accepted it and took a few sips before continuing on with her long story.

When she came to the part about meeting Luke, she tried to downplay his kidnapping her, and she told them he only wanted to protect her—which she knew was mostly true.

It wasn't until she got to the part about being bitten by the tiny, glowing creature in the forest that they stopped her.

"Where? Show us!" One of the men demanded, eagerly.

"You never told me about this," Salvatore said under his breath in her original language.

She lifted her hand and turned it so that the eight-pointed star could be seen. One of the elderly men stood and made his way toward her, while another one started rummaging through the scrolls nearest him. Alissia sensed excitement in the room.

The man lifted her hand and examined the scar, rubbing it beneath his own small thumb. Once satisfied, he released it and made his way back to his seat. "Tell us more, please."

Alissia cleared her throat and told of how she escaped from Luke and bonded with a wolf for protection. Talking about Fang brought up feelings of worry and guilt, and she could not help but wonder if he was still alive. She knew it was her fault he had left the safety of his pack.

Luke reached over and took her by the hand, and an unexpected surge of calmness began to seep into her. She glanced over to find his eyes closed, and she took a sip of her water before continuing with the details of being kidnapped by the two men.

Although part of her wanted to skip the horrible parts of her story, she wanted the Medicians to know the truth—Salvatore too. She was tired of the lies and secrets, and she wanted a release from it all.

She described how Ian had romanced her, and then she kept nothing back as she recalled everything that happened in the dungeon. She explained what she was thinking when she saved Luke's life, thus triggering the zeer bond.

Alissia did not know how long she talked, but everyone in the room seemed fully awake and interested in what she had to say—surprisingly, even Mia. Once finished, she lifted her drink and drained the last three sips of water. She then set the mug by her feet and sat back in her chair.

"How did you get pulled from another reality?" one of the ancients asked.

"I don't really know. I even met the man responsible, but he was not much help. He linked something like a magical rope to a journal of mine. When I touched it ten years later, it pulled me through the window, nearly killing me."

"How did the window get built?"

"The Eldership has something called Watchers, and they somehow use a jade to open small windows between our realities. This man wanted to enter my reality, but he couldn't find a way. He then got the idea to pull me through, thinking my body would make a big hole in the window."

"And did it?" he inquired.

"No, I squeezed through."

"So you know nothing of our relatives?" asked another ancient.

Alissia shook her head. "Only where to find them, and I was hoping I'd be able to return to them."

"Leave the island?" asked another ancient, in disbelief. "Even after all that's been done to you by the humans? Do you not see the danger?"

"I do, but I really want to understand and meet the ones who saved my life."

"Understand? What is it you don't understand?" he demanded loudly, causing Mia to flinch in Alissia's lap. "You're a mistake. The unfortunate couple that poured their energy into you assuredly regretted it the moment you were changed. Just the act of speaking into your mind that one time to warn you not to use your abilities drained them of their life."

"Kasim, that's enough!" The speaker stood and pointedly looked to each of the other ancients. "They made the choice to save her life, and that means they determined it worth saving. She's also been chosen by the guardians."

Kasim stood and said slowly and emphatically, "For the safety of our people, the guardians had to bless her to get her here. She's used her blessing. The danger's over."

Alissia noticed a few heads nodding in agreement, and then another ancient stood. "We don't need to have this discussion at the moment," he stated calmly. "We still need to hear Salvatore, and then we have another meeting. I believe we need a quick break before resuming, as we've been stuck in this room for hours. Let the girl and her half zeer go to their rooms."

Many of the others stood and nodded in agreement. Some grumbled about sitting still for so long.

Without waiting for direction, Alissia picked up Mia and stood, and Salvatore and Luke did the same. Salvatore put his hand on her shoulder and said reassuringly, in the modern language, "I'll see what I can do."

She avoided his eyes but nodded before pulling away and walking toward the door. The ancient that defended her was already there with his hand on the handle. He turned to her with a friendly smile.

"Please excuse the heightened emotions among my peers. We've never had this situation, and there's much confusion at the moment. It will settle, and you're welcome among my people."

Not trusting herself to speak, she nodded, praying he would open the door before she lost her control.

He turned the handle and held the door open, and she swiftly stepped through. She plastered a smile onto her face when she noticed Haku and Kawena get up from a bench and start walking toward her.

"How was it?" Kawena asked, much too cheerfully.

Alissia responded, "I did a lot of talking, and I'm exhausted. Can you please show Luke and me to our rooms? I'm just really tired right now."

"We can do that," Haku said, taking Kawena's hand.

As she and Luke followed the couple through various corridors, her mind raced with unpleasant thoughts. She kept both of her hands on Mia, not wanting Luke's touch. She knew he could feel her intense emotions, and it bothered her that he could see through the smile she tried to hide behind.

Alissia needed to be alone, or at least that was what she desperately wanted. She knew her tears would break free, and she did not want anyone to see that side of her—not even Luke.

She had been stupid! She had actually thought the people that changed her would accept her, and although these Medicians were not the ones that had saved her life, they were still Medicians.

The humans did not accept her as one of them, and the Medicians did not truly accept her as anything more than a mistake.

Her chest grew tight, and she could feel the tears trying to break free as a sudden thought entered her mind. She had never truly been accepted by anyone.

"That's not true!" Luke's voice boomed in her head, causing her to flinch. *"No matter what these people think of you, you're not alone. Stop hurting yourself."*

"Get out of my head!"

"I'm not in your head. You're emotions are pouring out of it like a volcano, and you're hurting."

"Here we are." Kawena stopped at a door. Haku turned the handle, and Alissia followed the couple through the entrance.

"We've given you one of our training suites so the three of you can stay together. We thought you'd want to be able to spend more time with Salvatore before he leaves," Kawena said.

"Leaves? When is he leaving?" asked Alissia.

"We don't know when," answered Haku. "We just know he'll eventually go back to the ship. He won't be staying here. You knew that, didn't you?"

"Yes," she answered, realizing how much she would miss him. She suddenly did not want to be left behind, as she now wanted off the island and away from the Medicians.

Hope flashed through her for a fleeting moment as she imagined her and Luke sneaking back to the ship, but she knew Captain Blackwell, and even Salvatore, would not defy any orders. They were bound by honor to be protectors of the Medicians.

During the tour of the rooms, Alissia learned the spacious suite was normally used to house apprentices, but there were none at the moment.

Unlike the formal décor of the lobby and meeting rooms, the suite was bursting with pillows, throws, and cozy studying nooks. The two bedrooms were filled with hanging beds made of reeds and ropes, as the Medicians did not like to cut down trees. Much of their furniture utilized the natural resources of the island.

They loved to be outdoors, and although the inside of the mountain was immaculate, the ancients usually held their meetings in an open hut beneath a cluster of palm trees. Haku explained that the mountain was mainly used as protection from the fierce storms that came their way. All of their scrolls and treasured resources were kept safe within the confines of the mountain, and when an occasional hurricane came their way, there was plenty of room for everyone to seek refuge within the solid walls.

Strategically placed openings in the upper portions of the walls allowed a fresh island breeze to enter the rooms, and Alissia was amazed by the advanced engineering used in the plumbing and cooling.

Unlike humans, the Medicians did not need to charge their glow stones in the sun each day. Instead, they charged them with a simple touch. The same went for heating stones used for cooking and cooling stones used to cool the rooms. Animals helped with the chores, and plants thrived around them.

With two bedrooms and attached bathrooms at opposite sides of the suite, a large, open room was in the middle. Half of the room held the dining area, which consisted of a long table with bench seats, cabinets, cooking stones, a sink with a faucet made of cane, and a cooling box for cold food storage.

The other half of the room looked like a comfortable den. It was filled with baskets, pillows, throws, and beautiful glowing, crystals. Oversized beanbag loungers in a variety of shimmery colors circled the open area, and a large ottoman was placed in the middle. Two reading nooks were carved into the upper portion of the walls, with a rope ladder leading to them.

Although Alissia's emotions were raging inside of her while she listened to Haku and Kawena give the tour, the room had a soothing effect on her, and she imagined herself hiding away in one of the reading nooks lit by the glowing crystals. She could easily picture the room filled with young apprentices studying in groups around the ottoman.

At the end of the tour, Kawena said, "Your meal is being prepared now, and there are snacks in the cooling box and cabinets. Is there anything else you need?"

Alissia shook her head. "No, I'm just really tired and want to get some rest. I'm sorry."

"Don't apologize," Kawena said.

Haku took his zeer's hand and gave it a slight tug. "We should fetch their meal and let them settle in."

Kawena nodded, and Alissia heaved a sigh of relief when they walked out, closing the door behind them.

"I'm going to the bathroom," she said.

Luke caught her by the hand as she went to pass. "We need to talk, Alissia, and I need to know what was said."

"I know. I'll hurry."

Once alone in the bathroom, she leaned her back against the locked door and closed her eyes. Knowing Luke was aware of the chaos within her, she decided against allowing herself to fall into self-pity. Instead of focusing on being called a mistake, she reminded herself that the ancients did not give her a chance to ask any questions.

That realization led to frustration, and she pushed that emotion to the surface.

When she walked out of the bathroom moments later, tears no longer threatened, and she was her old self again—cold and distant.

Chapter 25

As soon as Alissia stepped into the open room, Luke pulled her into his arms and held her tightly. When he finally pulled away, he picked up a mug and handed it to her. "It's good. Taste it."

She sipped the fruity drink and nodded in agreement. "It is good."

"Come," he said, walking toward one of the stuffed loungers. He sat down and patted the spot next to him.

Alissia smiled, remembering how thankful she was to have him in her life. "You're lucky you can fit on the furniture," she teased.

He nodded. "The bathroom and kitchen are a slight challenge, and I'd be in trouble if the ceiling were much lower."

She sat down next to him, and after a few more sips of her drink, she set it on the floor.

"I need for you to tell me everything you learned today," Luke said. "You have no idea what it's like to not know what anyone is saying. It's maddening."

She made herself comfortable in the cozy lounger, with her feet resting on the ottoman. Then Mia jumped into her lap and crawled onto her chest. Placing her tiny hands on each side of Alissia's face, she bent down and kissed her on the cheek.

"She's worried about you too," replied Luke.

Alissia asked, in the ancient language, "Did I kill the people who saved me?"

Mia removed her hands from Alissia's face and shook her head.

"Are they angry with me?"

Her friend shook her head fiercely.

"Did they make a mistake?" Alissia asked.

The tiny creature growled and shook her head again.

Alissia thought for a moment before asking, "Should I still try to go to them?"

Mia nodded and then made her way to the top of the beanbag, plopping down near Alissia's head.

Luke remained sitting, and he removed her glasses. "You really don't need these here, and I want to see your eyes." He set them aside before turning to face her. "Now, tell me everything, and don't leave out a single detail."

She nodded and told him everything she had learned, which was not much, as she had done most of the talking.

When finished, he replied, "Not all the ancients agreed with his words, and many seemed against him."

She frowned in disagreement. "How do you know? You don't even speak the language."

"That's why I focused on their expressions, and it was obvious many of them disapproved of what he said. They don't hate you, Alissia. I think they're divided, but I believe most of them don't agree with him."

"They won't let us leave the island," she stated, "and I want to meet the ones who changed me. I need to know how much it cost them. I keep hearing about a sacrifice."

A knock came at the door, and she sat up as Luke went to open it.

"We have warm food." Kawena strolled in with a basket in her hands. Haku followed with a larger one.

"The cooks prepared one of our island favorites. I hope you like it," Kawena said, setting the basket on the table. "We eat a lot of fruits, as they're more than abundant, and we grow our own vegetables. However, the trade ships supply us with much of our grains and spices."

Haku set his basket on the table as well. "Is there anything else you need? We've never had humans here, and I'm afraid we don't exactly know your ways."

Alissia stood. "We have everything. Thank you very much."

"Our pleasure," said Haku. "We'll soon get to show you around the island, and you'll see why we love it here so much."

"It's a beautiful place," Kawena added.

Haku looked at his zeer. "Well, we should let them eat and get some rest."

Kawena nodded and turned to Alissia. "We'll see you again tomorrow. Do you have any questions?"

Alissia had many questions. However, she was not in the mood for polite socializing. She smiled and said goodnight, telling herself she would get answers first thing in the morning.

The two Medicians left, and as Alissia and Luke were unloading the baskets, Salvatore walked in. Without even taking in his surroundings, he rushed to Alissia and pulled her into his arms.

"You didn't deserve any of those words." He squeezed her tightly.

Alissia stood awkwardly, her arms at her sides. When she glanced at Luke, she noticed the corner of his mouth turned up in amusement.

"Aren't you jealous of this?" she mentally asked.

His smile grew. *"As much as he compares you to Lita? He cares for you, Alissia, but it's much different than my feelings for you."*

"I should have said something, but I didn't know how to respond," Salvatore said, pulling away. "You didn't deserve that kind of treatment. It was wrong."

"I don't think they all feel that way toward her," Luke said.

"Oh, I know they don't!" Salvatore exclaimed. "They had some words about it after she left, and many of them weren't happy with his rudeness."

"Wow! Think they gave us enough food?" Alissia said, opening one of the containers. Her stomach grumbled, and she realized how hungry she was.

The three of them curiously tried each of the exotic food items, which all seemed to have a sweet flavor to them—some much too sweet for her taste.

The tall men seemed out of place sitting at the short table, and Alissia could not help but laugh at how they suddenly looked like giants in the kitchen area.

As they were putting the leftover food away and cleaning the dishes, Salvatore explained how he had overheard some of the ancients discussing Alissia during their short break. They were upset with how she had been treated and agreed her situation was not her fault.

After they finished their chores, Alissia went to her bedroom and prepared for bed. Her wardrobe trunk had been brought to the room during her meeting with the ancients.

When she walked back into the open room, Luke was sprawled out on one of the lounging chairs, with Salvatore doing the same on another. Luke lifted his arm as a gesture for her to join him, and she sprawled out next to him, with her face resting on his chest. He put his arm around her, and she looked at Salvatore.

"When are you leaving?"

"I don't know yet. We didn't talk about it. They asked me what I thought about you as a person and things like that. I assured them

I could get you to the other Medicians without you getting noticed, since I know that's what you truly want."

She nodded in agreement.

"What do you think about all this?" He looked at Luke.

"I think she should meet whoever saved her life. It's what she wants."

Alissia asked, "And you don't mind more sailing and horses?" She rolled her eyes. "Forget I mentioned sailing. I think you love it."

He laughed. "I enjoy learning new things, and I also don't have a problem with authority."

"Yeah, well I can't do anything on the ship but help in the kitchen and read books on deck. It's boring and a life I can do without." She looked at Salvatore. "And I'm stuck watching Lita make out with her boyfriend all the time."

Salvatore's eyes widened, and he asked cautiously, "What does make out mean?"

"A lot of heavy kissing," she answered.

"Is that boy sneaking into her room?" Salvatore asked. "His father will kill him if he finds out."

"It's both of them," she said. "I've seen Lita drag him into the room."

"Lucky them," Luke said under his breath.

Alissia lifted her head and looked into his eyes. "We can kiss too. You'll just lose your humanity," she said, with a grin.

He smiled back. "And every bit of it would be worth it."

"So you two have answers about why you can't kiss?"

She put her head back on Luke's chest. "Yeah, it seems I didn't heal Luke by doing a healing thing. When I healed him, I was kissing him and thinking how much I love him. That triggered some kind of zeer bond, but because we didn't... um... do anything else physically, the bond isn't complete."

"Oh," Salvatore said, his eyebrows lifted.

"If we ever do finish the bond, Luke will turn."

"Well, at least the two of you can be together."

After a moment of silence, Luke turned to Salvatore. "If we can't leave the island, I'd like to see if we can have a small wedding on the beach with Devon and the others there as witnesses. Do you think it would be possible?"

Alissia froze, as heat rushed to her face.

Salvatore looked into her eyes and grinned. "I think that could be arranged. I don't see why not. What do you think, Alissia?"

"Breathe, Alissia," Luke mentally said.

"Yeah, that would be nice," she heard herself answer.

Luke laughed, and Salvatore joined in. She did not trust herself to speak, and as the two men continued to talk, her mind traveled to thoughts she had never allowed herself to entertain.

She and Luke could marry and spend the rest of their lives together on an exotic island. Although she wanted to leave and meet the other Medicians, the idea of being married to Luke excited her in many ways.

Alissia soon fell asleep to the sound of Luke and Salvatore's voices, and unlike her usual nightmares consisting of Ian and her kidnappers coming back to life, her dreams were filled with laughter—along with images of her great longing for Luke finally being satisfied.

Chapter 26

"Good morning, Pixet." Luke kissed her forehead, and she smiled and opened her eyes. "How did you sleep?"

"Good. And you?"

"Best sleep I've ever had. I could get used to falling asleep with you in my arms."

"Where's Salvatore?" she asked, noticing his absence.

"He's getting dressed."

"What time is it?"

"I don't know, but we've had a long sleep."

She closed her eyes again, too relaxed to move.

"How do you think I'll look with purple hair and eyes?" he asked, causing her eyes to shoot open. "We'll match, although I'm much taller than you. Think that will change? Will I shrink? You said you didn't shrink. You've always been short."

Alissia blinked, her eyes staring straight ahead.

"Your pulse is rising again, Alissia. That seems to happen a lot. Is that a side effect of your change?"

"Okay, how do you do it?" she demanded, pulling herself from his arms and into a sitting position. "How come you can always feel me, but I hardly ever feel your emotions?"

Luke grinned smugly. "That's easy. I'm always calm and levelheaded. You, however, are a heap of emotions."

His grin faded, and he cocked his head. Staring up at her with a look that caused her heart to skip a beat, he reached up and stroked the side of her face. "That, and I make you a heated mess." He added roguishly, "You know you want me."

She rolled her eyes and knocked his hand from her face. Then she abruptly remembered something from the day before.

"Did you do something yesterday?" she asked, suddenly serious. "When you took my hand, I began to feel calm. I looked over at you, and your eyes were closed. What were you doing?"

"I wondered if it would work," he said, sitting up. "I could feel you getting upset, and since I couldn't understand your words, my emotions were flat and calm. We've sent images to each other, and we already know we can unwillingly transfer heightened emotions to each other. I got the idea that maybe I could send my emotion to you. So when I took your hand, I closed my eyes and focused on soothing you." He grinned mischievously, "Maybe I should've calmed you with images."

Alissia groaned and shook her head.

"I've missed this," he said softly.

"What?"

"Being alone. When was the last time we've been alone like this?"

"That's because single men and women aren't allowed to be alone together on Captain Blackwell's ship. Remember? The ship and captain you love so much."

"Nobody's ever alone on that ship."

"I thought you liked sailing," she challenged.

"I do. And I enjoy learning new things, but I don't exactly like spending every night in a packed room filled with sweaty men. That, and there doesn't seem to be a private spot anywhere on that ship."

His eyes went to her neck and stayed there for a moment. Then a sudden rush of longing went through her body—Luke's longing, not hers.

Alissia wanted to tease him about his heightened emotions, but her lips refused to move. Her own excitement began to rise inside of her, mixing with his.

His fingertips went to her ear and left a hot trail as they slowly made their way along her neck. They traveled to her lips, where they stopped before pulling away. She stared into his dark, intense eyes for a moment, her breathing heavy.

"You're not calm right now," she murmured.

"No, I'm not. I'm thinking how much I miss kissing you. I remember all too well what that's like." He bent down and placed his lips to her neck. "Remember?" She closed her eyes as his lips tenderly moved along her neck, stopping at her ear. "I can lose myself with you forever, Alissia," he whispered.

The sound of a door closing caused them both to jump. Luke pulled away, and they both looked to find Salvatore standing in front of the bedroom door. He was wearing fresh clothing, and his hair was wet.

"Interrupt anything?" he asked, with a grin.

Alissia quickly stood. "Uh… we were just talking about heightened emotions."

He nodded. "I can see that." He strolled to the same lounge chair he had sat in the night before, but as he went to sit down, a knock came at the door.

"I'll get it," he said, making his way to the door.

"Good morning," came Kawena's cheery voice. "We've brought some breakfast. How did everyone sleep?"

"Very well. Thank you," Alissia answered.

Haku and Kawena set two baskets on the table and began to pull out food. Kawena looked at Alissia. "How did you like our island food last night?"

"It's nice."

Haku set his empty basket aside. "You'll want a big breakfast. We have a lot planned for the day."

"You do?" Alissia asked, sitting down at the table.

He nodded. "Yes, the ancients will be meeting today among themselves to decide on some matters, and Kawena and I are to take you all on a hike and to a swimming spot."

Salvatore and Alissia's eyes met in a moment of confusion as he sat down beside her. "Am I to go back to the ship today?"

Kawena sat down across from him. "Not today. The ancients will know more by tomorrow. Today is for fun and relaxing."

Haku nodded and sat down beside his zeer. "My father told us what happened last night, and he—along with others—are ashamed of what was said. He wants you to see the beauty of the island today so you're not trapped inside while they're meeting."

"Are they considering letting me leave?" Alissia asked.

Haku and Kawena glanced at each other, and it was Haku who turned and said, "I don't know. They're meeting again with Selona and trying to make some decisions."

"She wants to start trade among the high races again. Am I right?"

"I believe so," Haku answered.

"And they're considering this?" Alissia asked in disbelief. "Did they not hear all that I told them happened to me and Luke? What her people are capable of? They're monsters. I mean, they're *real* monsters."

Kawena nodded, looking somewhat uncomfortable. "The poor woman did give up her life, though, to come here. She'll die soon, and the ancients take her sacrifice seriously."

"What do you mean she's going to die?" Salvatore asked.

Haku said, "Her people can't live outside their land for long. It's written in the scrolls that they need the nutrients from their bog to survive, and since she left her home, she's been eating human food and breathing fresh air. Her body can't survive that for long. It's toxic."

"Did she know that when she left?" Salvatore asked.

Haku nodded. "She did, and from what my father told me, she willingly gives her life for the cause at hand."

"Which is to reestablish the trade?" asked Salvatore.

"Yes," Haku answered.

"We don't know the details," Kawena said, "and no decisions have been made. Today will be a fun day. We're going to take a hike to one of our beautiful waterfalls, and you'll love it there." She turned to Alissia. "You can ask us questions about your change, and we'll try to answer them."

Haku nodded. "Kawena and I spoke about your situation last night, and we both can't imagine suddenly going through a change like you did and not having any answers."

"Dreadful," Kawena added. "And I'm sure you have plenty of questions for us."

As soon as Alissia finished eating, she went to her room and got ready for the day. She put on a bathing suit and a sarong as a cover. She then braided her hair and grabbed a pair of dark glasses.

Mia went with them, and they hiked along a heavily shaded trail through the exotic paradise. Their surroundings were beyond beautiful, with distant mountains, lush greenery, and the sound of birds and bizarre animals scurrying in the trees.

The thought of marrying Luke and living on the island lingered in the back of her mind, and she found herself looking at him more than usual. His smile told her he was enjoying their surroundings, along with a rare day free from danger and responsibilities.

They stopped at the bottom of a small waterfall, the water flowing into a clear pool. After arranging their towels along some large rocks, Kawena and Haku promised Alissia they would talk after everyone cooled off with a swim.

It felt strange for Alissia to be around people shorter than her. Being five feet tall, she was accustomed to looking up quite often, and the thin, fragile-looking frames of the Medicians were greatly foreign to her.

Kawena's pixie haircut was much shorter than Haku's shaggy mop, and both of their hair was lighter than Alissia's. While hers resembled that of a deep-colored plum, Kawena's was a beautiful lilac, and Haku's was a violet tone.

The small couple stripped down to their bathing suits and took off their dark glasses, and Alissia immediately noticed jades hanging from cords around their necks.

After motioning for the others to do the same, the Medicians took off running toward a cliff. Alissia watched as Kawena waved before diving into the water.

"I've missed this," Salvatore said with sadness in his voice. Alissia noticed the tears in his eyes.

"Is it like this on your side of the island?" she asked.

"It is." He sniffed. "This is what we left behind when she died. It just didn't seem the same without her."

"Oh, Salvatore." Alissia put her arms around him. She had never been one for hugs or affection, but she had no words to offer.

"I'm sorry," Luke said, putting his hand on Salvatore's shoulder.

Salvatore gently pulled away. "No, I'm sorry. You two go and enjoy your day. You deserve it, and if you get to leave the island, it will be a long time before you'll see anything like this again—if ever."

"But—" Alissia started.

He shook his head. "No, buts. Both of you, off you go!" He pushed Luke toward the cliff. "Show your woman your skills."

Luke hesitated for only a moment. Then he stripped down to his suit and headed for the rock.

"Are you okay?" Alissia asked.

"Shh! Look at your man. You know you want to ogle his body."

As Salvatore stripped to his suit, Luke waved at Alissia before taking an expert dive from the rock.

"Is there anything he can't do?" Salvatore asked.

"Kiss me," Alissia answered.

"Oh, right. I guess that makes up for everything else he can do."

Alissia laughed as Salvatore headed toward the cliff. She untied her sarong and set it on the towel before removing her sandals and glasses. Then she made her way toward the rock.

The water was the perfect temperature, and she and the others spent the rest of the morning swimming and playing. Mia seemed to enjoy diving into the water, as she spent most of her time climbing up a cliff, only to let go and drop back down.

After lunch, Salvatore and Luke went to a large rock near the edge of the water, where they sat and began a conversation. Haku rested on his towel, his dark glasses back in place, and Kawena sat next to him, with her back against him.

"What questions do you have for us?" she asked.

Alissia stared down thoughtfully at Mia, now relaxing at the end of Alissia's towel, and she suddenly wished she had made a list of questions.

"I guess I'll start with the ones about Luke and me. The surge of heat and my glowing blood when we kiss—what is that?"

Kawena said, "That's normal. In our culture, I believe we are much older than humans when we unite. We become promised to each other long before we participate in the ceremony, and the night of the zeer ceremony, we go away for a year of togetherness—away from others."

"You mean you spend a year together without anyone else around?"

"Yes, and it's a beautiful place." Kawena's eyes became dreamy.

"What do you do about work and money?"

Kawena shook her head. "Things are different among our people."

"I believe she means we're more relaxed than humans," Haku added. "Most of us make our own clothing, and we do a lot of bartering in our society."

"When we go away for a year," Kaweena said, "we spend our time getting to know each other without the distractions of our family."

"You make your own clothing?" Alissia asked. "Where do you get the shimmery material?"

Kawena smiled. "Our ancestors brought veolla bugs with them to the island."

"What are those?"

"They produce a thin, stringy material we dye and weave for our clothing." Kawena looked down and touched the top of her suit.

"We have veolla bug farmers," Haku added.

Alissia shook her head, reminding herself she had more important questions to ask. "All right, so if Luke and I kiss, what will happen?"

Haku answered, "You've already started the bond, so kissing would complete it. Which... well... it's not something you should do lightly."

"What do you mean?"

Kawena said, "It's powerful and very overwhelming. It's not just a kiss. It would be like..."

At her pause, Haku interjected, "Just don't do it until the right time."

"Exactly!" Kawena added. "It's very emotional, and it's a big experience."

"A beautiful experience, but not one to play with," Haku said. "The bond takes a lot of commitment. It ties the two of you together."

"We're already tied together. I feel his emotions, and when he had a burned hand, I felt his pain. I'm also told that if one of us dies, the other dies too."

"That's true," Kawena said. "But there's more to the bond. It's hard to explain. Take it slow and wait until the right moment. There's no rush."

"We can't even kiss each other, though," Alissia said, hating the whine in her voice.

Haku responded, "Love is more than the physical. This is your time to learn about each other in different ways."

"I know," Alissia said. "So when it happens, Luke's hair, eyes, and blood will turn? Does that mean he'll have the same abilities as me?"

"Yes," Haku answered, "he'll be like you."

"Will we be able to have children one day?"

Kawena said, "Yes, but our fertility is much limited compared to a human's, and you're not of the fertile age."

"But I'm twenty-nine."

Kawena smiled. "Not even zeer age when it comes to our kind. You're still but a small child."

"Does this mean I've got to go through puberty all over again?"

"What?" Kawena asked, looking confused.

"Never mind," said Alissia, shaking her head. "That's a human word."

She thought for a moment before saying, "I can bond with and heal animals. I can also tell them what to do. Is there anything else I need to know about my healing abilities?"

"We were created to be the healers of this world," Kawena said. "You now have that same power. Both plants and animals thrive from your touch. The animals sense it in you."

"Is that why they expect healing from me?"

Kawena nodded. "It's what we're here for."

"I can also charge solar stones. Does that mean I can make a jade?"

"It takes an entire lifetime to fully charge a jade stone," Haku said. "You could charge a stone, but you only get one stone."

"Why do you charge stones? What does it do for you?"

"It's a way to store extra power," replied Kawena.

"Why can't I bond with Mia and tell her what to do like the other animals?"

"Because she's considered one of the lower races," Haku answered. "It consists of humans, pixets, and other various complex creatures. They're not just animals. They have a soul."

"What makes the lower races different from the higher races?"

"We have many abilities the lower races do not," said Haku. "Humans would consider them magic, but we just consider them abilities."

"Other than being able to see in the dark, heal plants and animals, and charge things, do I have any other abilities I don't know about?"

Kawena said, "That's it. However, you'll likely live to be around three hundred years old. We have better vision than humans, and we can't—and would never want to—eat meat."

"You mentioned the people who changed me made sacrifices. What do you mean by that? Did it make them sick? Could it kill them?"

Haku said, "It's barely mentioned in the scrolls, as our people have always been against it. I don't believe it made them sick or depleted their strength—at least, not in a long-lasting way. They were probably weak for many days after using that much power, though. The scrolls mainly speak of the mental and emotional connection built. The ones that changed you probably feel your pain, joy, and many other emotions."

"Even now that I'm so far away?" she asked. "I mean, I can no longer feel them with me. When I was closer to where they live, I would wake up each morning feeling as if they had been in my head during the night. That feeling and connection seems to go away after a certain distance."

"I don't know," Haku said. "The scrolls didn't say anything about distance."

"Last night one of the ancients mentioned it probably killed them to mind speak to me the one time they did. Mia said it didn't kill them, but did it hurt them?"

Haku said, "I don't know that answer either. However, that would've taken an immense amount of power. It wasn't an easy task."

"And what do you know about the guardians?"

Kawena answered, "They're rarely seen, only by our race and only at great times in history. Their presence is a miracle in itself. You were chosen, and you were blessed."

"Can I heal people?"

"No," Haku said, somewhat firmly. "The ones that healed you made great sacrifices that we don't even know about. Humans have a soul. They have many thoughts and emotions. Wars, triumphs, and many other things come from them. You must never attempt to heal a human."

"It could kill you," Kawena added. "You didn't heal Luke. You gave him a zeer bond, and you can't do that but once in your lifetime. If Luke were not your true love, you'd still be stuck with him for the rest of your life. Only death breaks a zeer bond, and even then, you both die."

Alissia turned her eyes to Luke, still sitting on the rock talking to Salvatore. She tried to think of other questions. She knew she had more, but nothing came to mind at the moment.

Luke looked up, and they locked eyes for a short moment. Then he turned his attention back to Salvatore. The two men appeared to be in a deep conversation.

"Any other questions?" Kawena asked.

"I thought I had a lot more, but I can't think of any right now."

The sound of laughter came from the trail, and Alissia turned around to find a Medician couple and child heading toward them. The child looked too small to even be walking.

Kawena stood. "We should leave anyway. We wanted to show you some more of the island today."

Alissia nodded and mentally relayed their plans to Luke as she tied her sarong around her body.

They spent the rest of the day touring a cavern. She also got to play with some of the local animals and learned that if she and Luke stayed on the island, they would have a variety of choices in their living arrangements.

Although she had seen the tree houses in the village, there were also homes with a small piece of farmland, houses close to the beach, and houses built into the side of a mountain.

The day ended similar to the night before, as the three of them ate in their suite, got ready for bed, and then they met in the den and discussed what Alissia had learned that day. They steered clear of talking about the future, as everything seemed to depend on the decision of the ancients.

She fell asleep in Luke's arms for the second night in a row, and her dreams consisted of a wedding, a hut near the beach, and Luke.

Chapter 27

Alissia opened her eyes and blinked a few times before slowly and carefully lifting her head to find Salvatore no longer in the room.

Luke appeared to still be asleep, and she smiled, thinking it was a rare moment she awoke before him. As she stared down at his face, an overwhelming sense of affection came over her, nearly bringing tears with it.

His eyes fluttered for a moment before they shot open, and a smile filled his face. Alissia smiled back, and then she began to squirm until she was positioned with her head on his chest.

"Why'd you do that?" he asked. "I want to look into your eyes."

"No, I've got morning breath."

He laughed. "Is that what that's all about?" He swiftly pulled her body on top of his so that she faced him. "I want to spend the rest of my life waking up to your face, Alissia Roswell, and you're going to have to get over your little phobia."

She pulled her lips in tight and shook her head. A grin slowly filled his face, and she immediately knew she was somehow in trouble.

"You know," he said slowly, "I've never checked to see if you're ticklish, and I believe that's something I should know by now."

She lifted her chin defiantly, and her eyes narrowed. His hands began to travel along her body, grabbing and teasing, yet she remained in control of her emotions. After a while, he stopped and stared up at her thoughtfully.

Without warning, he rolled on top of her, and his mouth shot forward and burrowed into her neck. He began to blow on her skin, and when her hands came up to fight, he swiftly caught them and forced them down. Her attempt at a struggle got her nowhere, as his body pushed her into the lounge chair.

Alissia lost every bit of her control, and laughter shot out of her mouth. Luke triumphantly began to blow even harder.

"Stop it!" she screamed, when he slightly let up. Then laughter overtook her again as his mouth went back to continuing its torture.

After a while, he stopped blowing, and he began to place soft kisses along her neck. She was able to catch her breath before saying, "I'm going to kill you. You are so dead, Luke. You have no ideaahhhh!"

She screamed, and her entire body writhed beneath his, as his tongue playfully danced along her neck.

It seemed like ages before he lifted his head, and with a wild look in his eyes, he stared down at her. His body began to shake, and his head fell onto her chest, as he laughed heartily.

Between heavy breaths, she swore, "I will *so* be paying you back for that. You have no idea what you've started."

After a long laugh, his head came up. "It was worth it." Luke let go of her hands and rolled off of her.

"Are you two finished alerting everyone on this island of your presence?" Salvatore asked, now sitting in his usual seat across from them.

Alissia sat up and touched her neck, and her face scrunched up in disgust. "You slobbered all over me," she said, wiping her hand on Luke's shirt.

"So much for morning breath," he replied.

"Oh, you're so gross!" She grabbed the bottom of his shirt and bent down to mop her neck with it. She turned to Salvatore when she heard his laughter.

"What?" she asked, her forehead wrinkling.

He shook his head. "You two were made for each other."

Luke put his arm across her shoulders and pulled her in close. "Hear that? You were made for me, and I was made for you. That means I'm your blessing, and you're my blessing."

Alissia shook her head and rolled her eyes, "Curses are also made."

A knock came at the door, and Salvatore went to open it.

"Good morning," came Kawena's voice. "We've brought your breakfast and some news."

Luke and Alissia stood, staring expectantly for her to continue. After setting her basket down on the table, she said, "The Ancients want to meet with you this morning."

Haku added, "They've made their decision."

"What did they decide?" Alissia asked eagerly.

"We don't know," Haku answered. "My father didn't say."

Alissia barely heard anything else as she rushed through breakfast before hastily getting dressed. By the time they sat down in front of the ancients—with Mia in Alissia's lap—she had come to the conclusion that she and Luke would be forced to stay on the island. She had even already imagined a wedding and her yearlong honeymoon.

Selona was there as well. She was coughing and suddenly looked somewhat sick. Alissia studied her for a moment, wondering if she was faking.

"We've made our decision," said the ancient sitting in the middle, "and we believe it's one that will make everyone happy."

Many of the men nodded in agreement, and he continued, "Selona's people want to reestablish trade among the higher races once again, and we believe this to be the best interest of our people. Not only that, but we want to reestablish contact with our relatives now that Alissia knows where to find them.

"However, the first thing that must be done to open the trade again is to locate the Bontogs. They're another hidden race, and Selona tells us she knows where to find them."

Looking at Salvatore, he said, "You'll need to gather a small group of trusted people to go with you. Selona and Alissia will need to remain concealed from the humans. Will the threat of war among your people be a problem for this journey?"

Salvatore shook his head. "They're in negotiations, and I believe the threat of an actual war is minimal—however, not entirely impossible."

"Do you foresee a problem with this plan?" the ancient asked.

"No, I don't."

Alissia cleared her throat. "I'm sorry, but what is this higher race like? Forgive me for asking, but if you recall from what I told you the other day, you know that Selona's people tortured and nearly killed Luke and me. They despise humans, and they despise Luke and me even more for what we are.

"I also understand that we're not truly welcome by everyone here, and I understand why. However, I don't want to experience the same hate and prejudice I experienced by her people. They're a cruel and hateful race."

Selona coughed, and somehow it turned into a coughing fit. One of the ancients left his seat and poured her a cup of water. After taking a few sips, she looked at the ancients and said, in her raspy voice, "I apologize for the actions of some of my people. However, not all of them wanted harm to come to Alissia and her zeer. That was the cruel desire of one man."

The ancient in the middle looked at Alissia and said reassuringly, "This group of people is known for their inventions. They're a peaceful race, and I don't expect any harm to come to you or our human protectors.

"We'll be sending birds with you, as they'll need to learn the trade routes. When you meet with our friends, they'll have something to send back to us. Alissia, it would help if you would direct three birds back to us with the item. It's best they travel in a group."

Alissia nodded. "And then where are we to go?"

"Once your group has delivered the jade, you'll take Selona back to her home."

As Alissia started to speak, he lifted his hand. "You don't have to enter the bog, as we've already thought about your safety. Selona tells us you can leave her at the edge of the ancient trails, tie a note to one of our birds, and then instruct the bird to go to her people with the note. That way her people will come to her, and you can leave before they even receive the note."

He looked at Salvatore. "You never enter the bog or the ancient trails. Selona and her people understand the importance of Alissia taking you to our relatives, and they won't interfere. There's no danger with them, as they need the help of our relatives more than us."

Salvatore nodded. "I understand."

Alissia wanted to scream. Once again, she was being told what to do, and it was the opposite of what she wanted.

Luke took her hand, and she began to feel a calming sensation flow into her. She tried to pull away, in an attempt to keep her well-deserved anger. However, he held tight, and her heart rate soon began to go back to its normal pace.

The ancient said, "You'll need to leave immediately, as we fear Selona is already getting sick from being away from her home. Therefore, we've already begun sending supplies to your ship, and we expect your departure to be this afternoon, while there is enough sunlight for the crew to be able to see the rocks."

Looking at Salvatore, he added, "Selona knows where to go, and you'll need to discuss the location with her. Other than that, do you have any questions about this journey?"

"No."

"Thank you, Salvatore. Is this a job you would prefer us give to another protector? We understand you've been doing much travel these past years."

"No, thank you," Salvatore answered. "I prefer to be the one to stay with Alissia until she's safe with your relatives."

The ancient smiled and nodded. "That's what we expected. You'll be her protector, alongside her zeer."

He turned to Alissia. "Which reminds me, my dear. You must not complete the zeer bond until you are safely hidden with our relatives. I understand how difficult this will be—especially since the bond has already been triggered—but it's important for the sake of our entire race. Can you give us your word, along with that of his? You may ask him now."

Alissia turned to Luke. "They want us to do more traveling. First, we have to go to another hidden race. Then we have to return Selona to her bog, but we won't enter it. And finally, we'll be able to go to the mountains. He said we can't complete the zeer bond until we're with the other Medicians, and he wants us both to agree to this."

Luke looked at Salvatore. "Do you agree to all of this?"

He nodded. "It's the only way they'll let Alissia leave the island, and it seems important to them. Can the two of you keep your hands off each other—I mean your lips away from each other?"

Luke looked at the ancients thoughtfully and then turned back to Alissia. "You need to meet with the ones who changed you, or it will bother you for the rest of your life—which is a long time." He squeezed her hand. "This will only be a brief moment compared to how much time we have left with each other."

She forced a smile onto her face and nodded. "We can wait." Turning to the ancients, she said in their language, "We both give our word that we won't complete the zeer bond until we get to the other Medicians."

"Thank you," said the ancient. To Salvatore, he said, "You'll need to keep a diligent eye on them. The triggered bond—along with their natural desire—will be a strong temptation for them. It will only take one kiss to strengthen their bond."

"I will," agreed Salvatore.

"And little Mia," said the ancient, directing his attention to her. She sat up and stared back at him. "You serve your people well. I expect you already know the dangers of these two finishing the zeer bond while in the presence of humans. I've been told of your keen abilities at preventing it from happening, and I ask that you continue to watch over your charge, which now consists of two."

Mia nodded, and then she began to slowly move her fingers around. When she stopped, she turned her face toward Alissia, and all the ancients laughed. Alissia scowled down at her.

The ancients stood, and the middle one said, "If there are no more questions, you need to get back to the ship, and we will pray for your safety on your journey."

Chapter 28

"We'll be back soon to take you to the ship." Kawena opened the door to their suite. "I know the supplies are being loaded onto the boat, but do you need anything personal to take with you?"

"No. Thank you for your kindness," answered Salvatore. "We've enjoyed your company, along with the brief tour of the island."

Alissia stepped through the entrance and rushed toward her room, closing the door behind her. She unlocked her wardrobe trunk and began to throw what little clothing and personal hygiene products she had unpacked back into the trunk.

Once finished, she slammed it closed and locked it. She stared at the door for a moment before shaking her head and sitting down on the nearest swinging bed.

A knock came at the door, and she closed her eyes and frowned.

"Yes?" she called out, in a controlled voice. She opened her eyes. "I'm not dressed."

The handle began to turn slowly, and the door opened.

"I said I'm not dressed."

Luke stared back at her from the doorway. "And you lied, Alissia." Leaving the door open, he entered the room and sat down beside her.

"You're upset."

"I'm frustrated."

He took her by the hand and entwined his fingers with hers. While looking down at their hands, he said softly, "You know, yesterday was amazing, and the past two nights falling asleep with you in my arms has given me something to look forward to."

She could feel his own sadness seeping into her body, and when he looked into her eyes, she could also see it.

"We've been through a lot, and I know it feels like our moment will never come. But it will. And the wait will only make our moment even more special.

"Yesterday gave me a glimpse of our future. We now know that we can get married. You also said we can have a child. That's another answer we didn't have before."

He lifted her hand to his lips and kissed it. "We can still do the simple things," he said, lowering their hands back to his lap. "And we'll have many years together—more than humanly possible."

She nodded and let out a sigh. "I'm just tired of always being told what to do. First it was you, then it was the Elders, and now it's the ancients—not to mention Gore forcing us to take Selona."

Luke chuckled. "Ah, the problem with authority."

A knock came at the main door, and Luke stood. He pulled her up to stand next to him, and then he gave her a quick peck on her cheek.

"It's time to go, Pixet."

*****

"We'll miss you," Kawena said, and Haku nodded in agreement.

Alissia looked up at the tree houses above them as their carriage rode through the village.

"Maybe we'll see each other again," Kawena continued.

Although Alissia doubted that would ever happen, Kawena's voice sounded hopeful.

"That would be nice," she said politely.

"We have some things we want to give you so you don't forget us." Kawena picked up a pack at her feet and pulled out a deep blue, folded piece of shimmery cloth. Passing it to Alissia, she said, "Open it."

Alissia set the material on top of Mia, who was sitting in her lap, and began to unfold it.

"Oh, wow!" she exclaimed, staring down at a black pearl necklace and matching bracelet. Luke helped her to put them on, and Kawena grinned.

"Good! They fit. I added some more pearls to the strands this morning. You're not much bigger than us, but I still didn't think they'd fit without the extra pearls."

She picked up the material from Alissia's lap and unfolded it. Holding it up, she said, "I know this is too small for you to wear as a sarong, but you can still wear it over your shoulders as a wrap or even in your hair."

"It sparkles." Alissia touched the silky material. "It's lovely. I'll definitely use it—use all of it. Thank you very much. I wish I had something to give you."

Haku held up his hand. "We don't want gifts in return. Meeting you and your friends has brought great honor and joy to us, and it's been a pleasure to spend time with each of you."

Kawena handed Alissia the wrap, now neatly folded, then reached into the pack and pulled out what appeared to be a diamond prism attached to a cord necklace. The prism was about two inches long.

"This is for Luke, and I also have one for Salvatore." She touched the prism, and it began to glow brightly. "It's different from a normal glow stone, as it's made from the highest quality stone available and its light is very bright. It was mined from the mountains."

She touched the black material that attached the prism to the cord. "This was part of the mountain as well." Giving the prism a quick tug, it came loose from the cord to reveal a pointed end.

"This is one of the strongest stones, and it can cut through anything. So this prism will serve as a light and as a cutting tool."

More like a dagger knowing Luke, Alissia thought.

Kawena reattached the prism to the necklace and held it out for Luke. He accepted it with a smile, and then he surprised them all by thanking them in the ancient language. He then turned to Alissia. "Salvatore has been giving me lessons, and I know some of the basics."

"Why didn't you tell me?" she asked.

He shrugged. "I only know a few basic phrases."

Alissia turned to the two Medicians to explain. Shortly thereafter, the carriages stopped on the beach, and they said their goodbyes.

As she walked along the pier, Alissia realized she would miss Haku and Kawena, and she would also miss the beautiful island.

She had spent much of her childhood at the beach and had always loved the sound of the waves and palm trees blowing in the breeze. The island was the most beautiful and exotic place she had ever visited. It was also the last beach she would most likely ever see again.

A sense of sadness began to take hold as she realized she would probably never be allowed to leave the mountains once she found the other Medicians.

She and Luke would no longer be forced to hide while traveling, and they would finally be able to settle down. Yet unlike in her former reality, she could never pack up and take a beach vacation.

When she boarded the ship, she found Santo sitting in the women's section. Although his mind was clear, she learned that his body was still fatigued from the poison.

Captain Blackwell said he would allow Selona to sit in the women's section as they made their way out to sea, but he warned her that he would throw her overboard if she attempted to hurt any of his men. He let it be known that he disapproved of the pain she caused Salvatore's family by poisoning Santo.

When questioned, Selona assured Salvatore that Santo's body would recover and there would be no lasting side effects.

Alissia noticed the creature looked healthier than she had while in the meeting with the ancients, and she was not coughing anymore.

"Is it true you'll die since you left your home?"

"It's true," Selona answered solemnly. "My people can't survive away from our land."

"So how much time do you have left?"

Selona shrugged her shoulders. "I don't know. I no longer have meat from my home, but there are still some plants for me to chew on. They provide little—but not much—of what I need."

"And you chose to leave your home?" Alissia asked.

"Yes, I made the choice to sacrifice myself for the good of my people."

"Why would you do that just to reestablish the trade among the high races? What's so important to your people that you would die for it?"

Selona stood and looked down at Alissia. "Fresh air doesn't seem to be good for me, and I need to get away from it."

As she began to walk away, Alissia said, "I don't trust you, Selona."

The creature turned and smiled, revealing her filthy, pointed teeth. "Your opinion of me and my people is like a speck of sand at the bottom of this ocean. It means nothing to me, and it doesn't seem to matter to the Medicians either."

Alissia clenched her teeth as she watched Selona make her way to the stairs.

"Don't let her upset you," said Santo.

She pasted a smile onto her face and turned to him. "She doesn't." In an attempt to change the subject, she added, "So you know Duff and Lita are a couple now, don't you? How do you feel about that?"

"Lucky we finally found someone that will take her," he said wryly and smiled. "The Blackwells are good people, and Duff and Lita have known each other since they were children. In fact, the two of them would always get into trouble together. Although they're both the youngest in our families, they were the meanest and terrorized me and Duff's brothers."

He shook his head, staring out ahead of him, his mind in another place. "Have you heard about the time the two of them nearly got me thrown into the ocean?"

Chapter 29

lissia spent the rest of the afternoon listening to stories of Lita's wild childhood. Santo surprised her by talking about his mother as well. She could hear the fresh pain in his voice caused by the recent visions, and it hardened her heart toward Selona even more.

They ate dinner in the captain's quarters that evening and discussed their new journey. However, Alissia could not seem to focus on the conversation. Her mind kept drifting to Selona's reaction to her question, and the memory of Gafeen promising to see her again kept flashing through her mind.

At one point during their dinner, Luke put his hand on her shoulder and gave it a light squeeze. He leaned over and kissed her on the cheek and told her not to worry. Then his attention went back to the planning stages of the journey, and she knew he would be distracted and busy for the rest of their time aboard the ship.

The island had given her a glimpse of what life with him would be like if they weren't surrounded by danger. But, his main focus was back to keeping them both alive and safe.

She was glad when it was finally time for everyone to say good-night, and she was already in bed when Lita entered their room. The young woman plopped down on her bed and began to watch the door expectantly.

"What are you doing?" Alissia asked.

Lita turned, and a grin filled her face.

"Don't tell anyone yet," she said excitedly, "but Duff wants to marry me."

"But I thought you didn't want to live on a boat for the rest of your life."

Lita shook her head vigorously. "I don't, and I'm not. Duff is going with us. He's leaving the ship. Oh, and I didn't ask him to. It was all his idea."

At that moment, Duff slipped into the room. Without even glancing at Alissia, he looked down at Lita with a mischievous grin on his face.

"You're not sleeping in your brother's room tonight," he said.

Lita jumped up and met him at the door. "I've missed you."

"I've missed this," he responded, pulling her into his arms.

Alissia glared up at the ceiling. After a moment, she turned her eyes back to the young couple.

"Um… guys. Y'all, I'm in the room. Helloooo! Remember the freaky little nonhuman? I thought this reality was against public displays of affection."

The fact that she was being completely ignored greatly added to her list of frustrations, and her temper began to rise.

"You know what?" she asked, standing and picking up her pillow. "Now's a good time to let y'all know that I'm not going to spend the rest of the trip watching the two of you give face slurpies when I can't even kiss my own man."

She pelted Lita's back with the pillow, and then she did it again. Finally the couple's lips separated, and Lita glared back at her.

"What are you doing?" Lita snapped.

"I'm not watching this. I'm done! Go away!" Alissia flicked her hand at the door.

Lita turned to Duff and said sarcastically, "I'm sorry. It seems my roommate has gone mad."

He leaned down to kiss her again, and Alissia whacked them both with her pillow. Lita turned around and said warningly, "Don't make me take that pillow from your tiny little hands and throw you on your bed."

Something inside of Alissia snapped.

"You did *not* just challenge me," she said with a flash of rage in her eyes. "You think because I'm little I can't take you?" She tossed the pillow onto her bed. "You want to see what these tiny hands can do around your neck?"

"Are you threatening me?" Lita asked, glaring back at her.

"Oh, I don't have to threaten you. We both know I've already taken you down once before, and I can easily do it again."

"Girls," Duff whispered, "keep your voices down." He tried to grab Lita's arm, but she pulled away, her eyes never leaving Alissia's.

With her finger poking into Alissia's chest, Lita said, "You want to try doing that again, little one?"

Duff began to look desperate. "Lita, help me out of the room," he pleaded. "Go see if anyone's in the hall."

"Little one? You want to see what this little one can do?" Alissia fired back.

A look of panic instantly came over Duff. "Ladies, please."

Alissia shoved Lita and retorted, "Okay, let's do this!"

As Lita let out a raging scream, Duff opened the door and made his way out, only to bump into Salvatore.

"What's going on in here?" Salvatore demanded.

Lita swung, and Alissia ducked. With both hands, Alissia grabbed the younger woman's hair, yanking her head down as she lifted her knee. The two body parts made impact, and then she tossed Lita onto the nearest bed. She was about to pounce, when Salvatore grabbed her from behind.

With Salvatore holding onto Alissia, Lita was able to jump from the bed, and she went straight for Alissia's face, only to receive a solid blow to the stomach by the heel of Alissia's bare foot.

"Get in here, boy! Grab Lita!" Salvatore demanded. He struggled to keep ahold of Alissia, now frantically thrashing in his arms. Duff glanced anxiously toward his father's room, and Salvatore yelled, "I'm her father, and I'm telling you to enter this room and restrain my daughter."

As Duff went after Lita, Alissia's foot found the bed, and she was able to thrust her and Salvatore's bodies back. He struggled from falling onto Lita's bed, slamming into her nightstand instead.

Although under normal circumstances, Alissia would never try to hurt Salvatore, her only coherent thought at the moment was to teach Lita not to underestimate the power of a petite woman.

Lita must have had wild thoughts of her own, because she kicked Duff and threw multiple punches at him when he attempted to restrain her.

By the time Luke and the captain made their way into the room, Salvatore and Duff were struggling to maintain their hold on the two uncontrollable women. Blood was streaming from Lita's nose and smeared across her face, arms, and splattered all over Duff and the floor.

"What's the meaning of this?" roared Captain Blackwell. Power and authority reverberated into the room, and both women immediately stopped their thrashing.

The captain looked from Lita to Alissia. "I will not have this behavior on my ship, and the next person that throws a punch will find herself locked in a cell with Selona! Is that understood?"

Both women glared at each other for a moment, their breaths ragged, before they looked at the captain and nodded.

"What's this fight about?"

Lita's eyes locked onto Alissia's, and a pleading look took over.

Alissia frowned, letting her own rage subside. "We were fighting over the lights in the room. I wanted them off, and Lita wanted them on."

The captain studied her face for a moment, and Alissia didn't think he believed her. "Is it over now?"

Both women nodded, and Salvatore and Duff cautiously released them.

"Duff, go to your bunk and leave Lita here with her father." The captain turned to Luke. "Take Alissia above deck to give her some fresh air."

Duff's right eye looked red, as he stared anxiously at Lita for a moment. Then he turned and walked past his father, leaving the room.

Alissia turned around and gasped when she saw the gash in Salvatore's lip. With wide eyes, she said, "I'm *so* sorry. What did I do?"

Salvatore lightly touched his fingers to his mouth, in an attempt to assess the damage. "I think your head got me."

Alissia scrunched up her face in concern. "Is there something I can do? Should I help you clean it?"

Captain Blackwell's authoritative voice said, "Go with Luke. I'll have Debina look at the damage you two women have caused tonight."

At the sound of her name, Debina entered the room with a look of worry on her face.

Luke took Alissia by the hand and gave it a tug, and she grabbed her sandals before they made their way to the women's area on deck. He pulled a blanket from one of the storage sections in the bench seat and put it over them after they sat down. Then he put his arm around her and pulled her into his side.

"Do you want to tell me what really happened?" Alissia reflected on the fight for a moment before he prompted, "It had something to do with her calling you tiny."

"What?"

"That word screamed into my head, along with a rage that made my own hands shake. I could barely walk to your room without punching someone myself."

"Sorry." Alissia looked up at him sheepishly. "She thought she could beat me because I'm so little."

Luke nodded knowingly. "She challenged you."

"If that's what you want to call it."

He laughed and then leaned his head back and closed his eyes. After a short while, she asked, "Are you going to sleep?"

"No, I'm just trying to relax again. Just moments ago I felt like I wanted to kill someone." He opened his eyes and looked at her. "And you nearly killed Salvatore yourself."

"Lita and Duff are getting married, and he's going with us," she divulged. "Don't tell anyone. I think it's still a secret."

"And that's what angered you?"

"No, of course not! I got mad because he keeps sneaking into the room for their nightly kiss. Every. Single. Night. And I'm done with it!"

He nodded. "I believe it won't happen again. Salvatore will talk to Lita, and the captain is smart enough to know your fight wasn't about the lighting in the room." He shook his head. "Was that truly the best you could think of?"

A smile crept to her face. "I wasn't thinking clearly."

They both jumped when Mia pounced onto Alissia's lap. The tiny creature studied her ward's face for a moment, and Alissia suddenly became aware of the many loose strands of hair that had been pulled out of her braid. She wondered if Mia knew about the fight or where she had even been.

Mia shook her head, and Alissia thought she recognized a look of disappointment before her friend turned away and began to make herself comfortable on her lap.

"Are you ready for another adventure, Pixet?" Luke asked.

"I'm tired of adventure."

His body trembled as he let out a small laugh. "One day we'll have a lot of stories to tell our children and grandchildren."

She frowned. "I'd rather read them books."

"Ah, but why read them, when you can live them?"

Alissia rolled her eyes and shook her head. Then she snuggled against his side and rested her head upon his chest.

A smile began to spread across her face, and all the unknowns and fears that plagued her throughout the day began to drift away. In that moment, the walls around her heart were unguarded and down, and she allowed herself to savor being in Luke's arms.

An image of a little boy with purple eyes and the same mischievous grin as Luke came to mind, and telling herself it was just for the night, she allowed herself to dream of a happy ending filled with love and a family of her own.

Unexpected Beginning

Alissia Roswell: Book Four

Chapter 1

"No one's here!" Alissia Roswell hurled the knife in her hand and watched as it hit the practice target. Then she spun around to face Selona, sitting at the base of a large tree. "Gore was wrong, and it'll soon be winter. Is that your plan? Get us stuck out here so we'll freeze to death?"

The creature stared back at Alissia, her strange eyes resembling polished, black onyx. She gave a smug grin, revealing sharp, slimy teeth. It had been months since Lita had cut Selona's dark hair at the natural spring, and it now resembled a wild mop atop her head.

Although their base camp was at the edge of a clear stream, the swamp creature's hygiene was greatly lacking, and a mix of animal blood and dirt spotted her body and clothing.

Selona let out a sickly cough before responding in her natural raspy voice, "They're here somewhere, and our task is to find them."

Alissia snatched another knife from her boot and slung it at the target. It landed within an inch of the others, sticking out from the block of wood. Turning to Salvatore, she ignored Luke's request to only speak in the ancient language to help with his teaching. "We've been searching this forest for weeks without finding anything. How long are we planning to stay?"

The older man's weather-beaten face crinkled with unease, and Alissia thought she noticed some new grey streaks in his shaggy brown hair. His broad chest filled with air before he let out a long sigh.

"I've been assigned to finding these people, and we have to do a thorough search." He stood from his seat on one of the large roots protruding from the ground, and then he stretched his sore muscles.

Alissia could not remember if it had been three or four weeks since they had entered the dark forest, and although her body healed itself and she was not in any pain from all of the hiking, she could tell it was beginning to take its toll on Salvatore and Selona.

The creature was beginning to show signs of sickness from being away from her homeland for so long. The eerie bog was the perfect ecosystem for her people, with its unique algae and bacteria growing in the black swamp water.

Selona no longer carried any of the living plants and animals from her land, and she now filled her stomach with what was foraged from the forest.

The sound of Lita's laughter coming from behind a large tree caused Alissia to frown even more. She reached into her other boot to retrieve a knife, only to find it missing.

"Looking for this?"

Her face softened at the sight of Luke carrying her knives from the target. He placed them at her feet, leaving one in his hand. Holding it out, he said, "I see you lost count of how many you've thrown. I thought I told you to count your throws, even when distracted. In a heated battle, you'll need to always remember how many knives you have left on your body."

Alissia smiled sweetly and took the knife he offered. "I see you're doing an amazing job at learning the old language. I'm impressed at your fellziug myandar."

"You're right. I know enough to know when you're making up words, and it won't work on me this time." He shook his head. "You have a sadistic side to you. You know that, don't you?"

Having an assassin for a boyfriend often made it difficult to get the upper hand, especially when it came to anything physical. Although Luke had been teaching Alissia self-defense lessons since they first met and she had always been one to work out, she was completely powerless against him.

It had nothing to do with the fact that she was only five feet tall, while he was a whole foot taller. Luke had been training for his elite position within the league since he was a child, and by the time he was a teenager, he was undergoing secret missions for the Eldership and was a trained killer.

Every part of his olive-toned, lean body was pure muscle, and his dark, penetrating eyes and unruly black hair greatly matched his personality. Without saying a word, his presence was dominating and could put fear into those around him.

Alissia reveled in knowing she had been able to fool Luke a few times, and she grinned. "I prefer to think of it as extra training. Having you learn fake words broadened your memory capacity and helped to prepare you for the real ones."

They both turned at the sound of Santo's laughter. He stood from the fire he was tending and shook his head, staring at Alissia.

Although Santo could easily be recognized as Salvatore's son, with his brown eyes and shaggy hair and his chiseled facial features, he did not have the same broad frame as his father. He also had a playful disposition.

As he went to speak, his younger sister, Lita, ran into the clearing. Her husband, Duff, followed but stopped near the tree line. The younger woman grabbed her sword and turned to face him, a grin filling her face. "I think I can take you down today."

"Is that a challenge?" asked Duff.

"Yes. Get ready to battle."

The young man grinned, his blue eyes twinkling with mischief. He strolled over and put his hand over Lita's, covering the sword's grip. He was only a few inches taller than her, and the front of his blonde, shoulder length hair was pulled back.

Since becoming a bride, Lita had changed in many ways. At first, while aboard her father-in-law's ship, she had worn a bit of makeup and wore her long, honey-colored hair down. However, that changed as soon as they began to travel by horse. She immediately began to dress in her usual riding clothing, with her hair pulled into a braid.

The change was not drastic, but Alissia thought her friend looked best without all the extra work. Lita had a fiery spirit, and her natural look matched her personality.

Like Alissia, Lita traveled in riding boots, slim pants, and a poet's shirt. Both women hid many knives beneath their clothing, and wearing makeup and taking time to look in a mirror was not worth the trouble when they spent most of their time trudging through the forest wearing backpacks.

Lita raised her eyebrows, as if daring Duff to make another move. As he began to lean toward her, Alissia let out a frustrated sigh and threw the knife in her hand. It whizzed past the young couple, landing in the tree behind them.

Duff released his wife's hand, and they both turned their attention to Alissia.

"You could have hit us!" Lita accused.

"But I didn't."

The young woman set the sword against the tree and stomped over to Alissia. "That was over done!" She crossed her arms over her chest.

Alissia shrugged. "No PDA. Remember? We've talked about this."

"We weren't even going to kiss." Lita threw her hands in the air. "My father's standing right there!"

She shrugged again. "Then consider my knife a reminder."

The younger woman glared, her chest rising and falling rapidly beneath her shirt.

"Can't the two of you get your women under control?" asked Santo, glancing between Luke and Duff.

Lita swung around to face her brother. "What did you just say?"

"I said you two need to be tamed."

"Really?" asked Alissia, crossing her arms. "And you want to show us how that's done?"

Lita smiled over her shoulder at Alissia. "It has been a while since we've given my brother a lesson." She took a step toward Santo.

Alissia grinned and uncrossed her arms, challenging Santo with her eyes. "A good fight does sound like something I could use right about now."

Santo glanced expectantly at Duff and Luke.

Lita's husband lifted his hands and shook his head. "You did this to yourself. Again."

Luke smiled. "It's fun to watch Alissia in action."

She looked over her shoulder. "Should I try one of the new moves you taught me?"

He nodded. "But not the one involving the throat. It could kill him."

"The groin one then?"

Luke eyed Santo. "Do you think he deserves that much pain?"

She shrugged. "He's the one that thinks he can tame me." She grinned and turned back to face Santo, now giving Salvatore a desperate look.

"Father?"

The older man chuckled and shook his head. "You'll learn one day not to open your mouth around these two." He turned to Alissia.

"Just remember his body doesn't heal like yours, and he'll have to be able to hike tomorrow."

Alissia nodded, and she and Lita began to roll up their sleeves, both eyeing their prey. Santo let out a resigned sigh and took off his shirt, revealing his tribal tattoos. After throwing it on top of his pack, he stepped away from the fire and stared back at the two women.

"I'll go first."

Alissia slowly made her way toward her future victim. "Hmm... Where have I not hit you?" She stopped in front of him and frowned. "Luke taught me how to break a leg, but I guess I can't do that."

She went to poke him in the stomach with her finger for more taunting, but he grabbed her by the wrist. Without warning, her right hand flew up to his face, where the heel of her palm slammed into his nose.

He let go of her wrist and tried to take a step back, but she quickly tucked her leg around his, while both of her hands went to the side of his face. Pushing with her hands and leg, she forced his body to the ground.

Stepping back, she grinned triumphantly. "Am I tame yet?"

Santo sat up and touched the blood trickling from his nose. He frowned as a cloth landed on his chest.

"Thought you'd need that," said Luke.

Alissia turned to her boyfriend. "It worked!" She sprinted to him, grinning excitedly. "I can't believe it was so easy. Did you see that?"

Luke nodded, pride showing on his face. "Feel better?"

"Definitely!"

"You're not done yet," said Lita, holding out her hand to her brother. "I want to spar so grab your sword."

"Alissia, I'd like to talk to you if you don't mind."

She turned around to meet Salvatore's gaze. "Okay."

The two of them walked away from the clearing and found a seat on one of the many strange trees that filled the forest. Both ends of this particular kind of tree grew into the ground, and instead of standing upright, it was in an arched position.

She dangled her feet beneath her. "What's up?" she asked, using her American slang.

Salvatore gave one of his fatherly smiles she was used to getting from him. "I've noticed you seem stressed lately."

She looked down at her feet and began to chew on her bottom lip, knowing he was right. Once they left the Medicians on the island, they traveled by ship where Alissia watched Captain Blackwell oversee the marriage of his youngest son to Lita. Then they traveled to the northern border by carriages during the hot summer months.

When they reached the forest, they had to leave the carriages behind. They followed a stream as far as their horses could take them. After setting up a base camp in a clearing by the stream, they spent the past few weeks in groups of two backpacking through the forest. Every three days they returned to the base camp, hoping someone had found the creatures supposedly living in the forest.

But no one had found anything, not even Salvatore's two large dogs or Mia, the resourceful, little creature sent to her by the Medicians from the mountains.

While spending time with Luke on the island, Alissia got a taste of what life could be like for the two of them once they reached the mountains, where she could finally meet the Medicians who saved her life—changing her in the process.

The Medicians Alissia met on the island answered many of her questions about her transformation. They told her that Luke would change like her if they kissed. His jet-black hair would turn into a dark shade of purple, unlike her plum-colored, long curls. His eyes would turn purple and glow slightly. He would have purple blood, shimmery skin, and his body would naturally heal itself from wounds.

Then there were the special abilities she had acquired since her change. She could bond with animals, healing them in the process, and she could give them commands. Plants thrived from her touch, and she could charge solar-powered stones that were highly relied upon in this reality.

Night vision was an interesting side effect to the change, along with her inability to eat or even smell meat without getting sick. She also had to wear dark glasses, as sunlight burned her eyes.

She learned that when she saved Luke from near death, she unintentionally triggered a bond between them. That bond gifted them with the ability to mind speak to each other. It also meant they could not live without the other, and they would die together.

With the Eldership guards searching for her along the roads, Alissia and Selona had to constantly hide in the secret compartments in their carriages. The swamp creature continuously taunted Alissia with comments that made her uneasy about her future.

As young newlyweds, Lita and Duff spent most of their time wrapped up in each other, and although Alissia was truly happy for them, she could not help but feel envious of them as well. Where they were free to be together, she and Luke could not even share a kiss, although their bond made the temptation even stronger than normal.

She looked up and met Salvatore's eyes. "I just don't think we're going to find anything here."

He nodded. "Is that all that's bothering you? How are you and Luke doing?"

"We're fine." She gave a slight smile. "We've talked more than we ever have since entering this forest. He's taught me how to forage for food and shown me a variety of animal tracks." Her smile grew as she added, "I've even gotten to interact with animals I've never seen before."

Salvatore smiled with her, and she continued, "We finish most nights with a self-defense lesson or knife throwing practice, and it's been amazing sleeping in the hammocks we carry with us. The sound of the leaves beneath my feet and the unique beauty of this forest is mesmerizing."

After a pause between them, Salvatore rubbed his hands over his pants. Then he clasped them in his lap. "So you're not stressed?"

She looked down at her feet in thought. She was tired of their primitive lifestyle. It required a lot of work. She yearned for a cozy bed, delicious meal, and a long, hot bath, not the small portable container she got to use every three days.

Turning back to Salvatore, she said, "I'm just tired of all the traveling, and I still haven't met the Medicians that saved me. I've been in this reality for a year now, and it seems like all I've been doing is fighting and hiding. I just want this to finally be over, and I want Luke and my life to begin."

He nodded. "Is there anything I can do to help?"

"Get us out of here." She stared up at him, pleading with her eyes.

"We won't be here much longer, but we have to do a thorough search." He put his hand on her shoulder. "I know you and Luke have been through a lot, but it only makes your relationship stronger. One day all of this will a be distant memory that will remind you to never take each other for granted."

He gave her shoulder a light squeeze. "I know it bothers you that Lita and Duff get to be together, but you have to remember that you and Luke will probably live to be over three hundred years. You have much longer to enjoy each other. You just have to be patient."

His hand went back to his lap, and Alissia let out a sigh.

"I know. I guess I'm worried about traveling through the winter. I don't like cold weather."

The two of them nearly fell from the tree when a grey and black fur ball unexpectedly landed beside Alissia. Twitching her tiny black nose and scratching at one of her pointy ears, the tiny creature considered them with round, grey eyes.

Mia took her role as protector of Alissia very seriously. Although she was only two feet tall when standing on her back raccoon-like feet, she had already viciously killed a man threatening her ward, and her adorable appearance was very deceiving.

"Mia, you've got to stop doing that!" Alissia scolded.

The tiny creature blinked, apparently unimpressed.

Alissia let out a frustrated sigh and turned to Salvatore. "Sorry about that. I think she gets bored easily."

He stood and held out his hand. "Shall we join the others?"

As she went to accept his aid, she was startled by a voice in the ancient language coming from somewhere above.

"I believe you've been looking for us."

Dear reader,

I hope you're enjoying Alissia's adventure as much as I love writing it. Stay tuned, as the rest of her story is a wild ride you won't want to miss. *Unexpected Beginning*, the fourth book in the series, will take you to different places, introduce you to new creatures, and will be filled with many intriguing surprises along the way.

I enjoy hearing from each of my readers and am greatly honored by the kind words and support I've gotten. This book includes the names of two of my biggest fans as a way to thank them for their support.

Writing a novel is a passion that takes an immense amount of time and effort, and I ask that you consider leaving a review on Goodreads or Amazon for the books in this series. It is the best way you can show your support, especially for a new author such as myself.

If you would like to receive insights into the next book, you may want to subscribe to my newsletter by going to my website. I can be found at the following locations:

www.tiannaholley.com
https://www.facebook.com/authortiannaholley
https://www.google.com/+TiannaHolley
https://twitter.com/holley_tianna
https://instagram.com/tiannaholley/
http://tiannaholley.tumblr.com
https://www.goodreads.com/author/show/7140745.Tianna_Holley

Thank you for your support,

Tianna Holley
Writer of passionate, fantasy romance without the guilt.